POMP
AND
CHANCEY

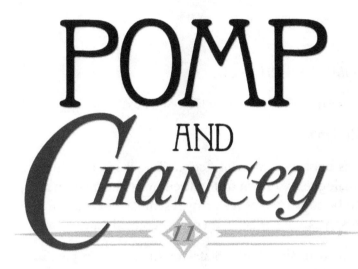

POMP AND CHANCEY

11

KAY DEW SHOSTAK

August South
PUBLISHING

POMP AND CHANCEY

ISBN: 978-1-7350991-7-0

SOUTHERN FICTION: Women's Fiction / Southern Fiction / Railroad / Bed & Breakfast / Mountains / Georgia / Family Fiction/ Small Town Fiction

Text Layout and Cover Design by Roseanna White Designs

Cover Images from www.Shutterstock.com

Author photo by Susan Eason with www.EasonGallery.com

Published by August South Publishing. You may contact the publisher at:

AugustSouthPublisher@gmail.com

Dedicated to
My Chancey family—
The fourteen children of Haskin and Levada Mann
Chancey, my grandparents.
They loved and laughed. They served and created.
They cried and learned.
And they loved stories.
The legacy from these fourteen has changed the world.

CHARACTER LIST

Jackson and Carolina Jessup – Moved to Chancey one year ago. Operate Crossings, a bed-and-breakfast for rail-fans in their home. They have three children: Will, 22; Savannah, 16; Bryan, 13. Will married Anna after the move and they have a new daughter, Frances. Carolina also runs the bookstore side of Blooming Books.

Jackson's family – Mother Etta lives at the beach in South Carolina. Father Hank is married to Shelby and lives in Kentucky. Two brothers, Emerson and Colt. Emerson is the oldest, and he and his wife have three daughters and live in Virginia. Colt is the youngest, is single, and moved to Chancey with his girlfriend Phoenix.

Carolina's family – Parents Goldie and Jack live in Tennessee. Carolina is an only child.

Missus Bedwell – Lifelong resident of Chancey. Recently widowed.

Peter and Delaney Bedwell, both 45 – newlyweds living in the Bedwell House with his mother.

Laney and Shaw Conner – Both from Chancey. Shaw owns an automotive dealership. Laney partners with Carolina in the B&B. They have three children: twins Angie and Jenna, 17; Cayden, 8 months.

Susan and Griffin Lyles – Susan is sister to Laney and manages the Lake Park. Griffin and Susan are recently divorced. They have three children: Leslie, 19; Susie Mae, 15; Grant, 13. Laney and Susan's mother is Gladys Troutman.

Gertie Samson – She has one child: Patty, 28, married to Andy Taylor. Gertie was raised in Chancey and returned after her daughter, Patty, settled there. She owns a lot of property in town. She lives in the house she, Patty, and Andy run their businesses out of.

Ruby Harden – Owns and runs Ruby's Café on the town square. Lifelong Chancey resident.

Libby Stone – Works with Ruby at the café and is married to Bill Stone. Daughter is Cathy.

Cathy Stone Cross – Libby and Bill's daughter is married to Stephen Cross, a teacher at the high school. They have a young son, Forrest.

Kendrick family – Moved to town for father Kyle to open new Dollar Store where he hired Anna Jessup as Assistant Manager. Wife Kimmy and their four children live in Chancey. Kyle's daughter, Zoe, from a previous marriage lives with Kimmy and cares for the younger three children.

Shannon Chilton – Operates florist part of Blooming Books. Lifelong Chancey resident. She's 30 and recently ended a relationship with Peter Bedwell. She is now married to Danny Kinnock and they live above the book store/ florist.

Bonnie Cuneo – Works in Blooming Books. Retired teacher who lives in Laurel Cove with husband, Cal.

Alex Carrera – Opened new restaurant on Main Street called AC's. He and his girlfriend, Angie Conner, live above it and run it.

Hey, y'all! Gertie here. Figuring y'all have had about as much of Missus's never-ending proclamations as I have, I'm hijacking this bit. Let me tell you, I've had that woman and her bossiness up to here! ("Here" being the very top of my head since you can't see where I'm pointing.) So I took the bull by the horns and replaced her three pages full of the stuff that comes out the other end of the bull where the horns ain't with this short rundown to catch you up on Chancey doings.

She ain't the boss of me.

First of all, just to get it out of the way real quick-like, me and Bill are getting married next week. We're doing it on a Thursday night, over in the gazebo since it looks like the weather is gonna hold. It will be the second week of May, so it shouldn't be too chilly. There's another good reason for me writing this—I didn't get a permit to have the wedding in the park. Didn't even apply for one because we all know Queen Shermania wouldn't've given me one, don't we?

Don't matter, though. By the time she reads this it'll all be over. Shoot, she probably wouldn't've even mentioned my nuptials in her diatribe, would she? Makes me mad just thinking about it. She'd skip right over it to blather on about something like her upcoming speech at the Chancey High graduation or the sinkhole that opened up downtown, right outside Laney's shop. (Thank goodness that crater didn't open when my son-in-law, Andy, was renting that place.)

Speaking of Andy, he and Patty are getting ready for our baby to come next month. June 15 is the due date, and that pushed up the timetable for my wedding, but babies don't keep no schedule. Patty keeps saying she doesn't think she'll feel like being in the wedding, but I think that's just silly. I'm gonna get her over there to do some exercising with that Phoenix. That girl's got plenty of energy to burn now that she's broken things off with Coach Colt. I hope he knows what he's doing, throwing in with Danny Kinnock's ex. Why, she's got three girls and a crazy mother he's going to have to deal with. With Phoenix he just had to deal with her dance studio, the juice bar, and her catering. Ya ask me, he's not thinking straight.

Plus Phoenix is a real good cook. I'm having her cater my wedding reception. I ain't told her yet that I've moved the reception from the Moonshine Cave to the park—don't want Missus to get a heads-up—but Phoenix is pretty flexible. (In more ways than one, if you know what I mean. Like I said, Coach Colt's messing up.) I am also going to change my flowers from the cut ones that just die like Shannon messes with to potted ones I got when I went by Silas's new place. He has planters and hanging baskets galore. I'm sure Shannon can figure out what to do to make it look all natural. I mean, flowers is flowers, right? I should make a note to tell her about the changes too.

Although if it's changes you want to talk about, that Shannon's been making them left and right. Why, it was just last Thanksgiving she was all hot and heavy with Peter Bedwell. Then, like she was picking a different hair bow, she was with Danny Kinnock. But don't matter how much you say it, a baby's daddy isn't something you can switch off and on like a light switch. Everyone knows that who the daddy is and I, for one, think it's right straight-up of Danny to step in. Ball is in Peter's court, but so far he's just ignoring it. Guess we'll all have a real show to watch when that young'un gets here in July.

Speaking of young'uns, I'm gonna have Susan Lyle's girl Susie Mae read a poem at my wedding. I've grown quite fond of her from when I'm over at Carolina's bookstore. She's not all highfalutin' like some of the other young women around here. Maybe with her momma spending every waking, and not-so-awake (get what I mean?), moment out there at Silas's nursery, maybe I can get a discount on the flowers. Although since I'm just borrowing the planters and such, I don't figure it'll cost much.

By the way, do you know anyone who does alterations? Carolina keeps telling me she doesn't sew, but doesn't she just seem like someone that would know how to hem my wedding dress? I'm dropping it off at her shop today, so if you know someone, just let her know. She'd probably appreciate the help. Plus with her Jackson just doing odd jobs around town now, maybe she should learn to sew. Pick up some extra cash. I mean, how busy could a B&B and a bookstore keep you? Never had much use for neither, sleeping in someone else's house or reading what some stranger wrote down. What's the point?

So, as you can see, nothing's really happening in

Chancey except for the big doings next Thursday. And don't spill the beans about the reception to Lord Lady Missus. Hopefully she'll stay preoccupied with that sinkhole and underground pipe mess. All I know is sinkhole, schminkhole—it better be fixed by next Thursday, 'cause you know, the wedding and all.

> *The soon-to-be,*
> *Mrs. William Purdy*

CHAPTER 1

"I can't believe you remembered!" Savannah repeats as she hugs me again. Her arms are tight around my neck, and for just a moment she rests her head on my shoulder. Oh, how many nights did I nestle against this head and breathe in my daughter. Those nights, I was her whole world. She gives me another moment, then pulls back with tears in her blue eyes and that crooked smile that acknowledges our rough patches. After all, we are mother and daughter. She's a teenager, and I'm a busy, stressed mom who doesn't know how my girl got so grown so fast.

With a nod and my own crooked smile, I chuckle. "Of course I remembered. You made me promise about a million times that summer we moved."

She steps back to lean against the kitchen counter. "But *I* kinda forgot. So they're really coming next weekend?"

"Yes. They get here that Friday after school, and you have the entire B&B wing both nights."

"But it's Mother's Day weekend. I thought there was the big brunch on Sunday like usual."

"There is. For your Marietta friends and their moms and your friends here and their moms."

Now I've truly stunned her. I've been planning this surprise for weeks now, but because it's normally a busy weekend for us, she didn't notice the differences. When we moved from Marietta up here to Chancey, I'd promised her she could have all her friends here for a weekend. One or two have come at different times, but I wanted something that would really stand out before she graduates.

"That'll be weird, won't it? I think of my friends here and there so differently." She chews on her bottom lip. "I don't know."

"Sweetie, I think they'll get along just great. Some of them are going to be at the same colleges next year. You might be helping create whole new friendships." I say this, but my breath catches a little. Bringing Savannah's Atlanta friends up here was such a fun and big idea that I didn't really think of what it would be like. The particulars. The individual women. Too late now. I step to the fridge and open it. "They'll all be together only for that afternoon. It'll be fun."

She doesn't answer me, so I peek out from behind the refrigerator door to catch her chewing on her thumbnail. "Savannah, stop overthinking it. Go back to being happy," I command.

She pushes away from the counter and hugs my shoulders from behind. "Yes, ma'am! And I am happy. I'm taking them hiking to at least one waterfall. Can we do a bonfire? Definitely muffins at Ruby's. What else should we do?"

"Whatever you want." I've put away the last container of leftovers so I take the drying towel from her hands. "I've got to go. Chamber meeting tonight, and we're talking about the sinkhole. You have much homework?"

"Not really. Just finishing up a couple of papers and projects. Grades for seniors have to be in next week." Her voice is soft, and I can tell her thoughts are already off on her big weekend. Jackson and I decided to tell her about the plan tonight at the end of dinner. This way she has time to talk it all to death with her friends. At the kitchen table I stick my phone in my purse, but as I go to put the strap over my shoulder, I'm hugged again.

"Thanks so much, Mom. Really." She dashes past me, heading for the stairs. "I'm going to call everyone!"

See? It's not so hard to have a loving, stress-free relationship with your teenage daughter.

For an hour, anyway.

CHAPTER 2

Laney flies to her feet. "I don't care, Missus! Just fix it!"

Susan tugs on her sister's belt and motions for me to pull Laney down from my side.

She's crazy—I'm not touching her. Shaking my head, I fold my arms tightly against my chest.

We are seated in the high school auditorium. Missus felt there would be a large crowd for the chamber meeting tonight since she opened it up to all citizens concerned about the sink-hole. However, I think the main reason we're meeting here is so that Missus has a stage. Lucky for her, Retta Bainbridge is laid up with a recent hip replacement, or Missus would've had to wrestle that gavel out of chamber chairwoman's hand. I can't complain, though. The cushioned, theater-style chairs are much better than the metal, folding ones we use at the book-store for chamber of commerce meetings.

Missus is up on the stage with the county engineer, the city maintenance director, and her son, Peter. No one knows why Peter is up there, not even his wife. Delaney Bedwell is seated on my other side, and her quasi-reasoning for why Peter is up there is, "Folks might have a legal question he can answer." Yes, she is still just as enthralled with him as ever.

As Laney gets louder, Susan's tugs get stronger until, finally, her sister turns around and slaps her hand away. Laney has on an orange jumpsuit. (I know, but it doesn't look like she's escaped lockup.) It's as businesslike as an orange jumpsuit can be, with a tortoiseshell belt and a leopard-print scarf. Her hair has grown out to shoulder length, but she's not brought back the massive pageant hair she had when I first met her. Tonight it's sleek, shiny, and straight. She's still rocking, and selling, the modern Southern belle vibe, and her shop is raking in money hand over fist.

Well, it was until last Friday, when the sidewalk outside her front door collapsed. No one was hurt because it happened in the wee hours of the morning.

The way she's going on about it, you'd think no other businesses were affected by the sinkhole, though I guess Laney's is the only one that didn't have a workaround. Phoenix closed her studio and juice bar to customers, but she was able to keep her catering going using her back door and her nearby house. Peter's law offices and the *Chancey Vedette* were also impacted, but until the sinkhole is fixed, Peter is working from home, and the *Vedette* is planning on printing from another small newspaper's facilities over in the town of Blue Ridge. Ruby took advantage of her block along Main Street being closed and shut her doors for a rare weekend off. Of course, that left the B&B scrambling for muffins, but Alex and Angie made scones for us. Like the bookstore, their bistro, AC's, is on the next block over from the sinkhole. We both have stayed open, with sawhorses sectioning off the unsafe parts of the sidewalk and street.

So, yes, Laney is the only one having a cow. And boy, is she good at it.

Missus is sputtering as Laney levels accusations of anything and everything at her—from Missus stealing the town's old copper pipes to sell for salvage, to robbers tunneling into the bank vault (even though there hasn't been a bank downtown for a couple of decades), to Peter trying to condemn the whole block so he can expand his law offices.

Delaney lets out a laugh and stands. "Laney, are you about through? Sit down and let the experts talk. This is not some massive plan to undo the success of your business. As far as I know, we *all* love shopping and hanging out there and can't wait for it to reopen."

On my right, Laney in her orange turns, mouth open and eyes fired up, and I'm so regretting my choice of a seat.

Delaney laughs again. "Seriously, girl, do you think anyone here wants to tangle with you? I've only been here a little while, but even I know the number one rule of living in Chancey is 'Keep Laney happy!'" She turns toward the stage. "Okay, so let's hear from the folks who wear hard hats. We'll sit down, and you let us know when we can get back to shopping at The Club."

She rolls her eyes in sympathy at Laney, then throws in a shrug for the rest of us. Then she sits down.

And so does Laney.

Susan and I don't risk eye contact over her head. Instead, I just pinch Delaney's thigh out of sight of my other neighbor and whisper, "That was incredible," out of the side of my mouth.

Peter encourages the county man next to him to stand and talk.

He lumbers to his feet, gives Laney a little smile, and explains, "Sorry, ma'am, but this is due to all the rain we had this past month. The storm water pipes were full, and where maybe there was a little slow leak before, the extra water caused a complete failure of the pipe. That wasn't noticed aboveground until it washed away all the underlying dirt, leaving a crater. With the water shut off, the crater won't get any larger. Now, this is a major repair, but not an especially difficult one. It shouldn't take more than a couple days." He sits down, but I notice he looks down at the floor and doesn't look back up. All around me are sighs of relief.

Missus, who is stationed behind the wooden lectern, leans to look toward the engineer who just delivered this news. "Well, that is good to hear. And I'm assuming work will begin in the morning?"

The man, still staring at the floor, pulls his finger and thumb down the length of his nose and takes a long breath in at the same time. He doesn't look her direction, but addresses his answer to the floor. "Well, now, Madam Mayor, that's a mite optimistic. You see, there's a little issue with some problems your town hasn't seen to in the past as requested."

The city maintenance man seated next to the county guy raises both hands. "I told the mayor. I told the police chief. I told everyone I could think of. No one wanted to deal with it until they had to. Well, now we have to."

Missus is back to sputtering. "What? You told me what?"

"Oh, no, ma'am. You and I haven't had a chance to speak yet. You've been quite busy with other things since you took office, or so I've been told whenever I've called trying to get a meeting. I meant Mayor Taylor. Well, now he's Principal Taylor." The man stands and looks out at the audience, pointing behind us. "Well, he was right there just a minute ago." Jed had welcomed us all to his relatively new domain of Chancey High when we arrived earlier. He took the job at the first of the year and so far, much like his mayoral reign, hasn't done anything much, good or bad. Jed is more a maintainer of the status quo of whatever he's in charge of.

Missus bends and picks up the leather binder that was laying on her chair. As she straightens she announces, "This meeting is adjourned. I'll get to the bottom of things once I find Jed. No worries; I will issue a proclamation with everything you need to know." She strides off the stage, leaving a stunned audience and the three men staring after her. Her son comes to his senses first. He jumps up, shakes the other two men's hands, then hurries to follow his mother behind the heavy curtain and down the side steps. Then probably out a side door straight to her getaway car.

Laney suddenly sits up tall in her seat and turns to scan the audience. "Where's Charles? He's got to be here somewhere." Then she shouts, "Charles! Wait right there for me." She waves for us to get up and move so she can get out.

Susan, Delaney, and I follow her down to the front row of seats, where Charles Spoon, editor of the *Vedette*, is seated. He's busily scribbling in his little notebook.

Laney plops into the seat next to him. "Charles, is this from before? Like, when I was treasurer?" She lowers her voice. "Remember all that about the pipes and money to fix them before it got catastrophic? I mean, I remember that word being used, but I thought they were exaggerating."

Charles taps his notebook, then looks up sideways at her from where he's slunk down in his seat. "Miss Laney, I think you might be right. You know, every city department always wants what little bit of money there is floating around for themselves. I wrote up the report back then, but it was pretty dry writing, so I can only imagine how dry the reading was. That was when we didn't have money for nothing, remember? Before your, you know, little income-producing deal."

Laney huffs. "My gambling, you mean, which could've saved the town. Holier-than-thou hypocrites didn't want my ill-gotten gains, and now look where it's got us! You know Jed never did want to spend money on stuff the public couldn't see."

Charles nods thoughtfully, then winks at her. "But, to be honest, neither did you, Madam Treasurer."

Tossing her head and straightening her scarf, she sniffs. "That was before I thought it might actually affect me."

Delaney, Susan, and I step back as the white-haired editor

comes to his feet. "It's gonna impact a lot more than just you. Can you imagine Chancey without Ruby's? I'm gonna have to go back and look at the articles from then, but I'm thinking they were talking about shutting down the road for a good month. Lord knows how long it'll take doing now with this sinkhole business included."

"Oh," I moan. "Who's going to tell Ruby she might be out of business for more than a weekend?"

Susan shakes her head. "I'd say let's make Missus tell her, but she'd enjoy it too much. You know, Ruby's house isn't too far from here. We could run by there on our way home. She asked me to let her know how the meeting went anyway."

"Okay," I say. "Laney, you want to come with us?"

"No, thank you! That house gives me the creeps." She shudders as she stands and loops her arm through Charles's. They start up the aisle, talking in low voices.

"The creeps? Why?" Delaney and I ask at nearly the same time.

Delaney then smiles and adds, "Maybe I should come with you two instead of going home with Peter. Sounds interesting."

As Susan heads out, she cryptically throws over her shoulder, "You're welcome to join us, but you do need to be aware there's a very good chance you'll end up with nightmares tonight."

As Delaney starts to frown, I grab her arm. "Oh, no, you don't! You're in this with me now. Come on!"

Chapter 3

The heavy April rains the engineer referenced earlier have delayed our spring. Skies thick with clouds and chilly temperatures kept the flowering tree buds closed tight, but then last week the clouds moved out and we had a solid five days of sunshine. The days are getting longer, and as we drive down the road behind the high school, we are greeted by swaying limbs, their white blossoms standing out in the deepening dusk. Turning into a gravel driveway, we are bordered on both sides by head-high azalea bushes, many in a light pink, which also shine in what's left of the daylight.

Ruby's house is a small one-story with a detached, metal carport under which no car has parked for many a year. It's full of stuff, some covered with old tarps or in boxes, but junk stacked almost to its roof. We park behind Ruby's uncovered car and get out. It's very quiet on her property, as large bushes and thick underbrush crowd right up to the house; no trimming or landscape work here. We walk up the old, broken sidewalk and then have to go single file up the three concrete steps because giant evergreen bushes, probably planted decades ago as small, decorative sentinels for the porch, have nearly taken it over. On the stoop, Susan pushes the lit-up doorbell.

The porch light, hanging beside the door, comes on. It's practically encased in dead bug carcasses, so the light is dim.

Delaney and I, right up next to Susan's back, due to lack of space on the rectangle of concrete—and due to our growing fear—make faces at each other. I whisper toward Susan's ear, "You're right. This is creepy."

As the door behind the screen creaks open, Susan whispers back, "We didn't mean the outside." Then she speaks up—louder and happier. "Hey, Ruby! We thought we'd come by and let you know how things went at the meeting."

Ruby pushes open the screen door. "Did ya have to bring the whole committee? Who all's out there? Never mind; come on in. My show is about to start so ya can't stay long."

Delaney follows Susan, and then I step up into the dim living room. The television is on, but muted. Light from the screen flickers to my left. Then, just as I start to look around, Delaney freezes in place, stiff as a board. I push on her back. "I'm only halfway in. Move."

She moves to my right and presses her back against the open wooden door. Shaking my head at her, I turn, and there are dozens eyes staring at me. Doll eyes. Dolls stand on every surface of the room. On top of cabinets and bookshelves, on the coffee table and wall nooks, they look down at us. The flickering television light makes their eyes come alive, and I might have had a small heart attack at first glance. Now I'm breathing more normally, but then Susan steps farther into the room, and I realize I have a death grip on the hem of her shirt. She pulls it out of my grasp, and I'm left with nothing between me and the legion of dolls.

"Come on in," Ruby growls at us. "Find a seat. Let me see if I can figure out how to tape my show, and y'all can stay longer."

I blurt out, "No! I mean, no, I can't stay. I have to get home." I close my eyes and feel my way a little farther into the room, keeping close to Susan. I open them, hoping to be looking only at Ruby, but she's sat down in her recliner. I find her, amidst all her doll friends, and do my darnedest to only focus on her.

"We just came to tell you you're going to be shut down longer than we thought. Something with the city not doing repairs before. We don't understand it all but wanted to tell you in person. Guess we should go now."

Before I can turn around, Susan yanks on my sleeve. "Sit down, Carolina. Delaney, you too."

Delaney hurries to sit on the love seat next to Susan, leaving me to walk across the crowded room and sit in the rocking chair on the other side of Ruby. The chair moves as I sit down, and the dolls on the tables on either side of me appear to be moving too. I close my eyes again. Who would've taken Ruby for a fan of dolls? Certainly not me.

Ruby sighs and sits back. "Can't say I'm surprised," she says, refocusing my attention on the reason for our visit. "Jed never was good at math, and none of them pencil pushers over there at city hall were interested in doing the *not-fun* stuff. They wanted to do the park, and the train station, and gardening folderol. So, when do they think I can open?"

The three of us shrug and share glances. Susan says, "Could be as long as a month."

Delaney leans forward from out of the deep love seat. "Maybe you can sell muffins and pies out the back door, like Phoenix is doing with her catering."

"Yeah, that's an idea," I chime in. "Although I just can't imagine not being able to drop in at Ruby's for coffee and talking. Surely this won't take so long?"

Ruby picks up her remote. "Don't bet on it." As she turns up the volume, she raises her voice. "Y'all are welcome to stay, but I'm not sure I recorded it, so we can just wait to talk during the commercials."

Delaney and I jump up.

"Oh, no problem," I say. "It's getting late. We should go."

Delaney beats me to the front door. We're both still saying our goodbyes as we hit the tiny porch and rush through the dark tunnel of bushes. Susan had locked the car, so we are both standing beside our doors waiting when she saunters out like those dolls aren't chasing her. I'm sure they were chasing me.

"Y'all are a couple of chickens. They're just dolls." She hits the button to unlock the car, and as we slide in, I immediately lock my door.

Delaney says from the back seat, after she's locked the doors on both sides, "If they're just dolls, why didn't you warn us?"

Susan grins. "Because I wasn't warned my first time. Although now that her daughter, Jewel, and the kids have moved out, she does seem to have added to her collection. That was a lot of dolls."

I shudder. "That's the creepiest thing I've ever seen. And dolls do not usually creep me out. But their eyes and the TV reflecting in them was awful." I shudder again and wrap my arms more tightly around myself. The car is quiet as we pass the road to the high school, and then I half turn in my seat. "Delaney, I wanted to invite you to a Mother's Day brunch up at Crossings. It's actually on Sunday, so I know you might already have plans with Gregory. But it's for Savannah and her friends and their moms, so it's not open to the public like we've done in the past."

She sniffs. I pause, but when she doesn't say anything, I slowly continue. "It's kind of a graduation present for Savannah, having her friends from Marietta up for the weekend, and then it ends on Sunday afternoon with the brunch." There are more sniffs from behind us, and Susan and I exchange a concerned look.

"Are you okay?" I gently ask.

She takes a moment, then, after another sniffle, quietly laughs. "That's the first time anyone has thought of me as a mother on Mother's Day. My family completely ignored it all these years, which is how I wanted it. Or thought I wanted it!" She pulls in a deep breath. "Can I get back to you on the brunch?"

"Sure," I say. After a moment or two, I hesitantly add, "But if you wait on Peter or Gregory to offer to do something, well, you might not want to wait on that. I know my guys are just not that good at remembering stuff. My mother told me long ago, 'If you're going to be disappointed if the man in your life doesn't get you a gift or a card, then you need to give them advanced notice or, well, plan to be disappointed.' And from my experience, sadly, she was right."

"Amen!" Susan says. "Girls are better, but even they forget you when there's anything else on their minds. I tell mine exactly what I'm wanting—even if it's just time alone to read, a certain plant, or going out to dinner. Griffin was always pretty good at remembering his mom, but that was because she was a holy terror if they dared to forget."

Delaney sighs. "Ugh, and I'm not good at being a holy terror. I'm more the 'wait and see if they notice' type. Which hasn't worked out too well so far!"

We all laugh and agree with her.

"Okay," she says with a smile. "Count me in for the brunch. If something else comes along with Gregory, I'll work around it. Thank you for the invite."

"You're welcome. It'll be fun."

Susan turns left, passes the triangle of daffodils, and starts up the hill toward my house. Down in the woods, where I'd never even known there was a house, there are now lights on.

"Augusta moved in over the weekend, I hear," Susan says, looking over in that direction.

"Did she?" Delaney mutters, as if Augusta is some random stranger and not the aunt who raised her son. "I haven't talked to her since she left at the beginning of April. Somehow she got my father to back down, which is unheard of. My mother doesn't know what happened either. She just says my dad reconsidered, and he has decreed we are to treat Gregory and Augusta as we did before."

So the family doesn't have any answers. Well, there isn't any further enlightenment coming from the front seat. Susan doesn't have any to give. And my lips are sealed.

The last time I spoke to Augusta Duvall was at the bookstore before spring break, when I gave her the phone number of a dancer friend of Phoenix's in Las Vegas. The dancer was very familiar with Delaney's father, Thompson LaMotte, and his habits—habits of all kinds, which were only on display when he visited Las Vegas—and she had tales to tell. Apparently that gave Augusta the leverage she needed to get out from under her brother's thumb and complete her move to Chancey. It has also given Thompson's grandson, Gregory, the freedom to leave college like he wants to and move to Chancey when his semester ends.

Delaney leans forward. "Neither of you know anything about what caused my father to change his mind, do you?"

Susan frowns and shakes her head. I kind of shake my head, then ask, "Do you plan on visiting Augusta in her new home any time soon?"

She sits back quickly. "I don't know. She raised Gregory. She probably doesn't want me around. What do y'all think?"

Susan shrugs. "I like her. A lot. I plan on helping her with her yard. She's reached out to Silas about taking some gardening classes."

I heartily add my opinion. "You know that I got along with her, so I'm sure we'll be friends. I think without your parents in the way, you and she will be fine. Just play it by ear."

We slowly cross the railroad tracks and pull up to my house. Susan says, "All looks quiet here tonight."

I huff and shake my head. "Except every light in the house is on like we're made of money! It doesn't matter how much you preach, they refuse to turn off lights. Anyway, I texted to see if Grant was here for you to give him a ride home, but Jackson said he isn't."

"No, he's at his dad's tonight. At least I think that's where he is." She lets out a huff of her own. "Both of us living in town, but in separate houses, is giving our kids way too much latitude. Grant goes wherever he wants, and neither one of us seems to be able to make them stick to any kind of a schedule. Neither of us wants to be the heavy. That son of mine is kind of a charmer, you might've noticed, and we all know Susie Mae needs a firm hand. As the temps warm, her clothing is getting skimpier and skimpier. But then look how Athena dresses. You should see what she wears just around the house."

"Athena?" I ask. "She dresses young, not provocatively."

"Whatever it is, she's bewitched Griffin. She's just not a good role model for either of my kids, but Griffin is unreasonable and is at her house with my kids every chance he gets." Susan hits the steering wheel. "She's got him playing daddy with her two babies. He always enjoyed the kids when they were little and was so good with them. I bet that's half her appeal for him. And she's getting a free babysitter. Well, maybe not exactly free, but she's obviously willing to pay the price. They act just like the perfect little family, but you know it's just an act!"

As she's ranting and I'm getting out of the front seat, Delaney and I make eye contact. The Lyle kids having way too much freedom since their parents separated has been something we've discussed, yet, as Susan just said, neither parent wants to put their foot down ,and none of their friends are going to do it for them.

I look at Susan. "Y'all need to sit down and talk about it, I think. As a couple and then with the kids."

"I know. You're right. But he'll probably want to include her. It's like they're joined at the hip. And things are so busy with school ending and everything. But, yeah, you're right. Of course. Talk to you later," she says as she puts the car into reverse. Her smile is tight at me as she looks out my still open door.

"Delaney, don't you want to get in the front seat?" I ask.

"Naw, I'm fine back here. Chauffeur! Take me home!"

I laugh as I close the door, then wave at the headlights that are pulling away. Turning and looking at the house, I can't help but think of the worries of my two friends. Both have tangles they know need to be worked out, but how can they do that without upsetting the folks they love most? I sigh for them both and turn toward the house, where not just one light, but *every* light, has been left on to welcome me home.

Funny, but all of a sudden a giant electric bill doesn't seem like a real problem.

CHAPTER 4

"Maybe we should start serving coffee," Shannon says as we look out over our store from behind the sales counter. "This morning is even busier than yesterday."

Apparently we're not the only ones missing Ruby's. The old men who usually gather at her diner to discuss the weather, politics, and basically keep the world on its axis are now gathering at our big table near the front windows. We're used to a couple of older men hanging out here, looking through Missus's late husband FM's books that we keep on display, but they are usually busy looking, not talking. Today, though, every chair is taken, the topics are wide-ranging, and the rarely used chess set is getting a workout. Matter of fact, one of the men added a cheap checkers game to the mix. He said it's for us to keep since not everyone "is hoity-toity and knows how to play chess."

As for the young moms who have made it a practice to stop in at Ruby's after dropping off their kids at the elementary school, they have now taken over the kids' book area. A couple of them have kids too young for school, and so they are all gathered there on the floor, corralling the babies in their midst and drinking coffee brought from home. We sold more kids' books yesterday than the entire two weeks before.

I turn to look at the big, open area at the rear of our store, behind Shannon's worktable. "Maybe we *should* serve coffee. Ruby could run it until she's able to open again. Just bring stuff over from her place through the back doors. We have room to put a few tables, but that's better than nothing."

Shannon grimaces. "Ruby? Here? Like, all morning? *Every* morning?"

I stop mid-thought and close my mouth. "You're right. What was I thinking?"

"There's Missus with a stack of proclamations." Shannon points out the mayor coming down the sidewalk. "I'm going back to my table before she gets here. Pregnant lady prerogative. You deal with her!"

Laughing, she hurries past the front of the counter. Her due date is now only seven weeks away, and since she's entered the third trimester she's gotten back some energy and is in a good mood almost all the time. Married life has been good for her and Danny. They are both calmer and more settled, and the way he's hovering over the moms and babies in their circle, it's obvious he can't wait for their own baby to get here. Well, theirs and Peter's, but that fact doesn't seem to diminish Danny's enthusiasm.

I shake my head as I remember he already has had three babies, his three daughters live full time with their mom here in town, but it's hard to believe Danny is their dad. Hopefully he was this excited for their births.

Hitting the front door, Madam Mayor causes the bell above it to signal her arrival. Since we've passed Easter she's back to her white gloves full-time, and in her white-gloved hands she's carrying a stack of magenta pages. Magenta is the color she's chosen for her proclamations. She's appalled at how unprofessional they look, but says when she did them in a stately cream, or official white, they were too often overlooked.

Color had nothing to do with it. And now we are subjected to 8½ x 11 magenta rectangles everywhere. *Everywhere.*

"Good morning, Missus," I greet her. "Interesting meeting last night."

"Maybe *you* call it interesting. I call it frustrating. To be left cleaning up Jed Taylor's mess once again. I had such high hopes for a term of exciting projects truly lifting Chancey out of the humdrum, backwoods existence we've been relegated to for so long; to see just how far we could fly, but no. I am being forced to squander my time and creativity on *groundwater runoff*. It's a travesty."

I shrug. "Well, such is life at the top. When will Ruby's be able to reopen?"

She thrusts a reddish-purple sheet at me. "Read the proclamation. It's all there. I must carry on." She tucks her stack of papers into the crook of her elbow and looks around. "Glad to see my efforts have caused a surge in business for you and Shannon. No need to thank me; it's my duty."

I don't look up at her, but roll my eyes anyway as I try to read the black writing on the dark paper. "Missus, there are no answers here. This is just to say you're holding another meeting!"

"Where there *will* be answers!" she belts as she sets the front door's bell ringing again.

With her gone, the counter area is quickly surrounded by everyone who'd been listening to Madam Mayor, but not venturing into her orbit. "Another meeting?" one of the men says in disgust as he folds his arms across his belly. "That woman will hold a meeting to determine if she's going to heaven or hades at the pearly gates!"

"I'm not getting another babysitter for her to stand up front and say nothing," one mom says, bouncing her toddler on her hip. "All I want to know is when Ruby's and Laney's club are going to reopen!"

"Yeah, when can we get back to normal?" another woman says. She is followed quickly by several echoes.

I hold up the paper. "The meeting is tomorrow in the park at three p.m. There's lots of writing and fancy words, but that's all it really says." I adopt Missus's high-and-mighty voice to add, "To determine if repairs will be approved."

Unfolding his arms, the man bangs a fist on the counter. "Approved? There ain't no decision to be made! Just get to doin' and cut out all this chitter-chatter!" He looks around at the nods and noisy agreement that follow.

The crowd seems to have found a ringleader, but shaking his head in disgust after exhaling a gruff harrumph, the man ambles back to the table to resume his chess game without another word to his would-be followers. The angry crowd follows his lead and melts back to whatever they were doing before Missus arrived.

We want Ruby's open, but apparently our mob action begins and ends there.

Chapter 5

"I'm taking the month off!" Laney declares, sailing into Blooming Books in the midafternoon. She's wearing a navy tennis skirt and a short-sleeve, navy-and-white-striped polo shirt. And the kicker? On her feet is a pair of real tennis shoes. Not cutesy shoes, but ones with real support and cushion, with real shoestrings. This is interesting. Laney's not big on useful or comfortable shoes.

I lean an elbow on the nearest bookshelf. "You taking up tennis?"

"I might! The outfit is from the line of vacation wear I'm carrying at The Club, and since no one else can buy it with me closed, I thought I'd try it on. I look good in skirts." She studies herself. "My legs are still really pale, but so are everyone else's. At least mine *will* tan, and now I'll have plenty of time to work on that. I've decided not to worry about all that sinkhole mess. Instead, I'm going to enjoy this last month with my daughters still in high school. I'm planning the biggest graduation party ever! It's going to be epic."

She's made all these statements while roaming around the front area of the store. Shannon and Danny are watching from near the flower table. I'm putting the kids' book area back together from the morning's rush and making a list of books needed to replenish our stock.

Laney bounds toward the worktable. "Shannon, you're looking just radiant! Do you know if you're having a boy or a girl? I'm sure Danny's hoping for a boy. I mean, you already have three of the cutest little girls ever, right?"

Danny pauses as if it's a trick question. Then, determining that it's safe to answer, he grins. "That's true, Miss Laney. However, another girl would just be a big ol' thrill! Right, babe?"

Shannon frowns, then nods, but she goes back to her flowers.

Laney looks from Shannon to Danny, then swirls around, raising her eyebrows at me. "Well, another thing I'm going to do with all my free time is read a book. What book should I read, Carolina? I trust your judgment."

Looking up, I peruse the window display. "*Where the Crawdads Sing* is really popular, and I'm enjoying it. We're discussing it at book club this month."

"Oh, so if I read it I can come to book club? I've never been in a book club, but I hear it's really just drinking wine and pretending to have read the book. That would be a great activity for my vacation time. I'm in!" She takes the book right out of the front window display, leaving an empty space, which Danny hurries to fill. People taking books out of the display is a pet peeve of his, but I've told him he has to ignore it. Most times, if folks take it from a display, they buy it.

However, I do say to the new lady of leisure, "Now, Laney. You can't just join the book club. They don't let everyone in."

That puts a stop to the swirling and twirling. "What do you mean? Y'all meet here in your store. Of course I'm welcome. You're funny," she says with a little laugh. But it's a dry laugh and she gives me a bit of side-eye with it.

She drops the book into her big, navy bag and heads for the door. "I'll be real careful with the book so you can resale it. I mean, that's what you do here, right? Sell used books?" At the door she turns. "Be watching for your invites to the big party. Bye now!"

And she's gone.

Shannon walks out in front of her worktable. "Well, you know what that means," she says.

"Yeah," Danny exclaims. "She took a brand-new book and is going to act like it's a used one!"

"That's okay, Danny. She's not going to even open it. When she returns it, it'll be just as new as it is today." Stepping closer to Shannon and we share a frown. "Yeah, it means she's up-to-her-neck guilty for the pipes disaster from her treasurer days."

Shannon snips off a dead leaf from the arrangement in front of her. "Oh yeah. She's way guilty." Then, with a smirk and a tipped-up eyebrow, she adds, "But I'm thinking Vacation Barbie is easier to live with than Burn-Down-City-Hall Barbie."

The slow afternoon made up for the busy morning, and without pie time at Ruby's, downtown was even slower than usual. I sent Shannon upstairs early, telling her that I could take down any orders and that she should take advantage of the rest. Mother's Day is always her busiest time, and after that she moves right into graduation flowers. Danny is training to join the volunteer firemen, so he'd already arranged to leave work early.

The warm, sunny day has the blossoms fading fast and the leaves unfurling on the trees in the square. I love the shadows on the fresh, green grass this time of year. Our spring decorations in the shop are looking dusty and tired, so I've started taking them down. They were so wonderful for the book festival and Easter, but now it's like taking down the Christmas decorations. Not fun, but everything feels more open and clean. Well, it will when I actually do some cleaning. We haven't really done summer decorating in the past that I can recall. Maybe red, white, and blue around the Fourth of July? Bonnie will be in tomorrow. She'll know what to do.

I step out the back door to shake out a rug, and I see Kimmy, Ruby, and Libby talking behind Ruby's Café. I hurry to let the door close before they can see me, but I hear Kimmy shout my name.

Okay. With a bracing sigh, I push the door back open. "Hey, y'all. What's going on?"

Kimmy is hurrying toward me, excitedly saying over her shoulder, "It's fine. We'll make it work. Carolina, look at this! Isn't it perfect? Not too far at all. We can smooth out the path." She reaches me and shoos me inside. "Here, open the door wider. See? No problem!"

Ruby and Libby eventually come in the back door. I don't even ask. I know what's coming. Kimmy lets the door fall closed behind us and spreads her arms. "See? Plenty of room. Matter of fact, I had no idea it was this big. Why, we can easily fit a half dozen of the small tables in here if we move that big table out of the way and block off this office area. Coffee can go there along the wall. Oh, it's perfect, right?"

The frowns on Ruby and Libby's faces clearly show their thoughts. I work on adopting a confused, unsupportive face. Kimmy should be no match for the three of us. We've all raised teenagers. We've crushed the dreams of people we gave birth to in between sips of coffee.

Ruby sighs. "Well, since it was Carolina's idea, I guess we should give it a try."

"My idea? None of this, whatever this is, was my idea! I don't even know what's going on." But then I remember that Kyle Kendrick is also training for the fire department. And although I can't remember where he was this morning, I'm sure Danny was listening to Shannon's and my discussion.

Libby puts an arm around my shoulders. "Sweetie, you're just so humble. It's just like you to want to help everyone out but not take the credit. It'll be a trial for all of us, but with you being so selfless, how can I not go along. I'll try to be as big about it as you are."

Kimmy swallows, and there are tears in her eyes. "It *is* just like you. Always thinking of others. I didn't know what I was going to do without the pie afternoons. I'm using the money to pay for the kids' summer camps. I was dreading telling them we'd have to cancel."

Ruby pshaws. "I don't know about all that. I think Carolina's just a good businesswoman and knows without Ruby's she's likely to lose her bookstore." She looks around at the wide open space with the black walls. "Besides, with all this space to brighten up, I can try out something I've always wanted to do. I have too many dolls for my little house. Can't display them properly. They'll be perfect here." She starts for the back door. "Yeah, that'll work out just great. You got a deal, Carolina. We'll start moving stuff in the morning."

Kimmy is bouncing in her joy as she looks around the area again, and she gives me an enthusiastic hug when she bounces by me. At the door she squeals, "Dolls? Oh, that'll be adorable!"

Chapter 6

"So you're moving Ruby's into Blooming Books?"

Jackson at least lets me get a foot on the first step of the porch before saying it.

Putting one foot in front of the other, I make it up onto the porch to flop into the rocking chair beside him. "Why do you already know this?"

"Don't you mean 'how'?"

"We live in a small town. 'How' is easy. 'How' is you answered your phone or passed one of our children in the hallway. 'Why' is what I want to know. You've been dragged into it, haven't you?"

He lays his head back and rocks his chair while grinning at me. "Yep. A load of gravel is needed in the morning to make a walkable path from the back of Ruby's to the back of Blooming Books. It has to be laid out by eight a.m. so the volunteers will have an easier time carrying everything." He holds up his phone. "Gravel will be waiting for me at seven. We're getting paid extra, so Will and I are putting this in front of tomorrow's other jobs. Besides, it sounds like half the town will be there to make it happen, so we might as well join the fun."

"Has anyone checked to see if Blooming Books will be open at eight a.m.?"

"Not my problem. Besides, Danny lives there, and from what I've heard, he's in charge of the volunteer firemen moving the furniture in."

"Good. Let him tell Shannon what's going on. I wasn't going to go upstairs and disturb her before I left." I rock for a minute. "Can you imagine having Ruby there every morning? And Kimmy is planning on moving Shannon's worktable and blocking off Bonnie's office." Taking a deep breath, I declare, "I'm glad I'm not involved."

Jackson laughs. "Oh, you're cute." He gets up. "And delusional. I'm going to be in the basement for a bit. Will and Francie will be here for dinner. Anna is working late. Savannah isn't home yet, and Bryan is down at the river."

"Bryan by himself?"

Pulling open the screen door, he shrugs. "Not sure. He just yelled down to me that was where he was going. I haven't seen any of the other guys."

"Okay. Dinner at six thirty. I'm excited that Francie's coming." I resume rocking as he goes inside. A bit more relaxed at the thought of spending time with my six-month-old granddaughter, I try to consider that having Ruby's in the store might be kind of fun. Tons of bookstores have cafes, don't they? It'll be different, that's for sure. It is concerning that it looks like this sinkhole mess isn't getting resolved any time soon, but maybe Missus will have real answers at her meeting tomorrow.

Yep.

I'm delusional. On more than one count.

Of course I wasn't letting all this happen without me. I might talk a big game, but I don't want to be left out. By eight o'clock the gravel path, three feet wide and stable, was done.

The low spots had been leveled out, and a small ramp had even been built outside our door to take care of the rather big step into the building. Kimmy, her daughter Zoe, and two of Zoe's friends got here at seven and cleaned our back area. Now the girls are headed off to school, each with a twenty-dollar bill and the promise of a free muffin in the future.

"Bye, girls! Have a good day at school," I say.

"Okay, Mrs. Jessup," Michelle, the tallest girl, responds. "Just call anytime you need some extra help." She waves at me, keys in her hand, as she holds open the door for the two younger girls.

"Thanks for the help, Michelle. I'll keep you in mind." I turn to Kimmy, who followed them to the front. "I didn't recognize the other girl."

"Pilar Estevan. She's new, a freshman like Zoe and Bryan."

"Oh, I see. It kind of threw me seeing Zoe with friends other than Bryan and Grant."

Kimmy rolls her eyes. "She's still got it bad for that Grant, and he's trouble. I know his momma is your friend, but that boy is too good-looking and too charming, and he knows it." She claps her hands. "Okay. Enough of a break. I've got to get back to it. First order of business is setting up the coffee station."

She dashes toward the back of our store just as some men arrive with their arms loaded down. Behind them comes Danny, who is also loaded down, but is giving them directions. "Just set everything there on that big table, and then we'll see where to go from there."

Shannon is slowly coming down the stairs. I watch as she sees her worktable filling up with boxes and machines. Her voice is low and menacing. "Danny. We talked about this."

"Hey, hon. I know. You are right; it's just for a moment. Gotta figure out what we're going to put the coffee on. The counter at Ruby's won't budge." He turns around as if hoping a counter will appear out of the wall. He grimaces at me, but leaves the grimace out of his voice, speaking light and cheerfully. "I'll have all this moved in no time." Then he adds, speaking more slowly, "Just a matter of minutes."

"There. That height is perfect. Just move that table to the wall," Ruby orders as she comes through the back door. "The other tables are too short."

Boy she sounds mean. What have we done?

Shannon moves toward the table with unsure steps and a choke in her voice. "This is my worktable. I have to have it." Uh-oh. I recognize those hormonal emotions seeping through.

"All of it?" Ruby scoffs, her wrinkles pull taut in skepticism, then sag as she scowls. "How much room can one bunch of flowers need? Can't work on more than one bunch at a time." She turns away, dismissing Shannon. "Here, move it this way along the wall." Ruby stands near the wall towards the back, showing with her outstretched arms where the table is to go. "See, Shannon? You'll have all this room to work."

"Facing the wall?" Shannon's voice trembles. "No. Carolina came up with this stupid idea to help you out. Not make our lives miserable. Danny... Don't move that table."

He has hold of one end of the table, and one of this buddies is holding the other. The newlywed husband grunts as he lifts his end. "We can try it. See how it works out. Everyone is making sacrifices, honey."

Sneaking a look at Shannon, I'm not sure if there's more of a chance of a torrent of tears or full-on fury. Hormones aren't real predictable, scientifically speaking.

She warns him, "I'm not facing the wall back there in the dark while I do my work."

Straining under his heavy load, Danny grunts, "All you have to do is turn your head and you won't be looking at the wall."

I was considering going to put my arm around Shannon to

calm her down, but well, now I think Danny deserves everything he's gonna get. No reason for me to get in the line of fire. That's apparently how everyone else in the store is feeling too. It gets very quiet, very tense, and when Danny turns around, he seems to realize his mistake. He places his hands on his hips and surveys the store. Then he dashes past his wife and into Bonnie's office. He comes out with the rolling desk chair and pushes it up to a shorter table for six that the guys have just brought in and placed near the flowers and books at the front. He studies the chair and table, then pulls it back out and rolls it to his short, very pregnant wife. "Your throne, My Grace?"

Shannon is blinking back tears of fury, but as her blinking gets faster she takes the offered seat. Then Danny waltzes her across the room to the table, facing the front. She'll be able to see everything—seated. "Does this work okay for you, honey?" he says, almost apologetically. "The doctor did say you need to stay off your feet."

He has one arm around the back of her chair and is leaning down to look into her face. "Shannon, you are my number one concern. I don't care about Ruby's or flowers, just you and the baby."

When Shannon's tears leak out, hers aren't the only damp eyes in the building. In the midst of this upheaval and all these sudden changes, her husband has made her another workstation, one better suited for her at this time. A couple of folks clear their throats, and we all busy ourselves with setting things up, giving the two newlyweds a bit of privacy.

I'm stepping to the front to turn the sign over to "Open" when Bonnie arrives at the back door. With her arms loaded with books and fabric, she heads straight to her office area. It's not *exactly* blocked off, but she has to twist and pivot to get past the tables and chairs in the way. She sighs loudly, but I'd texted her to alert her about Ruby's move, so she's not shocked.

I guess in the sweetness of Danny's actions we did miss one thing.

She sticks her head back out, eyes blinking and voice raised. "Where in the world is my chair?"

Chapter 7

"I just don't know why you'd call Michelle instead of me. I need extra money too. She thinks you're going to hire her." Susie Mae follows me to the front window. "Are you going to hire her? Don't you want me here anymore?"

"I told you, it wasn't my deal," I explain to my irate, teenage shop attendant. "Kimmy hired Zoe and a couple of her friends for an hour this morning. Look, there's a news truck from Atlanta." Missus's three-thirty announcement has become a press conference, and it looks like the press is complying as another news van pulls up.

Susie Mae continues frantically. "Did Michelle say anything about me or, uh, anything? So many of the girls at school think they are perfect. Just perfect."

I pause, then turn around to look at my young employee. "No. She seemed perfectly nice. I guess she's in this future-nurse's club with Zoe. Hon, what's going on? Why would she be talking about you?"

Finally getting my full attention causes Susie Mae to back up, look away, and shrug. "I don't know. Girls can just be so jealous. Anyway, are you going to Missus's thing out there?"

"Probably." I reach out and pull on her shoulder as she turns to walk away. "Susie Mae, are you okay? You look tired. What's going on?"

She shrugs again, and my hand falls away. "I'm fine. Just a lot of homework and stuff."

As she walks back to the shelves she'd been straightening, I resolve again to talk to Susan. *Really* talk to her about her kids. I'm afraid Susie Mae is falling back into her old habits. She's apparently been boy crazy since junior high, and it's led her to make some really unwise, too-adult decisions. I haven't seen her with any particular boys, but I think she's pretty good at sneaking around. I know I have to force a conversation with Susan... I just don't want to.

With a glance outside, I head to the counter and shout to Shannon, who is in the back at her new table. This seating arrangement makes it harder to communicate since I can't as easily make eye contact with her, but she's happy, so I'm happy. "Shannon, I'm going out to hear Missus."

"Okay!" she yells back.

Kimmy comes running up front, her red tennis shoes working double-time just like they do at Ruby's. "I'll step out with you. I got Libby to come in so I could go. It's kinda slow since it's our first day, but it's gone great, hasn't it?"

I have to agree, it really has. Ruby stayed down at the kitchen in her old place for the most part. Libby waited the new bookstore-based tables, and Kimmy ran back and forth between the two places. As for us at Blooming Books, we had fresh coffee and free muffins all morning, and now there's pie. Yeah, I realize that might become a problem for our waistlines, but for a first day it was good.

I pull the front door open and motion Kimmy through it. "It's not been as disruptive as I was afraid it would be. Plus, it smells so good. After Bonnie got her chair back and we bought Shannon her own, it's been kind of nice."

"What do you know about this sinkhole?" Kimmy asks me as she stops on the sidewalk to look that direction. "I did some googling and could it swallow like the whole town? I saw some that did that."

"No. Jackson explained this is just because of the pipe breaking not a natural one like they have in Florida sometimes. He says this is as big as it should get, however they're going to have to tear up more of the road and sidewalk he thinks." Bright orange cones and warning signs line the street. Behind them are two big pieces of equipment which arrived earlier today. There's also a stack of pipe on the grass in the park which is marked "off limits" with orange and white barrels and caution tape. It all feels very disruptive to our quiet little town. Behind the barricade Missus' house and Andy's Place peek over at us as if they're being held hostage. To get from there to here requires going behind the buildings on Main Street, like we are doing between Blooming Books and Ruby's, or crossing down the street at the other corner in front of the library and walking through the park. There's a steady stream of people crossing into the park from all directions so I prod Kimmy that we should get a move on.

Several rows of folding chairs have been set out, but they're already full. Kimmy and I join Alex Carrera and Phoenix beside a big tree at the back of the crowd.

Alex is sipping a smoothie from Phoenix's. He lifts it in greeting. "I ordered this for Phoenix to bring when she came. Figured it would help me keep my cool when Her Majesty starts talking."

Alex has fitted in so much better in Chancey than I could've ever expected. It's like his wealthy, city upbringing made him appreciate the simpler life.

I laugh at him. "We probably all need one, then, with a shot of something strong. Although I doubt she says anything except that she's trying to clean up everyone else's mess and that it'll be fixed as soon as is humanly possible now that she's in charge."

And that's pretty much how the next twenty minutes go. The Atlanta stations asked a few generic questions and got their generic answers, laced with tons of promises. The cameras got their shots of the Chancey mayor wearing her white gloves, which will play well in the city and suburbs. Just a small, Southern town with a classy grandmother at the helm. All in all, it was peaceful...

...until Charles stood up. At the same time, the young man next to him stood and began passing out sheets of typed paper covered in writing.

"Is that Bryan?" I ask, but it's only a rhetorical question. That most definitely is my son. "What's he doing here?"

Kimmy walks up to get a couple of the sheets of paper he's handing out. Bryan gives me a little smile and wave, but moves along with his duties.

"Wow. Look at this!" Kimmy gives Alex and Phoenix a sheet to share and lets me look on with her, but Charles's loud questioning distracts me.

"What do you say to the timetable put forth over a year ago for the repairs needed to the groundwater infrastructure? Is that still doable?"

Missus glares at him from the steps of the gazebo, where she's situated herself for the best possible photo op. "Charles, you and I can talk about this later. I don't even know where this alleged information came from."

"Then look at it. You'll see everything there is pulled right from the *Chancey Vedette* pages. All of it is public record. All of it has been ignored and has led to exactly the situation forecasted over a year ago. So, is that timetable still correct? Or will it be longer?"

The crowd gets louder as people peruse their sheets and find the aforementioned timetable.

"Six months!" I gasp.

Alex leans over, pointing even farther down on the page. "And look at the cost!"

Now everyone is talking and the news cameras have more to film than a stately-looking Southern mayor on the steps of her newly painted gazebo. Missus is flustered but still refuses to give any actual answers. She holds up both hands and declares the press conference over, then hurries to her car, cameras still rolling, reporters still asking questions. Once she's inside and pulling away, everything calms down. However, the reporters are still being filmed as they fill in their viewers on the "rapidly evolving situation." I don't think this will go away just because Madam Mayor left.

Phoenix is leaning against the huge tree trunk behind us. "Six months? Wonder if my insurance covers anything like this. Is it even safe for me to be in the studio or juice bar at all?" She straightens and looks around. "Where's Laney? She's got to be so upset. Poor thing!"

Kimmy, Alex, and Phoenix weren't here for the disastrous end of Laney's term as city treasurer, so they are allowed their innocence and their pity for their fellow business owner. They have no idea *poor* Laney isn't here for fear of fingers being pointed her direction.

And who am I to disturb their ignorant bliss?

"Well, I better get back to work," I say. "Y'all want to come have some pie?"

Kimmy jerks to life. "Yeah, I need to let all these people know!" She runs forward and shouts, "Ruby's pies are now available at Blooming Books. Chocolate, strawberry, and peanut are on the menu today, along with plenty of fresh, hot coffee. Come on over!"

We watch as the crowd does an actual swerve toward the front of our shop. Kimmy dashes ahead of the crowd, and I wave at Alex and Phoenix as I walk away. "Guess I better get over there."

"Mom!" Bryan yells as I start across the street. He catches up with me. "Can I get some pie?"

"Sure. What were you doing with Mr. Spoon?"

"I'm working on the school newspaper, and he needed some help."

"When did you start working on the school newspaper?"

We're almost to the sidewalk when he looks ahead and grins. "Susie Mae asked me to help out. You know she's on the school paper. Hey!" he shouts as his grins grows and he steps ahead of me.

I look up. Standing in the front window Susie Mae is waving at me. No, wait, not at me. At Bryan. And she's also smiling. Not in a cute friendly way, but a sexy, come-hither way.

Oh. Oh, no.

Oh, hell no!

Chapter 8

"It's not like I can say she needs to keep her daughter away from my son. I mean, she knows Susie Mae's past all too well. She's the one that told me about her and boys, but maybe it's not that. Maybe they're just friends; after all, he is two years younger than her. I know in some ways Susie Mae is very immature, so she doesn't seem that much older than Bryan, but she has been acting strange lately. What if he's just another feather in her cap? Just another boy for her trophy case? Not happening! Not. Happening!" Yelling at the windshield, since there's no one else in the car with me, is not very satisfying. After dropping Bryan off to help his dad at the day care remodeling, I'm driving on down the road to Silas's. Bryan talked a lot as we drove, but he said nothing important. He's good at that.

It is May. I do need some flowers. I also need to see if Susan is there, maybe feel Silas out for what's going on in their lives. I mean, I can't just rush headlong into a conversation like this with Susan about her daughter leading my young son astray. I've got to see the lay of the land. However, I am feeling a bit calmer, having yelled at the windshield.

Pulling onto the dirt road, I drive over the crest of the hill. I can see the greenhouses and the rows of potted plants and bushes outside, along with the nursery's truck and several cars. To my left I study Silas's house, a trailer set on a concrete slab, but it looks quiet. I creep the minivan forward, then turn toward the big building where most of the cars are parked.

This is where the market stalls and food court are going to be after the grand opening in a few weeks. Opening the glass doors to the building, I walk into an open, barnlike room with lots of shelves and display areas that had not been here the last time I visited. Toward the back corner of the room, next to the big windows overlooking the hill and the lake, is a kitchen with a counter and an empty space where I suppose chairs and tables will sit. Near the side door, talking to another man, I see Silas. He responds to my wave with a nod that says he'll be just a minute, so I walk over to the big windows. Outside, the hills are full of plants and people. Some are workers, but it also looks like there are buyers pulling wagons overloaded with plants behind them.

"Good to see you," Silas says when he joins me a while later. He places a hand on my shoulder and squeezes. "Can you believe this?"

"You've made it all happen." We're quiet for another moment, but then I can't wait. I inhale deeply and let it out on an exhale. "So what's with you and Susan? Is she here?"

He chuckles. "I knew there was something on your mind." He takes a step away, puts his hands in his front pockets, and looks at me. "She's at work, I assume. Her job, it's really keeping her busy. I wouldn't mind her working here, helping out some, but she never has time these days. Always working." He frowns. "And about our personal life, this is not like last time. I'm doing this right." He tips his chin up, then peers down his perfect, movie star nose to look me straight in the eyes. "I'm courting her. Her *and* her kids. I plan to be here for a long time, and I want a lasting relationship with her and her family. Her whole family."

Silas arrived with the movie crew last fall to shoot a made-for-TV movie in Chancey. Susan's marriage was unraveling, but instead of trying to hold the strings together, she dropped everything for the good-looking actor who fell in love with her and our town. She even wore his engagement ring for a bit before deciding she'd thrown her marriage away too quickly. But by that time Griffin had no interest in saving his marriage. Silas left, with his ring in his pocket, when the movie was over. But came back this winter to, as he says, "do it right."

"I thought you and Susan were back on track. Are you saying she's not spending all her time up here?"

"No. Actually, I rarely see her." He looks harder at me. "Why?"

"Her kids. Susie Mae and Grant are kind of on their own. Or seem to be. I kinda just assumed it was because their parents are preoccupied with their love lives. You know, you and her and Griffin and Athena." Athena moved to Chancey with her husband and a toddler and another baby on the way. However, they separated and divorced this past year. Griffin moved in across the street from her in the new-build neighborhood outside town, but they are definitely not *just* neighbors.

Silas lifts his hands. "That is not on me. Not this time. Like I said, if she wanted to work here some during the day, I'd be good with that. But as for dating we go out just the two of us one night a week, or at least I try to. She cancelled at the last minute last time. Then we spend one evening with the kids—again, when she can make time. Usually we just do dinner here as they like eating out on the deck and I'm really good at grilling steak. But that's it. No overnights."

"Really?" I can't help but repeat myself after no other response comes to mind. "I mean—really?"

"What do you mean the kids are on their own? Like when?" He leans against the window sash and folds his sun-browned arms. With the afternoon sun and hills behind him, it looks like a scene from one of his made-for-TV movies. His hair is longer than I've seen it before, but of course, it looks great on him.

I shake my head to try and clear my thoughts, but I can't make everything make sense. I throw up my hands. "You know, just forget it. Maybe I'm imagining things. I'm glad you're taking things slow. Ignore me." I lower my shoulders and breathe slowly as I look outside again. "So, when is the grand opening?"

"I don't really know yet. Everything is good with the plants, but this place, the shopping and eating area, is taking longer. That guy I was talking to is interested in parking food trucks here on the weekends, but if I'm going to have a kitchen here, I don't want to do that long-term. So many decisions to make and so much red tape to cut through." He grunts in frustration and stands up straight. "With acting I'm given my script, told where to stand and what to do. I mean, there's thought involved, of course, but not people standing around looking at me to make the big decisions. This being the boss thing is taking some getting used to. Honestly, I've been blaming Susan, but I don't have much free time either for social stuff."

"So Susan is okay with this taking-it-slow strategy?"

"Yeah, I guess. Especially since she's pretty upset with how much time Griffin is spending with Athena. That's why I was surprised when you said she's not smothering Susie Mae and Grant. It's weird for her to be blasting Griffin, then leaving them alone herself." He looks sheepishly down at the floor. "I guess we really aren't communicating that well. I just thought she was working more than usual."

"Maybe you're right." We walk to the big sliding doors on the side of the building, and we step out. "You do have an amazing piece of property with so many options. I'm sure it's overwhelming for one person to handle."

He looks over his domain as he nods in agreement. A man comes out of the first greenhouse and yells at Silas, then motions for him to come down there. Silas answers him, then turns to me. "It was good to see you. If I can help with anything, let me know." Then with a wave he jogs down the sloping gravel drive.

As I walk back to my van, I look at Silas's house, which has a great view of the nursery and the lake beyond. It is widely assumed that Susan is spending a good deal of time there. Like, pretty much every night. But Silas isn't a liar. It's easy to imagine an actor would be good at lying, and I'm sure some are, but he's not.

I lean against my open car door. It's been a rather warm day, and as the sun heads toward the horizon, it's cooling off nicely in the shade. None of this makes sense, and I need some time to think. A glass of wine on our deck sounds like the perfect space to think.

On the road headed back toward town one thought gets stronger and stronger.

Silas isn't a liar. But Susan?

Well…

Chapter 9

Looks like I won't be solo for my glass of wine on the deck. Laney is waiting on the front porch when I pull across the train tracks and up to our house.

"'Bout time you got here. You left town an hour ago." She's clearly disgusted with my failure to psychically discern her presence waiting on my porch.

Stopping on the steps to give her what I hope is the evil eye, I shake my head. "Where were you standing to spy on Missus's press conference? I knew you couldn't be far." I finish walking up the steps, but instead of joining her in my own rocker, I push the front door open. "Let's have some wine on the deck out back. It's too warm out here."

"That's why I'm out here. I was getting some sun on these pasty, white legs, but it's moving behind the branches. Well, I guess I can't have you drinking alone. Lead the way." She pushes out of the rocker and follows me in.

The house is quiet and warm. We don't have any guests booked until the weekend. Jackson and Bryan are still at work, and Savannah is at a friend's house. She's rarely home these days, as her senior year is winding down and her friends are all desperate to be together. Today was a much-too-early-in-the-year pool party.

"Jenna at Caitlin's?" I ask Laney.

"Yes. Her parents are actually paying to heat the pool for just today. They put in a heater, but it costs a fortune to run. Shaw says we ain't getting one. However, Caitlin getting into Georgia Tech called for a celebration, I suppose. Caitlin didn't want a whole big party with parents and all, just her friends. That's why I didn't ask Jenna and Angie's opinion on their party. I'm paying, so I get to do it how I want." She takes her filled glass and goes out on the porch.

I follow her out. "Savannah still says she's happy with a family dinner since all the grandparents are coming. Is Angie actually going to her own party?"

Angie and Jenna are twins, but that's where the similarities end. Jenna is going from a high school cheerleader and prom queen to the big state school at the University of Georgia. Angie, since turning eighteen in January, is living with her boyfriend, Alex, above the restaurant they run downtown, and she's very independent. I'm not sure how she's going to feel about a traditional graduation party. Jenna, on the other hand, loves a party, loves to be the center of attention, and loves presents, so we know she'll be there.

"Alex says they'll be there. You know, it started off rocky enough, but that boy is growing on me. I'm getting to that point you always hear about: 'If we break up, Momma and Daddy say they are keeping him, or her, instead of me.'" She sits up suddenly. "Oh, look! Goldfinches."

Down where my old garden stood, there are several bright yellow birds. They are picking at some weeds on the edge of the rest of the weeds.

She says softly, "You should get a feeder for them. I think it's thistle seed you put in it. They'll be all around."

I pick up my phone. "I'm going to put that on my list for Walmart. I've got to go out there sometime this week. My list just keeps growing! So, how did you know when I left downtown this afternoon? Where were you hiding and watching Missus's speech?"

"I wasn't hiding. I was visiting my daughter. Of course, she was still at school, so I was passing some time in their apartment. However, Alex was too busy with dinner preparations when he got back to talk. You know, to talk about the party. Of course that's why I was there."

"Of course," I say knowingly. "Just so happens their front windows look right over the park, but..."

"But I couldn't hear a darn thing she, or Charles, said. Did anyone mention my name?"

"You mean aside from all the folks saying, 'Poor Laney,' because of your shop being closed?" I drop the sympathy from my voice and go full sarcasm. "Funny, but those also happen to be people who weren't here for your term as treasurer."

She flounces in her chair and sniffs. "So I didn't want all my hard-earned winnings to go toward underground pipes. So what? I mean, it was a lot of work to win that much money." She flounces again, which is hard to do, unless you're Laney Conner in another new outfit I'm sure is from the stock of her store. The khaki shorts come almost to her knees, and her shirt is loose but tailored, with pleats at the shoulders. It's white with tiny stripes of red and khaki. Her shoes, once again a little too sensible for Laney, are red, canvas flats with woven hemp soles. She uncrosses her legs and looks down at them. "I think I've gotten a little sun. I'm really enjoying my time off."

I roll my eyes at her attempt to change the subject. "That's why you're sneaking around looking out second-story windows, right? Your role in the pipes not getting fixed?"

She snaps her head up. "Did she mention me or not?"

"No. Your name was not mentioned. Missus didn't say much of anything except she's going to fix everything. In private she's just like you, lamenting the fact that she has to waste her time and energy on mundane things like underground pipes. However"—I take a long sip of wine—"Charles Spoon was there with some old articles that say it could take as long as six months."

She groans and takes her own long drink. "See? That's why we didn't want to mess with it before."

"You knew? Y'all knew it was this bad?"

"Of course! You saw the article. It was in the paper, but I guess no one reads the paper anymore. And then about that time is when they found out where the money was coming from and I left city government. Jed's never really had a head for details, and well, it kind of just went away."

"Except it didn't."

She nods. "Except it didn't. And you're right. I miss my shop. I finally found something I really want to do, and I can't do it. I'm not good with being told 'I can't.'" With her big eyes wide, and a growing smirk, she looks at me. "However, I hear Ruby found a solution…"

"Temporary. A temporary solution."

We fall into silence, watching the goldfinches and other birds as we finish our wine. Laney scoots to the edge of her seat. "I'm going to take a few minutes to look over the B&B records. Quarterly taxes seem to be more like monthly with how fast they roll around. Then I need to pick Cayden up and get home to make dinner." She stands. "I forgot. I wanted to ask you if you had a chance to talk to Susan."

I stand, too, focusing on the birds. "No. Uh, have you two talked much lately? I mean, like, about her and Silas?"

"No," she says, wandering back into the kitchen. "Now that she's back hot and heavy with him, I don't ever see her. How's Susie Mae doing? I'm afraid she might be getting back into trouble, you know? At least that's what Jenna was saying. She said Susie Mae skipped out of school last week. Jenna covered for her, but I've told her not to do that anymore. Susie Mae's found herself another boy is my bet. Susan doesn't agree, though. She just blew me off, and I didn't want to get into it. My used-to-be-sensible sister, of course, has *other* things on her mind! It's like before: She's addicted to Silas." She growls under her breath and shakes her head.

Laney puts her glass in the sink and then walks back past me toward the little B&B office. All the while she's talking, so she hasn't noticed I've not said anything. Then she does. "Why are you just standing there?" she asks, taking a few steps back to look at me through the dining room doorway.

"I don't know. I'm not so sure—" But I get cut off by the front door opening.

"Hey, Mom. We're home!" Bryan yells, coming into the kitchen. "Dad told me to tell you Will is picking up barbecue for supper. Hey, Miss Laney!" He grabs a Gatorade out of the refrigerator.

"Where is your dad?" I ask.

"He's on the front porch on the phone. I'm going outside; it's hot in here. Why don't we have the air on?" He sails out the deck doors, leaving the stink of sweaty teen boy behind, when Laney's phone rings.

"Hello?" she answers. She listens for a moment, then hangs up and shoves it back in her pocket. "Cayden's running a fever. I'm sure he's just cutting a tooth, but Barb thinks I should pick him up. Did you know she's also watching a couple of other kids already? Your hubby needs to get finished building out that day care." Picking up her pocketbook from the kitchen table, she points a finger at me. "Talk to Susan and let me know what she says. I really don't want to get in the middle of her and Silas like I did before, but somebody has to. She won't get mad at you. Well, not *as* mad."

I hear her say hello to Jackson as she leaves, and I leave the kitchen to find my tired-looking husband leaning against the front door as it closes behind him. His work phone, as it often is these days, is clutched in his hand.

"What is it?" I ask him with a smile. "Who were you on the phone with?"

He looks down at the device and shakes his head. "Oh, that was nothing. Just placing an order at the hardware store. Bryan told you Will is bringing dinner?"

"Yeah."

"Well, Anna's coming too." He gives me a skeptical look. "They have something they want to talk to us about."

CHAPTER 10

"They couldn't just say, 'We'll bring over dinner,' and *then* tell us they had something to talk about *after* we've eaten? Nooo. They just *had* to get in a warning several hours in advance. Kids!"

I'm talking to my bathroom mirror this time. I seem to be talking to sheets of glass a lot today.

Jackson insists he has no idea what Will and Anna want to talk about. He said Will was fine while they were working, but that he did get a call as they were leaving. I wonder if Anna's pregnant again. They barely fit in their rural cabin with one baby, and wait till Francie starts crawling. She's not quite six months old and is already rocking on her hands and knees a little. Or, wait, is it too early for Anna to be pregnant again? What if she's being transferred? She's doing really well with the Dollar Store, and she's mentioned how she can't be a manager here, not with Kyle Kendrick filling that spot. I study my reflection and straighten another section of hair. I don't think he's moving. Or maybe he is moving, and she's going to be the manager here. Oh, but then Bryan will be devastated if Zoe moves away. Does he even like Zoe anymore? I was hoping he'd get interested in some other girl since Zoe is infatuated with Grant, but seeing the way Susie Mae looked at him, I'm fine with him liking Zoe. Man, was that *just* today?

It's been a very, very long day.

"Mom! They're here. We're eating!" Bryan yells from downstairs.

I look in the mirror. Only half my hair is straightened, and I'm not dressed. I blame the person in the mirror that kept me preoccupied. "I'll be right down!" I run the straightener through the other side, but only at the front, then hurry to put on jeans and a clean shirt. My work clothes are laying on the bed where I threw them earlier when I had plenty of time but was busy deciding what awful thing our son is coming to tell us. Why couldn't he just tell Jackson at work today? Why does he have to be so dramatic?

I catch a glimpse of the mirror on the inside of our closet door, and the woman there smirks at me. What is she trying to say? *I'm* not dramatic!

"I'm here; I'm here," I say, running down the stairs. "Grammy's here, Francie!"

Anna meets me at the kitchen door and gives me a hug. "She's showing her grandad her newest trick."

I peek in and see my clearly brilliant granddaughter seated on the table in front of Jackson, holding a sippy cup. "She's drinking from a cup?"

Anna laughs. "Kinda. She loves holding it and knows it's supposed to go in her mouth. One of the kids at the church's Mothers' Morning Out program had one just like that, and Francie was enthralled with it. I found her one, and it's her new favorite toy. There's just a bit of watered-down apple juice in it now, and every so often she actually gets a sip."

Will and Bryan come in from out back. My oldest, the one with news, says, "Hey, Mom. Did you see her with her cup? Isn't that great? We thought we could eat outside, but I think it's a little chilly. Well, it will be by the time we sit down. All we need are drinks. We went by Bobby Jack's and got barbecue, beans, cole slaw, and potato salad."

Jackson stands up while still holding Francie steady on the table. "Why don't I help with the drinks and Francie can show you her cup?"

The cutest face in the world watches her grandad get up, but she seems just fine with me taking his place. She pushes the cup at me like she wants me to take a sip. I laugh and pretend to drink, but my eyes are filling with tears. I can't believe they're going to move away. I'm going to miss everything with her. Her walking. Talking. Everything.

I pull my eyes from Francie long enough to examine Anna. She doesn't look pregnant, but then again, it could be too early to tell. She is wearing a roomy T-shirt, and her yoga pants stretch. "Oww!" The baby has bopped me, in my distraction, with her sippy cup, and I yelp loud enough to startle her. She puckers up, and I lift her to my chest. Yeah, I guess I should've been paying attention to her instead of missing her while she's still here.

Jackson's barely sat down at the dining room table before he's passing around the containers of food. "We don't eat at Bobby Jack's near enough. This all smells amazing." He bows his head, the rest of us follow suit, and he says a quick blessing over the shredded pork and fixings.

I'm having trouble concentrating on the prayer, though, too busy trying to figure out when and how I can ask what Will and Anna want to talk about. What if they say they want to wait until after we eat? Then how will I enjoy this? It does smell amazing. I catch the end of Jackson's prayer and mumble, "Amen," with the rest of my family.

Then Will lifts his glass of tea. "I'd like to propose a toast: to the newest science teacher at Chancey Middle School!" We all look at him, confused, so he adds, "Me! I'm talking about me."

Congratulations and laughter move around the table, which Francie accents by banging her cup on her high chair. Is this the end of their news? I'm feeling relieved, so I sure hope it is.

"I'll start in August when school starts," he says, "as a full-time teacher."

Anna speaks up. "Which gives us plenty of time to find a house!"

"Here?" I squeak. "A house here, in Chancey?"

They all look at me, confused all over again. Will finally says, "Of course. Where else would we go?"

I shrug and lean over to kiss my granddaughter's sticky, applesauce-covered face. "Of course Chancey. Right, sweetie?" She offers me her cup again, and I take a pretend sip. She's finished with me as she turns to her mama on her other side, but I bury my nose in her soft, fine hair and breathe in apple and baby shampoo.

Then, since I was too preoccupied to hear the blessing Jackson gave for our food, I say my own prayer under my breath. "Thank you. And well, sorry, God, for getting so far ahead of you. Again."

CHAPTER 11

"Of course I sew," Augusta answers. "Why?"

The newest resident of Chancey called me this morning, asking if she could take me to lunch. There is nothing I like better than lunch out on a Friday when I have the afternoon off, so I gave her an enthusiastic yes, and we are seated at AC's.

"Thank goodness," I respond. "Gertie wants me to hem her wedding dress. For some reason she assumes I can sew. I told her I can't and would be using duct tape, but she just laughed and called me a jokester before she left her dress at the store. Since then I've been trying to find someone that sews and has time. Have you met Gertie? She's a large lady, and this dress has a big skirt with a lace overlay. Duct tape will definitely not work."

Augusta laughs, hiding her mouthful of sandwich and her pink lipstick behind her hand. Yes, the nun look is gone. She's wearing lipstick, a little mascara, and her stick-straight bob is now a headful of curls. It's still gray, but she's thinking of dying it.

"I'll come by the store and look at it. I have met Gertie, and I think having her in my friend group could be a very good thing. I don't have my sewing stuff unpacked yet, but I can get it out this weekend. When is the wedding?"

I look around us. AC's is busy, but no one that would run

tattling to Missus is near us. Even so, I lower my voice, dip my head, and lean in her direction. "Next Thursday. A week from today."

"*A week*!? Is she eloping? And why are you whispering?"

"She's doing it, without permission, in the park. The gazebo. She and Missus have fought forever, and she doesn't think Madam Mayor would give her permission, so…"

"So better to ask forgiveness than permission."

I sit back. "Yeah, although I think it's more that she just wants to pull something over on Missus. I honestly think getting permission would be no problem, but I'm not getting involved."

"Except to hem her dress. By Thursday."

"Except that. Thank you for giving it a look. No pressure from me, but I sure hope you can do it. And thank you so much for lunch. This is delicious. How is unpacking going?"

"You're welcome for the hemming and lunch." August sets her sandwich down. "I wanted to thank you because, without your intercession, I would not be unpacking at all. I don't know how you got that woman's name and number, and I don't want to know—though I do have my suspicions, since she's a showgirl in Las Vegas and I think I remember a certain redhead here who used to work in Vegas. But I'm promptly forgetting that.

"Anyway, I wasn't sure if it would be enough to get my brother to let Gregory quit school and move here with me, but he folded almost immediately. I think he was actually looking for a way to back down without admitting he was wrong and giving in. His wife and daughter were working on him, I believe. I've always been good with Camille and Delaney." She closes her eyes and lets out a breath. "I barely got out of my mouth that I was planning on calling a friend of his from Las Vegas when he blustered that that wasn't necessary. He'd rethought his position, and if Gregory and I wanted to leave the life he'd lovingly created for us, he wasn't going to stop us."

When she reopens her eyes, they are so alive. So joyful. When she was here before, she'd been serious, focused. Now she seems lighter, possibly because she's shed her dark, nunlike clothing. She's wearing gray slacks and a light pink sweater. She has on bright, white tennis shoes and a pretty pearl-and-silver necklace.

"Can I ask why the change in your hair and your clothes?"

She looks down and smooths one hand down the arm of her soft, lightweight sweater. "When I moved to Aiken with a baby and no husband I came straight from the convent where I was in training, or whatever I thought I was doing. I'd left my fiancé practically at the altar, and his family was very well known in Charleston and Atlanta. I don't know if I would've become a nun, but I loved the peace and quiet and solitude after my crazy life and our huge engagement." She takes a quick sip of her iced tea. "He and I were the toast of the South, but I knew the whole time I didn't love him. That he didn't love me. We just kind of fell into it and then couldn't figure a way out. Everyone understood when I took a short trip to a convent for a weekend of solitude. They all just knew once I had a moment to breathe, I'd settle down and realize how fortunate I was to be marrying him. They were not so understanding when I stayed. Never went home, just mailed the ring back to him and... stayed."

She gives me a grimace. "Then Delaney got pregnant, and I was needed. Thompson set everything up, away from anyone we knew, and all I did was show up. Taking care of Gregory gave me a purpose, and wearing clothes like the sisters would wear was an extra layer of protection. No one in Aiken asked questions of a quasi-nun with a baby, and I carefully kept our distance from everyone. Of course we knew people, but… let's just say, I'm excited to make friends." She pats my hand. "Real friends."

The waiter comes to pick up our dishes, and we both order a cup of coffee. When he's gone, she pushes the sleeves of her lightweight sweater up and leans forward. "It was like my spirit was shut down until I came here last month. For the very first time, the dark clothes, the skirt, the black shoes, they all felt restrictive. Some of it is being out from underneath Thompson's thumb, I'm sure, but some of it is that I've done what I was supposed to do. I've raised a wonderful young man, and he is finally happy. I don't know that this writing project with Sally Blankenship is going to be everything he wants it to be, but it's a start."

"Yeah, about Sally Blankenship…"

She holds up a hand. "I believe I know who she is—well, who she has been. I hope, like me and Gregory, she's ready for another chapter in her life. I'm committed to being a person of second chances."

"Okay. Just keep an eye on her. She is well known in publishing circles," I admit, "so she can definitely help Gregory in that area."

Sally hasn't been back in town lately. She was staying with Silas when he got back together with Susan, so I thought that was why she left. Silas's trailer must have been a little crowded since Sally was actually sleeping with Susan's nephew Ronnie, who is at least twenty years younger than her, if I'm being generous. I really hope she hasn't set her sights on Gregory, but Augusta has been alerted, so I feel I've done all I can.

Our coffee arrives, and we both relax into the growing solitude of the restaurant. Others have left after their lunches, and the afternoon sunshine settles on our table.

"Enough about me," Augusta says. "I want to know how

you and Jackson ended up here and absolutely *everything* you know about Chancey."

I spurt out my first sip of coffee and then choke on my laughter. "You want to know *everything* I know about Chancey?" Laughing and coughing take over again before I pull in a long, calming breath and lay my hands flat on the table. I look her in the eye.

"No. You. Don't."

But I still told her enough over that cup of coffee and another. One story led to another and I think I gave her a pretty good overview of our time here. That and a couple good belly laughs. Then we strolled next door to Blooming Books, where the Friday afternoon pie rush was in full stride. I'd actually forgotten Ruby's had moved in until we opened the door and were hit with the sweet smells and loud chatter. It doesn't feel like my bookstore at all and that unsettles me a bit.

"Wow, this looks to be working out great," Augusta says. "So many book shoppers too."

Bonnie gives us a quick look from behind the counter. "You can say that again. Danny and I have been running our legs off. Susie Mae, too, once she got here." She gives me a pointed look. "She was late again."

Augusta motions that she's going toward the bookshelves, and I nod at her as I say to Bonnie, "I was just coming by to pick up something. Do you need me to stay?"

She hands the customer their bag, smiles at them, then turns her smile to me. "No. It's been manageable. Most people are just browsing and asking questions. Can't say what shape the shelves will be in tomorrow when you get here because they're carrying books around then leaving them wherever, so just be ready for that. I know I can't stay late to clean up, but maybe Danny—"

"No, he's got something with his girls tonight. It'll be fine tomorrow. I'll get here early." I go back to the office area, moving between diners and saying hi to Kimmy. She's really got this working smoothly. Then again, all she has to do is serve pie and coffee, and no one is ever in a real hurry. I mean, it's pie in the afternoon; it's the very definition of taking your time.

Gertie's dress is hanging from a shelf in our office area, and I'm struck again by how full the skirt is and how much fabric there is to be hemmed. It's solid pearl gray, both the underneath and the lace overlay, with three-quarter sleeves and a fitted, high waist that flares out to mid-calf. Well, I assume it's mid-calf, though she didn't try it on for me. She just pinned up a couple of places where she wants it hemmed to. I take it down, fold it over my arm, and hope, hope, hope Augusta says she can do it.

As I scoot out Bonnie's office door, I run right into Danny. "Oh, hey. I hear y'all have been super busy."

He nods quickly and sticks his hands in his back pockets. His hair falls into his eyes as he looks at me, bending down a bit. "Did you tell Ruby she could bring in those creepy dolls? She's got three tubs of them and wants me to help her put them around the whole place. Even up in the books."

"Oh, no way! They aren't going up in my area." I cringe. "Three tubs of them?"

He nods again, then lowers his voice. "And there's more where they came from, she says."

Shannon comes up behind him. "This about the dolls? Danny's a big scaredy-cat. I think they're great! I told her the more the merrier, and I've been the boss here longer than you, Carolina." She gives us both a disgusted look and goes back to her worktable.

Danny screws up his mouth with a sniff. "Well, that's not a good sign, is it?"

I move past him. "Nope, and if I were you, I'd start praying she's having a boy."

Chapter 12

"I'm not sure how we got out of going to Six Flags, but I sure am glad we did!" I say as I climb in our van to sit beside Laney on Sunday afternoon. Church service has just let out, and we offered to drive the Conners, so they are leaving their car behind as we head to a winery an hour or so away. Shaw and Jackson are in the front seats. The back seat is empty because all the kids are at Six Flags with the church youth group.

Shaw laughs. "I know how *we* got out of it: they no longer invite Laney. Not after she let the kids go swimming at Red Top Mountain when the beach was closed."

"It was hot!" she protests. "I was hot. We all had on shorts. What's the fun of being a chaperone if you can't make some of the rules?" She gets her seat belt buckled, then picks up a magazine she's brought along for the ride. "Besides, we've got Cayden to be involved with in a few years. I have to reserve my energy. Can you imagine how tired we're going to be then?" She shudders. "Mom's got him today. Now that he's with Barbara during the week, Mom enjoys having him occasionally. He was just too much for her more than one day at a time."

As we pull out of the church parking lot, Jackson looks at me in the rearview mirror. "You said Augusta doesn't need a ride?"

"Yep. She's riding with Gertie, and they left a while ago.

They wanted to get there earlier in case Bill and them needed any help setting up. I'd completely forgotten Bill played in a bluegrass band."

Laney chuckles. "I'm sure I never thought Gertie's mountain man was in a group worthy of playing at one of the wineries. The wineries around Dahlonega are classy—big money-makers with folks from Atlanta coming up here. It was so nice of Gertie to invite us."

Shaw turns in his seat to see us. "You said Gertie has a table for eight. Who besides us, Gertie, and Augusta is coming?"

Laney and I had already discussed that, so we shake our heads.

"Don't know," I say. "We tried to feel some people out, but no one said anything about a wine tasting. I thought it might be Susan and Silas. Did you see her at church today?"

Shaw's eyes flit to his wife's before he solidly turns back to face the windshield.

I lean toward my friend. "What's going on?"

She pulls her lips tight. "Susie Mae left school at lunch on Friday and didn't come back. Neither she nor her mother answered their phones. Griffin came down to the school, but he had no idea where his daughter was. I tracked my sister down finally, and she said she had been out of range for her phone, back in the mountains, looking at some property for the power company. Another green space thing." She waves a hand as though to dismiss this tidbit. "Anyway, she said she'd talk to Susie Mae about her delinquency, but she didn't seem concerned at all. It's like she's just given up on trying to corral her kids. Griffin acted befuddled, like he had no idea there was a problem. I'm beginning to wonder if she ever told him what all went on with Susie Mae in the past. I just don't know what's going on with her."

My stomach is not reacting well to riding on the curvy roads from the back seat. Or maybe it's—

"Bonnie said Susie Mae showed up late for work on Friday," I blurt out. "Was anyone else skipping school at the same time? You know, like, any boys?"

Laney slides her eyes at me. "Some boys were caught trying to duck out the other side of the football field, down toward the lake where the kids hang out."

I can't help it. I choke out, "Bryan?"

Her head snaps my direction, and I catch Jackson's eyes flying to mine in the rearview mirror. They both echo, "Bryan?"

Jackson adds, "*Our* Bryan?"

Laney shakes her head. "No. Bryan wasn't with them. It was seniors. Same guys as always. Why would you—"

She leaves her question hanging there, but Jackson adds, "Yeah, why did you ask about Bryan?"

It all spills out. "Susie Mae got him to join the school paper, and there was just something about the way she looked at him the other day. And the way he looked back. You know he doesn't seem as taken with Zoe as he was, and well, I'm worried. I don't know. I'm a mom. That's my job. To be suspicious. I like Susie Mae, I really, really do, but I don't trust her as far as I can throw her. Besides, she's two years older than him. He's just not ready for her." I gulp in a breath and turn away.

The ride is quiet for a while. The guys stare at the road ahead, Laney stares at the same page in her magazine, and I stare out the window, wishing I could cram all my fears back into my mouth.

Shaw clears his throat a couple of times, then finally lets out a sigh. "Guess a guys' night might be called for. You up for it, Jackson? I'll find out what works for Griffin and let you know."

Laney and I meet eyes and smile, but our smiles are only half ones.

If they're going to talk to Griffin, I guess that means we're supposed to fix Susan.

"Should've figured it was Patty and Andy," I whisper to Laney as we walk from the foyer of the stone lodge out onto the wide porch looking over the vineyard. We drove through rows and rows of grapevines, up to the top of the hill where the winery sits. One side is three stories high and looks to be where the work is done; the other side sprawls over the cap of the hill and terraces down a bit to offer fabulous views to guests. Porches, some open while other are covered, have comfortable seating for small groupings, with fire pits scattered throughout. The main level is for dining, and that's where we're being led to a solid, wood table for eight. Gertie, Augusta, Patty, and Andy are already seated when we arrive.

"Hello! We're here!" I say, and they turn away from watching the band setting up to greet us.

Gertie spreads her arms. "Welcome! So glad you could join us. Get your seats and we'll get started. The band doesn't start for a little bit."

As we get settled in, I mouth to Patty to ask if she's okay. She shrugs and nods weakly. She's eight months pregnant and looks so uncomfortable. Her yellow maternity dress seems cool enough, but there's a sheen of perspiration on her face. Andy looks like he's gained some sympathy weight, but he's beaming, full of energy. We have two babies due this summer with connection to our shop. Patti worked in the shop when she moved to town with her mother, who grew up here. Andy is the major supplier of our used books as well as the owner of Andy's Place where he resales all kinds of things. Savannah loves her job handling his computer sales. So much so she decided to major in computer graphics in college.

There are a few plucks of a banjo, and I look up toward the stage. I think I know which one is Bill, but three of the men are tall and lean with heads of gray hair, just like him. There's also a young woman and a younger, heavyset man.

I ask, "What's Bill play?"

"Banjo," Gertie says. "He's played since he was young. Real good at it. They're gonna play at the wedding, so I thought I'd invite some of y'all up here to get acquainted with the band. Gussie's idea."

Augusta—or Gussie, I imagine—is grinning. "Isn't this fun? I've never been to a winery. And I'm not sure I've ever heard bluegrass music live."

Gertie waves at a waiter as she says, "Figured we might as well make it a party. Now that Bill is moving to town, we need some friends our age to hang out with."

I feel rather than see Laney completely freeze at the thought that she's Gertie's age. Jackson can't choke back a laugh, so he covers it with a chest-racking cough. Thank goodness the waiter shows up, handing each of us cards with wines listed on them.

As we study our lists—well, I pretend to study mine; I really don't have any preferences when it comes to wine—I look around at the other tables. Beautiful charcuterie boards are on some of them, and I know we'll soon have one on ours. I can see a lower patio with fire pits, and one beyond it, dotted with empty picnic tables. Maybe it's for work retreats, or larger groups? There are people walking among the vines, and it's such a perfect scene. It reminds me of Silas's nursery, which returns me to my earlier, anxious wonderings: Where *is* Susan spending her time if not out at the nursery with Silas? Was she really at work Friday when Susie Mae skipped school? And where was Susie Mae? I can't buy that she was skipping school by herself. Should I call and make sure Bryan was there? They'd have already called me if my son skipped class, right?

I half-heartedly listen to the discussion at the table. Laney and Shaw have definite opinions on the wine. Jackson only knows what he doesn't like. Andy is throwing in little facts here and there, and I'm impressed by the general knowledge he's picked up since helping his mother-in-law with her moon-shine cave. Augusta and Gertie are talking low while looking at the band. Patty looks so exhausted she might as well be asleep.

The waiter comes back over, makes some suggestions, gets our requests, and then waves over a man carrying two huge boards of food.

Now I'm interested!

"It's fascinating how the wine truly does pair with certain foods," Augusta says.

There's a break in the music, so we're all talking. The boards are considerably emptier than they were when they were set down. It's a thought echoed by the others of us who thought all that pairing stuff was made up to sell wine. The wine, sunshine, food, and music have gotten us to a mellow state. Even Patty is enjoying herself. They brought her a non-alcoholic wine flight, and so she's gotten to share in our pairing talk. Plus, being fed usually makes a pregnant woman feel better.

Gertie has an empty glass of pinot in front of her and her chin tucked contemplatively on her fist. The band is taking a short break onstage, and she only has eyes for her fiancé.

"Isn't my Bill good-lookin'?" she coos.

Shaw lifts his glass. "And a mighty fine banjo picker. They are really, really good. We have some events coming up at the dealership I'd like to talk to them about. Have they played to-gether long?"

"Pretty near forever. They're all related somehow or 'nother. The one on the guitar? That's Joe, Bill's brother, and he's single."

She says "single" with a special lilt. I wonder what she's getting at until I realize Augusta is blushing.

"Augusta? What's going on here?" I ask with a grin.

I'm afraid she's going to crush her wineglass the way she's gripping the thin stem. She smiles and announces, "I have a date. A date with Joe."

Gertie nods. "Yep. We got to talkin' when she brought my wedding dress over to mark the hem." She looks to her side at her new friend. "That's what you call it, right? Markin' the hem? Anyway, I told her she needs to get out there and meet some men, so she's doing my hemming and I'm doing some matchmaking. There's a world of lonely men out there that are looking for a good woman, and I've got the skills to put 'em together!"

Then she puts a big arm on my shoulder while lifting her glass with her other hand. "Here's to good women and lonely men!" Our table is a little slow on the uptake, but her loud voice carries to the whole patio, and she's joined in a rousing cheer.

Jackson reaches for my hand under the table. Then, as he takes a drink, he says out of the side of his mouth, "Lord help us. Gertie Sampson is now a matchmaker."

The band starts up again, and I notice that Joe is sneaking a few smiles at Augusta as he plays. We finish the food on our table and have a round of coffee with tiramisu as we listen to the next set. Patty and Andy leave before the music ends as she's in need of a real nap, and then when the band begins packing up, we say our goodbyes to Gertie and Augusta. Apparently they're extending their afternoon at the winery so the date can happen here tonight. Augusta keeps grinning and looking at me with wide, excited eyes. I sure hope she has a good time. I never saw her being big buddies with Gertie, and well—never mind. I just hope she has a good time. Joe seems nice.

As we start back toward the main building, we see some

stone stairs leading down to the level where the couches and fire pits are.

Laney turns in that direction. "Let's check this out on our way to the car," she enthuses. We agree and begin to follow her, but at the bottom of the steps she stops, backs up a step, and turns to us. "On second thought, Griffin and Athena are down here, looking very romantic. Do we say hello or just go back the way we came?"

Both guys know they aren't being consulted, so they keep their mouths shut. I shrug, but say, "I think we should. Just real quick. Right?"

She thinks, then nods. "Yes. Otherwise, Gertie will probably see them and tell them we were here. Okay, we'll breeze by, but we'll say we have to leave to get Cayden. Let's go."

We end up chatting with Griffin and Athena less than five minutes before Laney moans. "Oh, we'd love to sit and talk with you, but we really have to get home to Cayden. Poor Grandma will be exhausted. He's getting to be a handful. You know how babies are!"

Back inside the building, Laney pulls her shawl over her bare arms. "Most times having a baby is a complete inconvenience," she observes. "It's nice when they can be an asset."

CHAPTER 13

I wasn't aware of the magenta proclamations plastering the whole of downtown until I saw the back of ours through Blooming Books' glass front door. As I slowly walk toward the shop, I have a feeling my peaceful, early Monday morning is about to be shot all to you-know-where.

When I say "early," I mean *really* early. Ruby isn't even here. The coffee hasn't been started. The sun is nowhere near the top of the mountains. But I couldn't sleep. Yesterday, after too much wine, food, and sun, I came home and fell asleep on the couch. I woke up long enough to welcome the kids home from Six Flags. Since they'd stopped for fast food and didn't need dinner, they retired to their rooms. They claimed they needed to do homework, but I think they went to bed early too. Jackson was in the basement, catching up on some work, so I fell back asleep on the couch, where I found myself near midnight, in a dark house, covered with a blanket. As I crawled into bed, Jackson mumbled that he had tried to wake me to come upstairs. No worries, I went straight back to sleep…

…until 3:30 a.m.

Knowing Ruby would be showing up at five, I decided to come to work for a little bit of peace and quiet. Now, there's this.

In bold, black lettering against vibrant purple, Missus's

proclamation reads: *Work is to begin on the drainage system this morning. There will be temporary water shutoffs, more road closures, and general discomfort, but all should be done—soon.*

Again, a whole lot of nothing.

"Nothing! She told us nothing! That woman ain't fit to run my grandma's pajama drawer!" Ruby declares to her latest table of customers. I don't even look up to see their confused expressions. Ruby keeps coming up with colorful things Missus isn't fit to run. They went from confusing to funny, to nerve-jangling.

"Her grandma's pajama drawer?" Danny shakes his head and laughs. "I'm writing that one down. She's funny." Then he turns to the task at hand. "Man, Andy sure brought us a bunch of books this week."

"Yes, he did, and I sure am missing our extra room to work."

I'm squeezed to the side and back of the main room. My card table is shoved against the wall between the store and Bonnie's office. I tried sitting with my back to the wall, but then I couldn't get out from behind it to help anyone when it was needed, and if I hit the table, the stack of books fell off it. It's pretty rickety, so being against the wall stabilizes it. That's something else I need at Walmart—a new card table. I mentally add it to my list since my phone is somewhere in the store where I can't reach it easily. My mind apparently doesn't do well with a three-thirty start, but I'm trying to muscle through these new books, even if Ruby's rants are not helping. Why can't she go bake some more muffins and leave a little bit of peace?

"What in the Sam Hill does this mean?" comes a roar from the front door. "Where's Carolina?"

"Back here, Gertie," I yell. "Go show her," I say to Danny. "And see if you can find my phone."

He unfolds from where he was bent down, organizing the new books to get them on the shelves. We spend so much time reshelving books now with the browsers and now we have to find places for all these.

"Here she comes," he says. "I'll leave y'all alone." Danny has admitted he's scared of Gertie, and I don't think he's not wrong to be—especially the way she sounds today. She's loudly grumbling all the way back here.

"There you are, Carolina. You know if you faced forward you could see what's going on? Here, let me show you," she says as she grabs the corner of the table. One shake and the stacks of books are crumbling. She stares at them for a moment, then shakes it off. "Sorry. But listen. What's this all mean for my wedding? It's in three days!"

I'm not surprised to see her holding her own piece of magenta paper. I stand and stretch, ignoring the books lying around me. "Gertie, you know as much as I do. You need to talk to Missus and find out."

"I can't talk to that woman. You know that! She's not got any business—"

I hold up a hand and stop her. "I know. Believe me, I know. I've listened to Ruby rant about her for the past two hours, and it's done nothing. I have work to do. Let me know what the mayor says."

Gertie whirls around and stomps off. Hmm, that's never worked before. Or have I never been so stern before? Maybe it's a new leaf for me. I need to stop worrying if people are going to be upset and handle things more firmly. I bend over to pick up the books I was working on, then stand, hands full, looking for a place to put them. This is just not workable. I've got to figure something out.

"Here. You need caffeine and sugar. Eat that." Gertie has set down a cup of coffee and a muffin in the one tiny open space to work on my table. She takes the books from my hands. "Sit down. I don't have all day. Now, what I'm thinking is you'll close early Thursday, and I'll use your shop for a staging area. What time does Ruby's pie stuff end? Wait—why am I asking you? I'll go ask her."

Then she's gone again, so I sit down, take a bite of muffin and a sip of coffee. Apparently I am easily, and cheaply, bought. But it's nice to be thought of. And she's right. The coffee and muffin do help.

She's back. "Four o'clock. That works good. You close then too. Bill and the band will park right here in front. I'm not sure how everyone is going to get from the park to Andy's Place and the Moonshine Cave for the reception, though, since the road is completely torn up between here and there. I mean, it's not impossible, but…" She pauses, and I wait because I know what's coming. I wait, and I eat my muffin. Cherry and lime, I think. I know that's one of Ruby's new flavors. Like a cherry limeade drink.

Gertie gets to the thought I knew was coming. "I know! We'll have the reception here! It's perfect, especially now that we have all the tables for Ruby's. This works even better. I'll go let Phoenix know. Thanks, Carolina. Oh, wait—do you know if Susie Mae has been practicing that poem? I'd like her to recite it from memory, not just read it. I tried to catch up with her up at the winery, but she slipped off 'fore I could get to her," she laments, already shuffling off. "Enjoy your muffin. I had Ruby put it on your tab."

Just as I decide I'm rid of the bridezilla, she's back. Leaning around the corner of a bookshelf, she give a little whistle to get my attention. "And get rid of them dolls before Thursday," she hisses. "Or at least tell Ruby to dress them up in fancy clothes.

One's wearing a cowboy getup." She shakes her head like she's never heard of anything so crazy.

She should stick around here a while longer if she really wants to see crazy.

And, wait, did she just say Susie Mae was at the winery?

CHAPTER 14

"You called that about the reception," Phoenix declares as she opens the front door of her house. "Come on in."

I haven't been to her house in a long time, but with her dance studio and juice bar closed, this is where she's doing business. And as I step inside, I have to admit it does look like a business. Her living room furniture has been shoved to the front corner of the room, and the big open space is lined with several folding tables.

"Welcome to catering central," she says. "It has everything I need to keep Chancey fed and, especially this week, Gertie happy." She folds her arms and fixes a grin at me. "How did you know the reception would end up at your place?"

"It always does. Besides, Savannah, who works over at Andy's Place, said Andy hadn't even begun clearing the main floor like Gertie wanted. With the road torn up, it actually does make sense. Has it thrown a wrench in your plans for the reception?"

She laughs and points me to a barstool in her kitchen. "No. I guess we're both getting used to the Chancey way. I set up catering with Bobby Jack's for barbecue the first day she asked me to do the food—that's what Bill wants for the reception. I'll be doing the serving and setting up, but there's no way I can make barbecue that good. I'm taking care of the chocolate fountain, and she knows I don't do cakes, so we're ordering one. It's not too hard working with these people if you ignore all the blustering and do what you know needs to be done."

I frown at the delicate cup of tea she's handed me. "I think I need coffee."

"No, you don't. You need to drink this, go home, and lie down for an hour." She points to a foil-covered pan on the bar next to me. "There is your dinner for tonight. Chicken fettucine, and I have a salad in the small refrigerator by the front door with your name on it. No charge. Now drink your tea."

I open my mouth to object to her charity, but she frowns at me, clearly thinking back to the slight meltdown I had—fueled by too little sleep and too much to do—when she stopped into Blooming Books earlier. I take a sip of the warm tea. "That's good," I admit. "So did you just want me to stop by to give us dinner, or can I help you with something?"

She grabs a dish towel and wipes her hands, then twists the towel nervously. "How's Colt? I care about him, but I know I can't contact him since I broke it off, and I—well, I was wondering how he's doing."

"You never did tell him?" I ask. "Never gave him the chance to decide?"

"No. No one should have to give up having kids when they don't have to. He wants kids; I can't have them. He shouldn't be saddled with my shortcomings."

"Phoenix," I chide her softly. "Let him make that decision."

She shakes her head. "I just want to know how he is. He still dating Alison Kinnock?"

I relent with a sigh. "As far as I know, but I haven't seen him much. He's back in an apartment, you know. You should have a real talk with him. Treat him like a grown-up, and don't make his decisions for him. You've had some space from each other, but you are not going to have any peace until you tell him why you broke up. Talk to him. *I* can barely talk to him now because he'll figure out that I know more than I'm saying." I finish my tea and stand up. "I need to get going. The tea was perfect. Thank you so much for our dinner, but seriously, let me pay you."

Her partial smile is tight, and sadness exudes from her whole body. "No. This one is on the house. Next time you can be a paying customer."

At the door she reaches down to pull a salad out of the small refrigerator, and I notice there are other containers marked with names.

"Looks like your business is going well," I say.

"It is. And I'm doing well too. I was just lonely earlier. I shouldn't have asked you about Colt. That's all in the past."

I step onto the porch with my bag of food. "If you say so. But you know what I think?" I lift my bag. "Colt would love one of your home-cooked meals. Maybe show up on his doorstep with food and talk. That's all. Just talk."

She folds her arms against her stomach and leans against the doorjamb. "Maybe. So I'll definitely see you Thursday for the wedding?"

"Definitely! Then again this weekend. I'm so glad you're helping with dinner for Savannah's friends on Friday night. Your salads will be so great with the pizza. And then you're coming up for the brunch Sunday, right?"

"Wouldn't miss it!" she says this as though she's intentionally trying to brighten her mood. "Now, you go take a nap."

The car is warm, and the tea has made me feel all cozy. Checking my texts I see that Savannah is working until seven over at Andy's Place. He not only brings in a lot of books for me on his weekend scavenging trips, he picks up a lot for their resale store. Savannah does the online cataloging, so she often works later on Mondays. Bryan is helping Colt at baseball practice, so he won't be home until after six.

Poor Colt. He doesn't have a clue why Phoenix broke up

with him. It's just so sad to watch them both be lonely. I know he doesn't look too lonely with cute, blonde little Alison all over him, but I liked him better with Phoenix. So I'm pretty sure he's lonely.

As I start up our hill, I tell my phone to call Jackson.

"Hey," I say when he picks up. "You at home?"

"Yep, just got off a call, so I'm finished for the day. Where are you?"

"Headed that way." I grin and speed up. "You feel like taking a nap, Mr. Jessup?"

There's no reason for everyone to be lonely.

CHAPTER 15

It's hot. Almost going to be ninety degrees today, and it's only mid-May. It's rare for us to get much above eighty during May, but yesterday a pocket of hot air billowed up from the South, and it's supposed to last through the weekend. Savannah is thrilled to have this weather for her girls' weekend as she's got plans to go kayaking, creek-walking, and generally spend every moment outside, introducing her Marietta friends to life in the mountains.

Gertie is less than thrilled.

She's come up with more ways to say she's hot than Ruby came up with for saying how inept Missus is at being mayor, but I actually have sympathy for Gertie—today is her wedding day. The air is not only hot; it's thick and muggy. There's no real threat of rain, but we're just not used to being hot yet this year, so we're all pretty miserable.

"We didn't really have to worry about closing at four for the wedding," Kimmy says, walking up to where I'm looking out Blooming Books' front window. "We ain't had hardly any customers except those construction guys who are here every chance they get. Folks are staying home where it's cool."

"I know. And even though the air conditioner is working its little heart out, it's still so muggy in here." I turn at the sound of scissors being slammed down on Shannon's worktable. "Poor Shannon. I hated being pregnant in the summer."

Kimmy gives me a nod. "It is not bringing out her better side. She's got Danny apologizing for breathing."

I lower my voice. "Doesn't help that Gertie keeps adding things for her to do with the flowers. I told her to tell her no, but she won't. She thinks it's a reflection on her limitations from being pregnant, not that her client is a bully. I think her mother is making her feel like she can't possibly deal with work once she has the baby."

Kimmy's mouth pops open. "What? It'll work out. We'll all help." She peters out, though, as she stares at Shannon. "Except she won't let anyone help." She cuts her eyes back at me. "Oh, no. Carolina, she might have a problem. She won't hire any help, will she?"

"Nope. I've tried on several occasions." I take a step toward the counter, saying, "One thing parenthood has taught me: accepting help is not a weakness." I swish around and whisper, "But I'm not offering it again. I almost got my head bit off already once today!"

Oh, and in case you were wondering how it went telling Ruby to either dress the dolls fancier or get rid of them? Well, I didn't mention it.

Did you really think I would?

"If you'd submitted the appropriate forms, I would've made sure the request for overtime work would've been rejected." Missus pulls off one white glove, then the other, lays them across her knees, and then reaches for her glass of iced tea. It's sweating onto the table on her front porch, and she shakes it to let the dribble run off before she lifts it to her mouth.

I'm standing close to the table; I think it's best to stay between her and the red-faced bride. Gertie's not blushing. And her red face most likely isn't even from the heat. It's pure anger.

Her plan to thwart Madam Mayor didn't work.

She yells from behind me, "Now you see here, Shermania! You shut off them machines this minute. Why, I can't even hear my own self talk; how am I to hear my wedding vows? And look at all this dust!"

The hot, heavy air now has a tinge of orange and tastes like clay. When the street work didn't stop at its normal time, we thought they were just trying to finish something up. But then five thirty came and went, so Gertie sent Andy down to ask what was going on. He found out the workers had been given permission to work overtime until nine p.m. After reporting this back to his mother-in-law, who was getting dressed in her rooms at Andy's Place, next door to Missus's house, he called me at the shop and said she was threatening to rush out, wearing only her robe, and confront Missus at her house. I flew out the back door of the shop and down behind the shops to get to Missus's first. Turns out anger makes Gertie fast. I got there only to find Gertie huffing up the front steps, barefoot and clad in a short, silky, lilac robe. I was also huffing, but was able to get to the porch first, where Missus was sitting, watching over her kingdom.

Missus sighs. "Yes, the dust is something awful." She takes a nice, long drink of her tea while Gertie and I try to control our ragged breathing. "Oh! I'd offer you ladies a glass, but I know you have a wedding to attend."

I turn and pat Gertie's arm. "She's right. You go finish getting ready, and I'll figure something out." I notice the growing looks we're getting, not only from those arriving for the wedding, but from the work crew. I'd lower my voice, but I can't and be heard over the machinery. "You don't want Bill to show up to see you out here in your robe, do you?"

She looks down, and her hands fly to pulling the two sides together. A look behind her at the watching workmen hastens her decision to leave, but not before she scowls at her nemesis. "This is just mean. Just pure-D meanness!"

One of Madam Mayor's eyebrows arches. "Rules apply to all. I was elected to uphold the rules that keep Chancey functioning," she states loudly as Gertie hurries back down the porch steps.

"Missus, you know—"

She stops me with a raised hand until Gertie is on the sidewalk headed home. "Of course the machines will be stopped in time for the wedding. You see the gentleman on the top of that yellow thing with the front bucket? In the blue hardhat?"

I see who she means. "Yes."

"He's waiting on my signal." She waves the hand she stopped me with. The hard hat nods at her. He turns to the crew below him, and the sound stops. The half-dozen men all begin wandering off the jobsite. The silence is a relief, and it's like I can already feel the grit leaving the air.

"They aren't working until nine?" I clarify.

"Of course not." She stands. "Now, I need a bath and dinner, and you have a wedding to get on with."

At the bottom of the porch stairs, I'm nearly run over by Andy, who is practically in tears. "I'm going to beg Missus; that's what I'll do! Whatever she wants, whatever I can do for her!"

"Andy, stop. It's over. The workers are going home."

He looks from me to Missus's closed front door and then back at me again. He takes in the quiet work scene with some appreciation. "That's why I called you, Miss Carolina. You're the only one she'll listen to."

He starts, scurrying back down the sidewalk, and I call after him. "Andy, that's not what happened..."

"Yes, it is! Miracle worker, that's what you are!" Him yelling into the fresh silence seems especially loud. At the stairs to his shop, he turns back to me and shouts, "That's what I'm going to call you from now on—the Missus Whisperer!"

"So do we *all* have to call you the Missus Whisperer now?" Jackson slyly asks. I slide into the seat beside him and roll my eyes at his quip.

Everyone is seated in the park facing the gazebo. Augusta and I were helping Gertie and Patty get ready to come down the aisle. Now I hear the fiddle start to play the song that means it's time for Patty, so we turn to watch her progress down the aisle.

The poor thing looks so hot, and that pink dress isn't helping. It's not a great color with her peaches-and-cream fairness, and it just makes her full cheeks look fevered. She's even more pregnant than Shannon and is moving really slowly. She tried everything but early labor to get out of being in the wedding, but we all know how that ended. She gets to the gazebo, where Andy is waiting to perform the ceremony for his mother-in-law. He's accompanied by the groom, Bill, wearing a gray suit and tie, and his brother Joe, who is serving as best man. Patty takes her place on the bridesmaid side of the aisle as the music shifts to the wedding march, and we all stand.

Gertie stands at the bottom of the aisle. Her pearl gray dress falls to mid-calf, just as I guessed, and the full skirt sways in the merciful evening breeze. It is a good style on her, and Augusta got her to wear makeup, which I don't believe I've ever seen on Gertie. Her short, steel-gray hair couldn't have given Augusta much to work with, but it's puffed up a bit, and she's wearing a kind of headpiece, not quite a tiara, but there are silver and pearls. It's tasteful and actually kind of pretty.

When Gertie gets to Bill, their smile is private and sweet.

I sit down, and even though I'm burning up, I weave my arm around Jackson's, leaning so my lips reach his ear. "Yes," I say.

"Yes, you'd marry me again?" he asks with a wink.

"Yes, you have to call me the Missus Whisperer."

Chapter 16

"Why didn't you come down last night?" I ask Shannon as I ease up to her worktable.

She's sitting down but already looks tired and doesn't answer me.

"We missed you at the reception," I try again, adding a big smile. "The flowers were just stunning. Everyone said so."

She sighs. "Thanks. It sounded fun, but I went straight upstairs after the wedding because I knew I had all this waiting for me." She's bent down, and all I can see is the top of her head shaking back and forth. Her voice is husky. "What's wrong with me doing a wedding the week of Mother's Day? I'm an idiot!"

It's kind of hard to see her behind the piles of ribbon, oasis foam, containers, and greenery on the table. "You're not an idiot, but yeah, it is a lot." I pause, then bravely ask, "Is there anything I can do to help? I'm here all morning."

She shakes her head again. "My mom's coming, and, well, I finally bit the bullet. I hired Brittani Bennett to help out this afternoon."

I groan, and apparently that's the sound to make if I want her head to snap up. "Oh, get over it. So she and Bryan have a history. You live in a small town now. Get used to having a history with everyone and everyone else knowing all about it." She looks back at the ribbon she's tying and grumbles, her voice growing thick, "And throwing it in your face every chance they get."

Could this be about Peter and the baby? I wait, but she's quiet. "Can I get you a muffin?" I offer. "Libby just brought in a big box of them. I bet they're warm. Some tea, maybe?"

She nods quickly without looking up. I move toward the back, where Libby is working. I do my best to avoid actually looking at the dolls, which hover just above eye level. They are rigged to hang on the walls without a shelf, and it makes them look creepier than normal.

Eyes straight ahead, I say to Libby, "Good morning. Those smell delicious."

"We're calling these Berry Blast," she announces for all to hear. "Ruby's bringing some over in a bit with a cinnamon sugar drizzle on them. If I were you, I'd wait on one of them."

"Maybe I will, but can I get one of these for Shannon? And a cup of tea. Mother's Day week is rough for a florist." I speak softly, trying to get across to Libby that she doesn't have to yell. She's decided to just yell all the time it seems and not wait for the construction noise.

"And being pregnant on top of it," Libby commiserates. "Whew! Sure, let me get that. Oh, and your order for the weekend will be ready soon. Didn't want you to think we'd forgot."

"Thanks, Libby. Pies, too?" I'm practically whispering and add hand signals trying to get her to talk quieter. To no avail.

"Yep. And the peach cobblers for Sunday will be ready to be picked up tomorrow afternoon." She grins as jack hammers begin in the middle of her sentence, adding, "See? Saves me from having to repeat myself!"

"Perfect. Just perfect." I open a tea bag and set it in the cup so she can pour boiling water over it. Then I yell, too, "I think I have all the food covered for the girls—mostly junk food and some healthy snacks. The pies will be dessert all weekend. For Sunday's brunch I have quiches in the freezer that I picked up in Canton a couple of weeks ago. Phoenix is doing the pizza and salad for Saturday." I add a smile to my rundown. "I can't help but think how something like this weekend would've been so beyond me when I first moved here."

She laughs. "But we wouldn't let you off the hook. I remember carting my wedding dishes up to your house and getting there early to make the coffee for some such event we forced you to host."

I join her laughing. "I couldn't believe people actually owned those huge thirty-cup coffee makers! And now I have my very own." I take the cup and small plate. "Thanks, Libby. This looks perfect."

She stops me with a grip on my arm. "Aren't you worried about having all them girls up there at your place this weekend? What with us having a Peeping Tom now?"

Well, this is entirely unwelcome news. "What? Where?"

"Been seen several places is what Ruby was saying. She has a police scanner, you know. They didn't catch him." She shakes her head, then nods at the plate in my hand. "Better take that before the butter completely melts."

Walking through the tables I see everyone heard Libby's talk of the Peeping Tom and I see a lot of surprise on faces. I guess it's not common news. Well, it wasn't...

Things seem just as dire as before at the flower workstation, and I choke back my desire to ask what Shannon might know about the Peeping Tom. Hard to believe she didn't hear Libby, but she looks preoccupied. "Here you go. A Berry Blast muffin." I set the plate and cup down where she's cleaned off a spot. "Libby put a pat of butter on each half. Lots of berries, I guess, this time of year."

She sighs. "Yeah. I can't believe it's into May. The baby will be here soon, won't it?"

I lean over the end of the table, my head close to hers so we can hear each other. "Yeah. And I know it's scary, but you'll do just fine. We all want to help if you'll let us."

A tear drops into her tea. "It's a mess, isn't it? How can we have a baby upstairs? How can I keep working? But if I don't work, how will we live?" She peeks up at me. "Danny is, well, sweet, but..." She shrugs and pinches a bite off her muffin. She puts it in her mouth and then mumbles, almost as if she hopes the muffin will hide what she's saying. One word is clear, and it confirms what I was wondering. She repeats it with a shudder in her bottom lip: "Peter."

"Have you and he talked?"

She shakes her head, then whispers, "My parents don't know that he's the, uh, the..."

"Oh, come on." I get loud. "They have to. I mean, every—" I interrupt myself and clear my throat, lowering my voice again. "Well, then maybe you should talk to them before someone else does. Look how well Danny is handling it all. He'll help you talk to them.

When the upstairs door slams and we hear Danny coming down, we stop talking. Shannon takes a deep breath and says loudly, "Thanks, Carolina, but I've got it all under control. Everything is fine!"

Having been dismissed, I walk toward the front of the shop as Danny joins his wife and takes a bite of the muffin, exclaiming in his enthusiastic way how good it is. Shannon's parents do have a tendency to stick their heads in the sand, but surely in their hearts they know who the baby's daddy is. Shannon was living with Peter Bedwell when she got pregnant. Everyone knows the baby is his. Although, now that I think about it, apparently everyone knows but them—and Peter. The one time I asked Peter about it, he said that until Shannon tells him, he isn't thinking about it.

Wonder if he knows that Missus is already planning a paternity test?

"I'm surprised you're here. Aren't Savannah's friends coming today?" Laney says as she bustles through the shop, headed back to Ruby's. "Come have coffee with me?"

I chuckle at my friend's mile-a-minute banter. "For a second," I say as I follow her. "I'm just here for the morning—I'm taking the rest of today and all of tomorrow off. Listen, do you know anything about the police getting called for a Peeping Tom last night? Libby says, according to Ruby's police scanner, he was seen in several places. I just heard from Savannah that Amanda's mom and dad saw him! Of course he was gone by the time the police got there."

Laney perks up. "In their neighborhood? She lives out where Griffins lives, right? I haven't heard a thing."

We move through the tables as we talk. I try to keep it quiet as I say, "No one else has heard anything either." Luckily sound from the construction crew has ceased. Probably because four of the men are seated at a table enjoying big mugs of coffee and muffins. They have become regulars and Libby loves talking to them. They don't stop in the bookstore yet so I haven't gotten to know them.

"Well, that's creepy," Laney murmurs, "but it's probably some misguided boy with a crush on Amanda. Although it's not like when we were growing up and boys didn't have any other way to see girls except getting their hands on a girlie magazine. With the internet they don't have to risk getting caught by a dad with a shotgun." Her smile grows. "We had a couple of Peeping Toms when I was growing up. I didn't mind; I always did like an audience." She winks, then says more loudly, "Speaking of having an audience, what's up with the dolls? You seriously let Ruby bring these serial killer dolls in here and hang them on the walls?"

100

"Please don't talk about them. I'm ignoring them. They don't exist. I hadn't thought about it but we also had Peeping Toms when I was growing up and we never worried about them. It was always some neighborhood boy, but now it's scares me. " I take a deep breath and shake it off—for now. "What are you out and about so early for?"

"Party planning. Invites are going out today." She sits, then plops a big shopping bag on the chair next to her and starts digging in it. "Here, I'll just give you yours. A week from to-morrow. It's going to be huge!"

I open the shiny, white envelope with the hot pink lining. Of course, the table is instantly decorated with silver and gold confetti in the shape of graduation caps and stars. "Laney. You did the confetti? You hate this stuff."

She gives me a smug smile. "I figure if I have to clean it out of my own carpet, I'll return the favor. Besides, it makes the invitation so festive. Read it!"

"Wait. There's, like, two different cards?" I look up. "Is it two parties? On the same day?"

She's beaming. "Yes, siree! We'll have a pig roast in the af-ternoon, then a break for everyone to change clothes and rest, and then a DJ and dancing all night! How about that for the biggest graduation party ever?"

"So we'll go home to change?"

She snatches the cards out of my hand. "No, silly. Look right here: It says there will be lounging by the pool, a slumber tent for resting, and changing rooms in the house. It's like a house party."

I gape at her. "It's like *Gone with the Wind*. You're thinking of *Gone with the Wind*. Remember who my parents are? *Gone with the Wind* fanatics, so you can't fool me, Scarlett. Does Shaw have any idea what you are planning?"

She clouds up like only a Southern belle beauty queen can. "I deserve this. My girls deserve this. A whole day for them, and a night too." Her eyes drift off. "Just imagine: the white tents on the grass, everyone full from barbecue, men playing horseshoes with drinks in hand while the ladies take a rest and gossip."

"Aww, yes, ma'am," I say, deepening my accent. "We will get a respite from our corsets and crinolines. Why, Miss Scarlett, it's so nice of you to provide us a little time away from the gentlemen."

Her eyes slide back to me and my fake Southern accent. "Are you making fun of me?"

"I'm trying to get you to come back to your senses." I lower my voice. "This will cost a fortune. To heck with Shaw, do the *girls* know what you're planning?"

She tosses a hand out, fiddle-dee-dee style. "Oh, they're too busy to get involved. Besides, I'm throwing it *for* them, not *with* them."

Danny shouts my name from up front, where some bookstore customers are waiting.

I push away from the table. "Listen," I tell Laney, "I've got to go help him out, but you need to think about this and talk to Shaw. And the girls! Do not send out these invites." Before I walk away, I look down at the cards again. "A week from tomorrow? Can you even get all that together in just a week?"

She bites her lip, and I see the first blush of doubt cross her face. "I already did. I already paid deposits."

I shake my head and walk toward Danny and his frantically waving hand.

Shaw is going to kill her.

But the rest of us will have fun.

CHAPTER 17

By the looks of our backyard on this perfect Saturday night, Savannah's concerns about her friends mixing have been marked null and void.

Friday the girls from Marietta arrived and closed themselves into the B&B wing. They occasionally ventured out for another tub of ice cream or sodas and a family-size bag of chips. There were sporadic shrieks of laughter or bumps on the walls followed by screams. The threat of a Peeping Tom has proven absolutely titillating to the girls, so there are lots of screams as they walk past windows or peek through curtains, followed by more laughter. After the first set of extra-loud bumps, Jackson, Bryan, and I determined they were doing cheerleading stunts and dancing. There are five girls, including Savannah, and they are her closest friends from her growing up years in Marietta.

One is going to the University of Georgia, but the other three are rooming together at Kennesaw State, a large university near Marietta. It's grown tremendously in the last ten years, now having over forty thousand students and two large, sprawling campuses.

We have no idea what time the girls went to bed on Friday night because they weren't even sure themselves when they finally rolled out late this morning to sit on the deck in the sunshine and have coffee and Ruby's muffins. That lasted the better part of an hour before they were up and scurrying around to go exploring for the day. Savannah had arranged kayaking on the river north of a mountain town called Blue Ridge along with shopping in Blue Ridge's downtown boutiques.

Laney would've been so jealous with how they piled back in the house looking for afternoon naps. (It's all the rage, I've heard.) I even found myself with a quiet hour to read on the porch. Jackson and Bryan were working with Colt in town, purposely staying away from the house until it was time for hot dogs in the backyard.

Now the bonfire is going strong, and every teenager in town seems to be around it. Luckily the older guys, namely Ricky, his brother, Ronnie, and their friends have not shown up. I'm glad Bryan stayed in town with Grant. We've made sure they are sleeping at Griffin's and not pulling any shenanigans. Shaw and Jackson haven't talked to Griffin yet about the issues with the kids, but Jackson says Griffin understands the boys are his responsibility tonight. They also think the Peeping Tom is a huge joke, and last I heard, they were talking about laying traps for him.

I lean my head on Jackson's shoulder as we stand by the back window, looking out over the backyard. "It's great to see her so happy. She's having a blast."

He nods, pointing out our daughter throwing her head back in genuine laughter. "She said they were all enthralled with the mountains and that kayaking was great. They saw the train take off in Blue Ridge, and now they want to know all about it. Maybe come up and ride it one day."

"We need to ride it again soon," I say and earn a squeeze from my husband.

"Everything set for your brunch tomorrow?" he asks.

"I think so." I tick my to-do list off my fingers. "Phoenix made extra salads to go with the quiche. You picked up the cobblers from Ruby's. All that's left is setting the tables tomorrow." I pull away from him and head to the living room. "Want to put on a movie? I figure we'll have some kids out there to send home around eleven thirty, but I'm not planning on making the girls come in until they want. It's going to be a long night for us."

He joins me on the couch. "We probably need an action movie to keep us awake, right?"

"Sure. Put on whatever you want." I can't help but grin at how tickled he looks. I stretch to give him a kiss. "I love how easy you are to please!"

That earns me another squeeze as Bruce Willis appears on the screen. Jackson kisses my ear and whispers, "And there are five Die Hard movies, so we'll be good for a long, long time!"

"I can't believe how smoothly this weekend has gone," I say as I take my seat next to Phoenix out on our deck on Sunday afternoon. Across from me at our table for four is one of the moms from Marietta, Jean, and across from Phoenix is Missus. Delaney called earlier to see if she could invite Missus. Delaney realized only this morning that Missus hadn't been invited and she was having trouble coming up with a way to get out of the house without her. I'm having trouble convincing Missus I simply forgot to invite her, but I honestly did. I meant to invite her. I promise!

"I can't eat any of the peach cobbler, although it looks delicious," Missus says. "My son and grandson are taking us out for dinner later. For Mother's Day, you know. It's Gregory's first one to spend with us."

"Really?" my friend from Marietta says. "That sounds like an interesting story."

"It is. But it's private," Missus responds with barely a look at her. "Carolina, your garden looks a mess. What are your plans for it? It's quite unattractive for someone trying to run a business."

"I don't have any plans for it," I say as I get up from my seat. Okay, so maybe I didn't *forget* to invite her.

"Oh, quit being so sensitive," she protests. "You should have all that worked out by now. We don't hide behind masks and prettied-up words like they do down in the suburbs." She leans to my friend, Jean. "It's a different world up here. You wouldn't understand."

Jean's mouth drops open, but Phoenix gives her a sympathetic look. "Ignore her. We all do."

"Except in all this supposed ignoring, my townsfolk overwhelmingly elected me mayor." Missus sniffs. "I think I'll use the powder room." She stands and then says to the next table, "I might as well go now as I can't have dessert. My son and grandson are taking me out to dinner." Delaney, who is at that table, just shakes her head.

"Delaney," I join in, "would you help me serve the cobbler? I mean, since you can't eat dessert as your son is taking you out for dinner," I say as we walk into the kitchen. We laugh, and she peeks down the hall to make sure Missus isn't in earshot.

"She's being insufferable, isn't she? But about our upcoming dinner, I took to heart what you and Laney said, and I point-blank asked Peter what he planned to do for his mother. It was one of the few times I've seen him speechless. Then I got really bold and said he should check in with Gregory, as he might be planning something for me. That took even longer for him to connect." She rolls her eyes and pinches off half a croissant, which is sitting on the pan where I'd toasted them. She spits, "Men!" as she takes a bite.

"Well, it's made Missus's week. Her year. But thanks for bringing her. I should've remembered to invite her, but I had the girls and their moms on my mind." I have my back to her as I arrange the bowls of cobbler on a tray.

"And the ones you felt sorry for," she adds, "me and Phoenix."

I startle and stumble on my words, but she gives me a quick hug from behind. "I appreciate it. It's hard being a mom but not being a mom, you know? Anyway, what's Phoenix's story? I know I'm being nosy, but something seems different about her."

Turning around, I shake my head at her. "Nope. Nothing. Nothing's different. Here, take that tray outside, please."

Delaney cocks her head at me, then shrugs. "Sorry. It's really none of my business."

I pick up my own tray. "No apology necessary. Seriously. There's nothing to be sorry about."

I follow her outside, and we make our way around the tables, passing out dessert. It's hot, but we're in the shade, and a breeze has developed this afternoon, probably ushering in thunderstorms later tonight. Some of the storms are going to be severe, so I want to make sure everyone gets on the road and home before the clouds open up.

Plus, although it's been a wonderful, fairly easy weekend... I'm exhausted.

CHAPTER 18

"This *is* our Mother's Day gift," Susan says with a laugh as she pulls the fitted sheet off the bed in the Chessie room. As I said goodbye to the moms from Marietta and the girls all got their bags in their cars, Laney and Susan cleaned the kitchen. By the time I got inside and closed the front door, they'd moved on to the B&B rooms.

"What? Cleaning up my house is what your kids gave you?" I ask as I grab a pillow and take the case off.

"Nope, the rest of the day. We're going to get all this cleaned up, then hang with you." Susan smiles as she passes me in the hall, her arms full of linens. "Jackson has been instructed to not come home until later with Bryan. They are all out at the lake fishing with Griffin and Grant. Savannah won't be a problem; as you know, she's probably already asleep upstairs."

Laney hollers from the dining room. "I'm going to put a load in the washer. Just throw the other linens down the basement stairs."

"Well, thanks," I tell Susan. "This is a huge help, and I'd love nothing better than to sit and visit with you two. Come on, there's peach cobbler and pie left." What a great chance this will be to have a heart-to-heart with Susan. No interruptions and we're all in a mellow mood.

The rooms are really not that messy. The girls did some

policing as they packed this morning, since they knew their moms would want to look at the B&B rooms. Susan carries a full basket of linens downstairs while I put on a pot of coffee. The rain is starting, so there'll be no sitting on the deck. I put away the dishes my friends have washed and left out to dry, then start the very full dishwasher, pull out the leftover pie and cobbler, and set out some disposable bowls—the best kind of dishes to use on Mother's Day.

"Oh, that coffee smells wonderful," Laney says as she and Susan come up the basement staircase. "It's been too long since we've gotten to just sit and visit." With a couple whispers while working, Laney and I had agreed it's a perfect time to talk to Susan. So we're on the same page.

A rumble of thunder from far away greets us as we carry our dessert and coffee into the living room. "Just ignore me if I fall asleep," I say, sitting on one end of the couch. "We were up late. We sent the local kids home a little before midnight, but then we stayed up until we were sure the girls were settled in. They weren't nearly as rambunctious last night as they were Friday. I think the long day had them tired."

Laney puts her feet up on the coffee table. "Sweet girls. Their moms too. What a great idea to get us all together. Jenna really hit it off with the girl also going to UGA. Susie Mae seemed to feel a little out of place since she's only a junior," she says, as innocently as she can. "How's she doing?"

Susan shrugs and plays with the crust on the tiny piece of pie she chose. "Okay, I guess. Don't see much of her since she's working so much."

"But—" I begin to object. Susie Mae isn't working as much as I'd like her to, and when she does, she comes in late.

However, Laney gives me a "shut up" look as she asks, "So it's work? Not a new boyfriend?"

Susan looks away from her pie and at her sister. "Why? What have you heard?"

"Me?" Laney says. "Nothing much, just wondering if she's seeing someone new and what you think of him." Susan's frown deepens and her shoulders stiffen so Laney pulls back and changes direction. "Susie Mae did a lovely job with the reading at Gertie's wedding. I was surprised she was asked."

"Me too," Susan agrees after a pause in which her face softens and she takes a breath. "She told me she and Gertie talk at the shop? I guess I didn't realize Gertie comes into the bookstore that much."

I nod. "Gertie listens to the true crime podcasts, and I guess there's one Susie Mae follows, too, or whatever you do with a podcast. They are forever going on about it. That's really all Gertie would stop in for before Ruby's moved in." I take a bite of cobbler and decide to try again. "Susie Mae seems to enjoy talking to adults. She and Augusta have hit it off, too. Why do you—"

"Which reminds me," Susan interrupts me, sitting her uneaten pie on the side table. "That's another strange friendship, Gertie and Augusta. Drinking wine and giggling with their dates like schoolgirls on break. I'm surprised Augusta wasn't here today."

"I invited her, but she said she was busy."

"Really? With what?" Laney asks as she sets her empty plate to the side.

"Didn't say. I've noticed she doesn't feel a need to explain. She just says, 'No,' and that's it." I sigh. "I sure would love to develop that secret power. Maybe it's a former almost-nun thing. Can you imagine not feeling like you have to explain yourself?"

Laney grins. "I just lie. So no worries there."

"We know," her sister says with an eye roll. "I don't have to make up excuses or explain these days. I'm too busy to say yes to much of anything."

"Busy with Silas?" Laney jumps in.

"Sure," Susan answers with a shrug.

Laney frowns. "And where did you see Augusta and Gertie drinking wine and giggling? I mean, other than up at the winery? But you weren't there that day."

Susan starts, then shakes her head. "Oh, I don't know. So you had fun at the winery?"

"*Were* you at the winery?" Laney pounces with that sibling radar I've heard about. "Sounds like you were there."

"Why would I be there? I told you, I'm busy," she snaps. She looks down at her cup, running her finger along the rim.

I wait a minute, but she doesn't say anything else. This is too much on top of my full stomach and heavy eyes. She obviously doesn't want to talk about the kids or her and Silas. "So you're too busy to get involved with my garden this year, right? Missus was ragging on me at lunch today. It does look awful."

Susan settles her head back against her chair. "It doesn't look as awful as Athena Markham's. She planted four flats of impatiens last week, and they all got bit by that frost." Her eyes are closed, but she smiles. "Just brown mush now. You never plant before Mother's Day."

Laney and I exchange a look, and then she says very softly, all accusation gone from her voice, "You and Athena been talking more since the trip to North Carolina?"

Susan doesn't open her eyes but kind of sighs out, "Nope. Not at all."

In an even softer tone, Laney asks, "How's Silas?"

A frown crosses the drowsing woman's face, and she murmurs, "Poor Silas. Poor..." Then her face eases and she's asleep.

Laney and I share another look and a shrug before we settle our heads back and relax. We didn't get any answers and as frustrating as that is, I'm just too tired to care. Besides...

Nothing like dozing to the sound of rain.

"Griffin sure has his hands full," Jackson says that night as we're getting ready for bed.

"With what? We all know it's not his kids." I spit my toothpaste into the sink. "How was he with Grant today?"

"Fine. They seemed fine. I mean, they didn't really talk to each other, but I don't know how much Bryan and I would talk if we didn't work together for the business. But also, you know Bryan. If he's thinking it, he's saying it. Grant's a more private kid, like Will was." He walks out of the bathroom, but his voice carries back to me. "Griffin is consumed with work. The power company is having some personnel shifts, and he's pretty much the newest hire."

I come quickly out to the bedroom. "Is he afraid they'll let him go?"

Griffin left a very poor-paying job in Chancey last year to take a job with Mountain Power when they opened a new plant near here. His salary and responsibilities took huge jumps, leading to his buying the fancy house in Laurel Cove and the eventual end of his marriage to Susan. If he were to lose his job, I don't know what he'd find to do around here. His new house isn't as fancy as the one up on the mountain, but it's a new build, one of the larger houses in the magazine-perfect subdivision just outside of town.

"I don't know," Jackson says as I join him in bed, "but it sounds like he's helping Athena out a lot, too, with her kids and around her house."

I huff and turn out my light. "I just can't believe they are still together. She's so young. She has babies!"

"Yeah. I was glad it rained. We were supposed to take her toddler fishing with us."

I turn my light back on. "Wait, what? Today? With Grant and Bryan? Why?"

He pulls up the covers, then rests his head on his crossed arms. "Something about her having work to do. Or maybe he was just trying to give her a break on Mother's Day, like we did for you and Susan."

"Because you're the fathers of our kids. Where's her ex-husband?"

Jackson's eyes open, and he seems to realize this isn't a topic we should be discussing before bed. He smiles and reaches out a hand to hold my arm. "I don't know enough about it to talk about it. I'm just glad our weekend here went so great. Aren't you?"

"Yes. Yes, it was really good. So, no other Peeping Tom sightings?"

He pauses, his hand reaching for his light. "Nope. Griffin hadn't even heard about it until I mentioned it. He said he thinks they may have just imagined seeing someone in the dark. It's pretty dark out there since there's no streetlights in that subdivision. Speaking of lights, I'm too tired to even read. Good night," he says as he turns out his lamp.

I turn out mine, too, and settle into the covers, just in time for a knock on our bedroom door. Savannah pushes it open, letting light from the hall slice into the dark room.

"Mom? Dad? You awake? I saw your light under the door."

"Sure. What is it?" I say.

She steps in so that we can see her in the hall light. "I just wanted to say thanks for everything. It really was great and, well, can we talk tomorrow? I have something to tell you."

I lean up, mom radar on, and reach for my light. "Come on in. What is it?"

"No, not tonight. I'm so tired. Tomorrow will be good. Love you. Good night."

She's out the door, and our room is dark again.

We both lie still for a minute. Then I wriggle in frustration and blurt out, "Why in the world would she do that? How are we supposed to sleep now? What do you think it is?"

Jackson answers with a snore.

Happy Mother's Day to me.

CHAPTER 19

"If she doesn't come down right now, we won't be able to talk before she has to leave."

Savannah is taking her own sweet time getting downstairs this morning. I even heated her a muffin left over from the weekend and have her lunch finished so we can chat. What does she want to tell us? Jackson is already downstairs working, but she can at least give me a hint, right?

Bryan, on the other hand, won't shut up. His father had it right yesterday when he said if it's on Bryan's mind, it's coming out of his mouth. We got a few months of silent treatment when Bryan first became a teenager, but I remember Will's lasting a couple of years when he hit high school. Bryan's topics this morning, while he eats bowl after bowl of cereal, have been: a football camp he wants to go to this summer; Grant's new fishing rod; the construction project he, his dad, and uncle are starting this week; and the school newspaper. The details have just washed over and past me, but I've kept an ear open for certain keywords like "Susie Mae" or "Brittani" or "Zoe."

I know. I'm a little hyper-focused, but these girls…

Like the one I birthed, who is driving me crazy. She's probably hanging out in her room until the last minute so we can't talk this morning. I can feel it.

"Savannah! Come on!" I yell.

"Sheesh, Mom!" Bryan says as he puts his bowl in the sink. "She's in the living room. Didn't you hear her just yell at me to come on?"

"Oh. No, I didn't." I grab her lunch bag and move toward the kitchen door. She meets me there.

"Hey, Mom. So it's Monday, and I'll be late. I'm going to go out for supper with Jenna and Angie. Need to talk to them, you know." She smiles at me, takes her lunch, and swirls around, her hair flying out at me.

"What about needing to talk to me and Daddy?"

"Yeah. Tonight, right? Come on, Bry. We're late."

The front door closes. I watch them run down the porch steps, climb in her car, and they are off. The house is so quiet and still after such a full weekend. I huff as I lean against the kitchen doorframe. Of course she wasn't going to talk about whatever it is this morning. Jackson told me that but, well, I don't want to wait all day!

I guess I don't have a choice.

The text from Andy came after I was already dressed and heading out the door. He and Patty spent time finishing up the nursery and shopping for their new addition which will be here soon. Since he didn't go scavenging this weekend, there are no books waiting on me at the shop to check into our inventory. I probably should've anticipated this, as it sounds like they took advantage of Gertie being out of town on her honeymoon to do some things their way.

Good thinking.

Standing on the front porch, Jackson already kissed goodbye and back to work downstairs, the front door locked behind me, and a free hour to myself, I make a call.

"Morning!" I say. "How do you feel about an impromptu visitor?"

Getting the answer I expected, I get in the car and start down the hill. The early drive is beautiful. Full leaves are filling in where just a few weeks ago I could see the sky. It's not the deep shade of June and July because the leaves, although full-sized, are still a brighter, lighter green. They're not yet the thick, seasoned leaves that get us through the hot summer with that impenetrable shade the South is known for.

Before I leave the tree-covered road, I do something unusual, though I think it's something I'll be getting used to—I turn right onto a hidden gravel drive. Through the woods, I can see the white-brick house and Augusta waiting on its front stoop. She's wearing black capris, black sandals, and a white, long-sleeved tunic. She waves from the time she sees me until I'm standing beside her.

"You're here! Isn't this just a lovely morning? I'm so glad you came by." She takes my arm, pulling me in the front door. "Do you want coffee or tea?"

"You know, tea sounds right for being here with you. Oh, look at the floors!" I exclaim as I walk over the hardwood. I haven't seen Augusta's place since right after she moved in, and I love how she's spruced it up.

"There are a few places that are discolored, but for the most part they are good. I was so glad to get rid of that awful carpet." She laughs, then wrinkles her nose. "And that smell."

I follow her through the mostly empty room into the kitchen, where she fills a tea kettle. "As you can see, I didn't bring a lot of furniture with me. I brought our bedroom furniture and that table there but not much else. I don't know what I want, but I'm really not in any hurry. I did pick up chairs for the patio, though."

"Yes, you did talk about drinking tea beside the river." I step to the kitchen window beside the back door. Augusta hums as she fixes our tea cups. The click of spoons on china, the sound of water beginning to boil, the river outside, all add to the peacefulness. This was such a good idea.

"If you'll open the door, I'll carry the tray," Augusta says, and I realize that in my daydreaming several minutes have passed. I remember that's one of the things I so enjoyed about Augusta—she doesn't have to fill every minute with chatter. She's comfortable with silence.

"Sure." I open the door and step out to hold it wide. Augusta carries the serving tray with our cups and a plate of strawberries and blueberries past me. The new set of four patio chairs she bought have thick cushions and surround a circular, glass-topped table.

"Watch your step. This old concrete has some cracks and unlevel places." She puts the tray down and steps to the edge of the patio. "Isn't this perfect?" Her voice is low, reverential, and my breathing slows to match her cadence.

The patio is a foot above the ground, which then slopes gently to the riverbank. There are little bits of grass, patches of moss, lots of roots, and areas of red dirt, but no flowers and very little undergrowth.

Augusta lays a hand on my arm, then points to the edge of her yard. "See over there? That patch of ferns? I'm sure I can get those to spread along the edge of the patio to soften this drop-off. But that's really all I want to do back here." She squeezes my arm, then turns back to the table. "Our tea should be cool by now. Let's sit."

As we settle in, my first sip of tea is a surprise. "Is there orange, or maybe lemon, in this?"

She beams. "Lemon, and there is caffeine in it, so no worries about it putting you to sleep. Now. How did Savannah's friend weekend go?"

"Tiring, but so good. It's hard to believe these girls are all graduating."

"It goes so fast. Gregory will be moving here this week. Talk about things going fast!" She lifts her cup and settles back against the cushion. "We're going to be happy here."

I fight the urge to quirk my brow. "But Gregory and Peter took Delaney and Missus to dinner yesterday. I thought maybe he was already here."

"No, they met halfway. He has two more exams, one today and one tomorrow, and then he's finished. When Peter suggested it, he thought it was important to mark this first Mother's Day with Delaney and Missus. Get the whole family thing rolling."

"And you didn't go?"

Her smile is as peaceful as always, and once again, I'm glad she's moved here. "I was invited, which was very kind, but I'm ready for this new chapter too. I want to be Gregory's aunt, friend, roommate even, but not his mother. I went to church and then had a very peaceful day here."

"You're so grown-up!" I say with a laugh. "Speaking of *grown-ups*, how did your date with Bill's brother, Joe, go?"

She gives me a bit of side-eye over her tea cup. "Oh, it was fun. He's so much like Bill, quiet and watchful. Gertie was definitely the life of the party on our date, which was just fine with me. And I meant to tell you: we ran into Griffin and Athena that day at the winery. They were down on the level with the fire pits." She sniffs, but I don't think it's to smell the tea. "She seems awfully young."

"She *is* young"—I give her a wink—"but I like her anyway. Uh, you didn't happen to see anyone else from Chancey up there, did you? Susan or even her daughter, Susie Mae?"

"I didn't, but Gertie was certain she saw Susie Mae driving off. Said she was in a mad tear. At first she was just mad because the driver was being reckless, but then she saw it was Susie Mae. She even called her on our way home and left a really long message about her being more careful. Could she have been there with her father and that young woman?"

"No. At least," I add, "I don't think so. I really have no idea why she would be there, except I think her mom was there too. Those two are keeping the rest of us guessing, and I'm getting really tired of that game!" I pat the table. "Anyway, back to you and Joe?"

"Oh." She hesitates. "Joe... well, it was more to get my feet wet. And it was fun. He's a little hard to talk to, but that may have been because Gertie was all wound up about the wedding and the rest of us didn't get a chance to talk much. I like Gertie. I don't know that I've known anyone like her before. She really doesn't apologize for who she is, does she?"

"Not at all. Which, now that you mention it, is kind of refreshing. When it's not exhausting!"

She laughs in appreciation. "I don't feel like I have to be on guard or listening for hidden meanings like I do with Missus and Peter. Delaney even has her guard up most of the time these days. She used to be much more of an open book."

"Really? I never knew the Delaney that wasn't in the middle of all the Peter drama. As for Gertie, I don't know, I feel like her lack of a guard means I have to be ready to fend her off so I don't get run over!"

Augusta tilts her head toward me. "Oh, I'm never in fear of getting run over. I just step to the side and let them run on by!" We laugh and sip our tea, and then she tips her head toward the water. "Look how the light is on the river now, with all the ripples."

The river here is choppier than it is up near our house and the rail bridge. It narrows and flows faster here before it widens again, moving out past the high school. Sparkles light up the water, and we watch as we finish our tea and eat some berries. Never being in fear of getting run over keeps running through my head. Augusta never fears getting run over. That stirs something in me, and I want to think on it more, but it's time to get to the shop.

"This was so nice. I'll try to not make it a habit, but you know you are right on my way to, well, anywhere," I say as I stand. "I'm so glad you're all moved in and that Gregory will be here soon."

We collect the cups onto the tray and she says, "Be sure and tell Savannah. He'll be wanting to connect with his friends."

"Argh. Savannah. I'm trying *not* to think about her. She has something she wants to talk to me and Jackson about, but she's got school and work, so we can't talk until later." I pull open the door for Augusta. "And I'm not good at waiting."

She climbs the two steps, carrying the tray into her homey kitchen. "Oh, honey. Waiting is part of life. The more you lean into it and get good at it, the happier you're going to be." As I join her in the kitchen, she points out the window. "Think about how long I waited to get here." She sighs and turns to me. "The most important thing? Don't only get good at waiting. Learn to enjoy it."

My smile is tight. "Yeah, well. That sounds good in theory."

She laughs. "No, it *is* good." She pulls me into a hug. "And you, like all of us, are a work in process. Oh, I'm going to love it here!"

We walk through the living room, and she tugs open the old front door, which has stuck in the day's growing humidity. She follows me onto the porch and watches me walk down the broken sidewalk and get into my car. She waves as I turn around in the gravel drive.

Well, there you have it.

Yoda now lives in Chancey.

CHAPTER 20

The party is on—like Donkey Kong! Wait, is that even a saying? It felt like I've heard the kids say it, and it felt right until I actually said it. Anyway...

The party is on.

The whole party, or should I say, the two parties. According to Laney, an unbiased source, Shaw agreed with her that the girls deserve the biggest party in town. He even added some clients to the guest list and is having a putting green put in the yard.

"It's a temporary one, since it's short notice, but the company will start putting in the actual green as soon as the party is over." Laney is talking and writing while we share a table in Ruby's area of the bookshop.

I'm also writing a to-do list, but I don't do well trying to talk and write at the same time. Plus there's so much around me to watch. Two construction workers are arguing about our street project so I'm listening for a completion date. Libby is talking the ear off a couple who asked about real estate in the area. I think she said her daughter Cathy is getting her real estate license or something? I find it hard to concentrate in our store these days. Which makes work really frustrating. Laney clears her throat and I pull myself back to our conversation.

I lay my pen down. I can't think here. "A putting green? I don't think I've ever known anyone with one in their yard."

"He says it'll give Cayden an early start on being a golf prodigy and a place for them to bond. Plus, once I added it to the party list, he was all on board. This ain't my first rodeo." She lifts her clipboard. "There. I figured if we were adding his clients, I might as well add a few more people. Do you have your outfits for the party? Want to come shopping at The Club?" She licks her lips so that they shine as much as her eyes. "With the sinkhole, it's like those shops they have in New York City where you shop by appointment. I have a thriving business going on out of the back door." She leans forward and whispers, "Jenna is handling it. She has the keys and is letting ladies in only two at a time."

"Did you okay this with the city? I thought they said you could only go inside for an emergency."

"It's my store." She shrugs. "It's not like the whole thing is going to collapse."

"Well, what if it does?" A blast of a jackhammer punctuates my sentence and everyone stops talking. However, after that one blast, it goes quiet and the noise inside picks right back up.

"Oh, Carolina, you're so dramatic. So, when do you want to go shopping? I'll take *you* personally!"

"No, I'm on a budget. I'm sure I'll find something suitable in my very own closet." I stretch to make sure Danny is still okay up front without me. "Listen, did you know Savannah is going to dinner tonight with your girls?"

"Oh, yeah, Jenna did say something about it. Angie, too? But then I guess AC's isn't open for dinner on Mondays, so that makes sense."

My foot starts bouncing. "Okay. So what did Jenna say?"

"I think they're going out to the blacktop. Sushi place there."

"No! What are they going to talk about?"

"Oh, that." She pulls her notes back in front of her and starts writing. "Well, come on, you know what they're going to talk about."

"No. I don't. What?" I urge. "She didn't tell us a thing!"

Laney writes and ignores me for a moment, so I slap out at her arm. "What?"

"Oh, you know. The party. What else? Unless you've heard something more about that Peeping Tom? That's made me nervous. We live out there with no neighbors, so I don't really worry about closing my curtains. But I told Jenna she's got to get used to living in a dorm room and pull her shades down." She shakes her head, lips pursed in disgust. Then her eyes slant up at me like she's thinking something.

I fall back in my chair. "No, I haven't heard anything more. But it is super creepy." I make a mental note to pay more attention to our curtains. "What? What are you thinking?"

She leans forward on her folded arms, causing me to also lean in. "This Peeping Tom thing is suspicious. Boys now days have all kinds of ways to see half-dressed girls. Not like back in our day when they had to get their hands on a girlie magazine or find an open curtain. There's something else going on." She straightens up. "I'm thinking on it. You think about it, too. But right now I've got other things on my mind."

She's right. Something is off, but I can see that topic is closed for now. I scoot my chair out to get up and get back to work. "Oh, I stopped by Augusta's this morning. Gregory will be moving in this week, so you might want to add him to the guest list."

She doesn't look up. "Already on there. Did I tell you I hired a secretary?"

I sit back down. "Really? Who?"

Libby has obviously been listening to our conversation, and she interjects from two tables away, where she's pouring coffee, "And you won't be sorry! She lives for this kind of thing."

My head swivels from Libby to my tablemate, and I try to

keep my tone neutral. Folks are obviously listening. "You hired Cathy Stone?"

"Cathy Cross. She says she's dropping her maiden name." Libby is a table closer now, but still talking loudly enough for us, and everyone else, to hear. "She says it's better in her professional admin positions to use Cathy Cross. Then when she's in sales mode for her lingerie business, she'll continue to use Cathy Stone. Me and my Bill have lived here so long she needs a little distinction so folks don't *just* think of her as our daughter."

Laney rolls her eyes at me and fights a grin, but she doesn't lower her voice. "As if that's what she needs distinction from."

I stand back up as Libby gets to our table, her hand outstretched and holding business cards. "Here ya go," she says as she shoves one under my nose. "She had these cards made up. Ya never know when you'll need a little help with, well, ya can see right there she'll help with a bunch of stuff."

Sure enough, the card is packed border to border with a bulleted list of things Cathy Cross can help us with. Like filing documents. And dog-walking. "Thanks, Libby. I'll keep her in mind."

"And here's a couple more. Give one to Jackson and that Colt. They're running a business and might need some service Cathy can provide." She shifts the half-full coffee pot to her other hand, plunges into her other pocket, and brings out the bright pink cards I've seen before. "You might as well take a couple of these too. She's still doing the lingerie sales shows."

I take those cards with their curlicue script and the name "Cathy Stone" on the front. "Thanks, Libby. She's lucky to have such a good promoter as a mother."

The old waitress pauses, sets the coffee pot on our table, and then leans one hand on her hip. "She's a handful. Always has been. But she and Stephen are back together and raising my grandson, which is what I prayed for so hard. I know God don't need my help, but I like thinking I'm in on his plan." She brightens up and winks at us. "He might know more than me!" She cackles and turns around, walking back to the coffee station.

Smiling at Laney, I start back to my books, saying, "Hmm, that's something to think about."

Laney looks up. "What?"

"What Libby was saying. About getting in line with God's plan. Not worrying so much about *my* plan."

She frowns and gives me a dismissive wave of her hand. "Yeah, as long as God is planning good weather for Saturday. If not, he and I are going to have issues."

Like God doesn't already know he has issues with Laney.

"What is she doing here?" Shannon drawls.

Her jaw hangs open and her eyes follow Cathy Stone Cross as she sashays through our store, back to where Laney is waving at her and calling her over. Laney returned this afternoon, once again commandeering one of Ruby's tables for a desk. Shannon and I are passing a boring afternoon cleaning out the counter area while Danny dusts. The up and down noise and activity level now that Ruby's has moved in, makes me irritable. Plus when they're not busy back there in the mornings, Libby wanders up here and bothers us. Well, she bothers me. She doesn't mess with Shannon and Danny seems to love talking to her. So while I'm bored, I'm also on edge when Cathy Stone Cross arrives.

"She's Laney's secretary now. Apparently she's starting a new business." I pull out one of the cards Libby gave me this morning. "Here."

Shannon reads the card, and her mouth not only closes, but

it forms a grimace. She stares at her husband, who is looking in our direction. He shrugs and smiles before moving over to the fiction shelves with his feather duster.

She clinches her fist, crunching Cathy's card. "I'd say you should warn Laney that Cathy is trouble, but I'm sure she knows. Besides, Shaw has plenty of chances to wander if he wants to."

"What? He wouldn't give Cathy the time of day." I say this much more confidently than I feel it. I don't know if it's that Shaw is a car dealer and kind of a flirt, but I've always... no. "I'm sure Laney can handle her."

"Well, I'm sure not handling her. She better stay well and away from Danny. I'll tear her eyeballs out!" Shannon rips the crumpled card in half, then tries to rip those two pieces in half again, but they won't tear. She finally throws them in the wastebasket before marching over to Danny and giving him an earful, strident but too quiet to hear.

"Hey, Carolina!" a new voice greets me.

I startle in response. "Oh! Cathy, I didn't see you come back up here."

She turns, leans one hip against the counter, and looks back at Shannon and Danny. "Ol' Shannon has got her work cut out for her if she thinks she's going to keep that sweet Danny on a short leash. Some men are just easy to sway, and if you got one of them, you're better off letting them loose and not worrying about it." She flips back around to face me, as though she hasn't just insulted two of my favorite people in town. But then she has known all these people her whole life. "So. Laney says Momma gave you some of my cards to give to Jackson and Colt? I'm sure I could help take their business to a new level. Add some professionalism to the whole thing." She pulls out her phone and presses it to life. "Give me Colt's number, and I'll reach out to him personally."

"Uh, I think they're fine for now. I'll give them your card. I will. I promise." I'm lying.

She smiles and puts her phone back in her purse. "No worries, Carolina. I can get a hold of them anytime. It's not that big of a town."

She steps away from the counter and looks back over again to where Danny is now working alone, his back to us. She walks to the front door, but once there she stops and says loudly, "Danny! We should catch up sometime. Talk about the old days!"

He fumbles around with the feather duster, then waves it in her direction, but he never actually looks at her, even as the door swings shut behind her.

I'm still standing behind the counter, not sure what is going on, when Laney comes bustling by. "See ya later, Carolina! If you decide you do want to go shopping at The Club, just let me know."

I say in a low voice, "So, were Cathy and Danny a thing at some point?"

Like any good piece of gossip, this stops Laney's hustle and bustle in its tracks. "Of course. The four of them, he and his wife, Alison, and Cathy and Stephen, were the wild kids at Chancey High back in the day. Then Alison and Stephen went off to college. Cathy and Danny were left here to make the most of things." She waggles her eyebrows at me, then leans across the counter. "Lots of folks figure Forest is Danny's, especially Stephen's high-falutin' mama. But Stephen married Cathy before his mama could get a paternity test done. Alison was already pregnant, and her wedding to Danny was about to happen, so everyone backed off. Anyway"—she blows me an air kiss—"I gotta go. Talk to you later!"

Yeah… I didn't really follow all that. But it does not sound good for peace and quiet in Chancey Place. Get it? Like Peyton Place?

Laney hurries out the door, and the store falls quiet. Danny is over in the shelves, dusting. Shannon is sulking at her work-table. Kimmy yelled that she was going over to the actual café for a bit, and there's not a customer in sight. We've noticed that late Monday afternoons quiet down since AC's isn't open for dinner. Kimmy has said she's going to stop opening on Mondays and Tuesdays for pie after this week, and we've talked about actually closing our store early on Mondays.

The store may be quiet, but there's so much tension in the air. A supposedly restful bookstore and florist is shimmering with past mistakes and secrets. Down every street, in every direction, behind every door, you'll find the same.

Small towns are nothing but well-disguised minefields.

Chapter 21

"I can't believe we let Will move here. Now he's going to be enmeshed in all this drama. I mean, he and Anna didn't go to high school here, but it looks like they plan to spend their lives here. Everyone will know everything that went on with them getting married and then, you know, their troubles. It can't be good for everyone to know everything about you!"

Jackson hasn't even sat down on the deck after dinner when I hit him with all this. I'd stewed on the scene from the shop and then got to thinking about what will happen between Shannon and Peter when the baby comes. Jackson worked until dinner, which was just the two of us since Bryan is at Grant's—as far as I know. Jackson came upstairs to eat and started talking about a work project, which allowed me to stew even more as we ate, because Lord knows I wasn't listening. Then, when he came out on the deck after dinner with his glass of iced tea, he made the mistake of asking what I was thinking about.

So I told him. He stares at me, holding his glass and not moving toward his chair. "Oh. I figured you were thinking about Savannah."

"Savannah?" It takes me a second to remember. "Oh yeah. What *does* she want to talk about? You have any idea?"

He laughs and sits down. "No idea at all. So, what is all the drama you're talking about?"

I fill him in on the tangled web of Danny, Alison, Stephen, and Cathy. "So do not even think about hiring her. And don't let Colt within ten feet of her!"

"Honey. I know Cathy Stone, or Cross, or whatever she calls herself. She only goes after low-hanging fruit, so that's no problem with me. As for Colt, I'm not getting into his personal business. We have thought about getting someone to deal with our scheduling, though. Maybe Colt should reach out to her." He holds up a hand to stave off my next protest. "For work! Nothing else."

I growl, "Does fruit get any lower-hanging than your brother?"

"Well, he is single." He turns to the side. "I think I heard a car door."

It's not long before we hear Savannah coming in the front door and calling out that she's home. Jackson gets up and waves at her through the doors. Then, sitting back down, he says, "She motioned that she'd be out here in a minute."

I sip my iced tea and wait. It's funny that the drama from this afternoon made me forget to worry about Savannah. I guess that's one advantage of all the skeletons here not having closets to hide in.

"Hey." She walks out and pulls a chair from under the patio table to sit in. She's on her daddy's side of the table, and he and I turn our chairs around so we can see her.

"How were Angie and Jenna?" I ask, resisting the temptation to launch into the third degree. "Excited about their party on Saturday?"

She chuckles and rolls her eyes. "They actually are. They were going on about their mom being over the top, but I could tell they were really looking forward to it. Angie says she's surprised how well she's getting along with her mom and dad and that they want to include her in everything. But I also think she's thinking about moving out of Alex's, so she needs to stay on good terms with them."

I'm startled by this news. "What?"

Savannah cocks her head to one side. "Don't say anything, Mom. Promise. She's just not sure she's ready to settle down, and he kinda is."

"But they have the restaurant together," Jackson says.

"Yeah, she's not really thought it through. Anyway. I wanted to talk to y'all about something." She clears her throat and shakes her head. "I know I have everything lined up for working here and going to school in Dalton in the fall, but, well…" After a quick pause she rushes on. "The girls from Marietta who are going to Kennesaw State had a girl drop out of their apartment. They can only keep the four-bedroom apartment, which is bigger, if they can fill the spot, but they'd prefer it to not be a stranger." Her big, blue eyes look up at us. "I know I can get in. I actually talked to admissions this morning, and they sent an email this afternoon saying it's all set if I want it to happen."

Jackson leans out of his chair and squeezes our daughter to him with one arm. "Congratulations, sweetie! I'm shocked, but I'm happy if you're happy. We will definitely miss you around here, though."

She hugs him back. "I really liked being with the girls over the weekend, and it felt right." She pauses and looks at me. "What are you thinking, Mom?"

I draw in a long breath. It's a calm, peaceful breath, and I realize that I feel good about this. Letting the breath out, I smile. "That it's a great idea, Savannah. Yes, get away from here. Meet new people. There's no need to be stuck in this little town." The scene from this afternoon and all my muddled thinking that I've been doing over the last few hours make this sound like the best idea ever. "Yes. By all means. Let's do this!" I get up and meet her on the other side of the table for a full hug. "And congratulations on already getting accepted. I guess they really want to get their fall classes lined up. We'll have such fun getting you ready—I've heard it's a beautiful campus!"

Savannah pulls back and tucks her hair behind her ears on both sides, then folds her arms. "Well, it's actually not for fall. The only way it'll work is if I move in this summer. They've already got the apartment, and the girls are taking summer classes."

"Summer?" I start to mull this over as I return to my seat. "Wow, we've got a lot to do, but we can make it work. Might have to move our vacation up from July, but since it's at your grandmother's beach cottage, I'm sure she won't have a problem."

Jackson leans back in his seat to more fully see his daughter. "Naw, Mom will be fine with whenever we want to come. But we'll have a lot to get done."

Savannah clears her throat again. "Well, actually I'm doing two four-week classes. I start May 30."

I stare at her. Her daddy stares at her.

I finally say, "But that's in a couple weeks."

"Yep. Two weeks from tomorrow. Graduation is on that Friday, with our big family lunch on Saturday, and so I'll have Sunday to move in. Monday I have orientation stuff."

"Oh," is all I manage.

Jackson doesn't even get that much out. He stands up and steps to the railing, facing down the hill toward the river. Then he turns to face us with a big, fake smile in place. "We're going to need to look into this. Um, don't they want money before they let you move in?"

"Not for classes. And rent for the apartment isn't due until June 1." She stands, and I follow her, but my legs feel a little shaky. Meanwhile, Savannah's beaming. "Listen, I have to call the girls in Marietta and tell them it's all set." She gives us quick hugs and then, as she pulls open the door, she squeals, "They don't even know yet!"

She runs inside, the glass door slamming behind her.

I fall into Jackson's chair. "Imagine that. They don't even know yet."

Chapter 22

"I'm moving into Savannah's bedroom," Bryan announces.

Between mouthfuls of cereal.

Before I've even had coffee.

"No, you're not," his sister says from her perch beside the coffee pot. She rolls her eyes and announces as I walk into the kitchen, "No one made coffee yet. That's why we're having to wait."

Bryan keeps talking. "You get a cool new apartment *and* the best room in the house? No way. You can have my room."

"Not happening. Your room smells, and I don't have time to move my stuff down there. Oh, that's cool," she says as I show her how to stop the flow just long enough to pour a cup of coffee. "I didn't know it would do that."

Oh, all the stuff she doesn't know how to do. "Where's your dad? Already downstairs?"

"Yup." Bryan decides to talk while he chews, primarily to goad his sister into a lather. "I'm moving up there as soon as you're gone, and you can't stop me."

I pause before my first sip. "But *I* can." This is *one* thing I can keep off my plate. "You are not moving into Savannah's bedroom… yet. We'll see how it goes."

Savannah whirls out of the open refrigerator. "Are you joking? He can't have my room. Ever!"

"No. I'm not doing this. Y'all fix your lunches. You have time, and I'm not awake yet." I make it to the living room couch and plunk myself down, cradling my coffee and a massive headache. "Bring me the ibuprofen," I say loud enough to be heard over their bickering.

Jackson got up way too early, which I thought might let me go back to sleep since he wouldn't be tossing and turning beside me. But then the dreams started, about some boat Savannah was on or that I was on. It was sailing, and we didn't have our luggage yet. I couldn't find it. Then there was a bird. I'm not sure what the bird was doing, but Savannah was screaming at it. There was a dance on the deck, and Laney was there. I was, too, but I had on a nightgown. An old, worn-out nightgown. Laney kept telling me to go change, but again I couldn't find my luggage.

It was a rough night.

"Here," Savannah says as she hands me the bottle of pills. She stops at the end of the couch, one knee up on the arm. "Daddy seemed grouchy. Is he upset about me leaving?"

"It was just a big surprise. We haven't been thinking of paying for your housing, since we thought you'd be living here and commuting to Dalton, but we'll manage. It was just a surprise. Dad's not good with surprises. I'm not either." I look at her and smile. "If we didn't like surprises, I guess we shouldn't have had three kids, huh?"

She smiles, then frowns, a pretty, pouty frown of pink lip gloss. "I guess I did kind of spring it on y'all. Y'all just always take things so easy I didn't think about it being a problem. Is it a problem?"

Her dark hair is shiny and held back with a white hair band. She's wearing a white button-down shirt, long, navy shorts, and tennis shoes. I let out a little sigh. She's going to love college. "No, sweetie. It's no problem at all. We're just going to miss you. And—it was a surprise."

She lets out a breath I didn't realize she was holding. "I'll be home all the time." Then, after she offers up that olive branch, she steps back and yells, "Come on, Bry. We need to go!"

Before I can get a couple of ibuprofen down, they are both bustling toward the door. I struggle up and meet them there. Hugging Bryan is like hugging a tree. Savannah, however, leans into me. "Thanks, Mom. You make everything easy." Then she's out the door, and they are both jogging to her car.

I hear Jackson come up the basement stairs, and I wait for him to find me. He's there just as the car bounces over the tracks. He hugs my shoulders from behind, and we watch them drive away. "How did this happen so fast?"

"I have no idea. She said that we always take things easy and that we make things easy. That's all right, isn't it? Did we make their lives too easy?"

He turns me around and hugs me. "No. But we'll make this work too. I was awake half the night worried about the money. It'll be rough, but we will be fine. And she's a hard worker. It's worth our investment."

I snuffle into his shoulder, then wipe my nose on the sleeve of my old robe. "But I'm going to miss her."

He tightens his hug and also snuffles. "I know. Me too."

"So she's moving the weekend after graduation, and I don't know what to do," I say to my mom on the phone. I'm so glad I'm off today to try and make sense of the next two weeks. I'm still in my robe and just made a fresh pot of coffee.

"That will be pretty hectic with us there," she says, "but we won't get in the way. Why don't I see if I can get a camping reservation near there? Then we won't be parked in your drive-way and can stay out of your hair. What about Jackson's folks?"

"Etta is coming, but we still don't have an answer from Hank and Shelby. I'm hoping they're on the road with this speaking events and can't come for long, but who knows. They'll probably blow in here the day of graduation, wanting the best room and all the trimmings."

She clucks in her throat. "Let me get off here. I've got a hair appointment soon, but I've got a couple of minutes to look for a camping space. Don't mention it to your daddy—he's got his heart set on staying there with you all—but if it makes his darling Savannah's life easier, he'll get on board. I mean, I guess we all will, won't we?"

My mother and I get along pretty well. I've always considered myself a daddy's girl, but honestly, she and I have the same mindset most the time. We make things move along, keep the flow going. Daddy does have a tendency to bluster at times, but she'll handle him.

I already called Jackson's mom, Etta. She gets up earlier than my mom does. Etta lives down at the beach since she and Jackson's dad divorced a couple of years ago. She's very happy to be on her own and out of the Hillbilly Hank universe. My father-in-law has written a series of books, more like pamphlets, and does speaking engagements all over the South, mostly at senior living centers. His new wife, Shelby, is one of my least favorite people in the world, and that has nothing to do with the fact that she was married to Jackson for about a minute when he and I broke up one summer in college. They got a quick divorce, but she hung around as Hank's secretary. Yes, air quotes and raised eyebrows are definitely implied when I call her his secretary. Our first Christmas in Chancey, Etta finally admitted what had been going on for years. She took some recently inherited money and moved to a beach cottage in South Carolina.

Hank and Shelby are still at the homestead in Kentucky. Hopefully they're too busy to come long for graduation, but who knows? I'm not calling them. I put that squarely on Jackson's to-do list.

Savannah hasn't wanted a big graduation party, just a family weekend, which is why I put together the brunch for her and her friends and their mothers. I've booked a big lunch on graduation Saturday at AC's for all of the family. However, since last night, our family weekend has become a moving weekend. Well, I've done all I can about that. We'll help her pack as much as possible before our company starts arriving.

Now, this house is still a wreck from the *previous* weekend, and this is my only day off this week. Before I can get up from the couch, though, my phone rings. It's Susan.

"I heard the news," she says. "Savannah is moving to Kennesaw right after graduation?"

"Yep. We're still kind of reeling with it all over here. Now, on top of graduation stuff, we have this to make happen. I've got to go over to Silas's today and get some flowers for the front pots. You want to come?"

"I do have a job, you know, and things to do," she blurts out. Then she seems to take a breath. "But if you can make it late afternoon, I can do it. I'd like to see what he's done with the place."

"Are you really not seeing him these days?"

"We're playing it cool. You know, not rushing things like we did before. All for the kids. Besides, I've been really busy."

I wait for her to explain what has kept her so busy. However, she waits me out, so I answer, "Okay. I'll meet you out there around four?"

"Sounds good," she says and hangs up.

I get up from the couch before I can get bogged down with thinking again.

"I'm going to get some answers from her today," I declare. "Something is going on with Miss Susan."

"Have you had lunch?" Jackson asks as he comes to the top of the basement stairs.

I lean on the mop handle and shake my head. "Nope, but I'm not eating until the mopping is done, and you're not either if you plan to use the kitchen at all. It's kind of early for you, isn't it?"

He leans against the stairwell's doorjamb. "Yeah, but well, Dad called back."

I lean even heavier on the mop. "They're coming, aren't they?"

"Yeah, and well, he's got some shows in the area. Wanted to know if we had a room available this upcoming weekend through graduation weekend."

"You told him no, right?"

"I was honest when he texted this morning and told him I didn't know. But, well, that's why he was calling back. He, uh, he called Laney because he remembered you told him she handled the bookings."

"Yeah, that was back when I didn't want to tell them there was no room for them the last time they came through. Let me guess: Laney told him we had a room open."

"So she *is* still doing the bookings? When I told him to call her, I didn't think she was, so I thought it was safe. Sorry."

At least he has the decency to look sheepish.

"No worries. But she didn't want to leave me with everything. When will they be here?"

"He doesn't have a show until Wednesday of the next week, but Laney invited them to the girls' graduation party on Saturday."

"Of course. They wouldn't want to miss that."

"Nope," Jackson echoes. "They wouldn't want to miss that. They'll be here on Friday."

As he walks off, I consider stabbing the mop handle through my chest, then decide against it. That'd just be more to clean up.

Chapter 23

"Well, I thought I was going to have some help!" Silas snaps at Susan.

She gives him a dirty look and he gives her an even worse one right back.

Don't judge him too harshly. Susan is being awful. I don't love being in the crossfire, so I walk outside to the porch of the barnlike building, where the shops and café are going to be.

I can still hear their vicious sniping.

"If you didn't think you could handle it, you shouldn't have taken it on!" Susan yells. "Who ever heard of going from acting to running a business in a matter of weeks? No one told you to move here!"

"Yes, you did! *You* literally told me I should move here!"

"*Should* move! I didn't force you."

"You're being so juvenile!" he snarls. As he joins me on the porch, he passes a shaking hand over his face. "What is *up* with her?" he whispers.

Looking to make sure she didn't follow him, I add in my own whisper, "I don't know. Honestly. Neither Laney nor I have a clue. Sorry. She *is* being ugly to you. Have y'all been fighting before today? This didn't feel like a repeat.

"How can we fight? We never see each other. She's always got an excuse."

"Same here when I try to talk to her. As a matter of fact, that's why I invited her today, to find out what's going on."

"What do you think?"

I shrug. I have some thoughts, and the way she's avoiding Silas gives them legs. But I'm running them by Susan first and hoping it's just a new guy she's interested in. My other thoughts are too crazy. "I love your place, Silas. Are things going as well as it looks?"

"It's running me ragged. I'm trying to not hire anyone to help me manage it because"—he motions with his head behind us—"I want to do this with her. That was always the plan."

I lay a friendly hand on his arm. "It's your first year. Just do what you can and remember you're building for next year." Walking to the end of the porch, I look down on his busy venture. People and trucks are everywhere. He's hired lots of workers. I can identify them by their sky-blue shirts, which match the one he's wearing.

"I like everything you've done," I tell him.

"But why is she doing this? I mean, don't get me wrong. I love this place. All of it. I'm here to stay. This is my home. But I just pictured…"

"So much more. I know."

We sigh together, then turn when we hear footsteps behind us.

"So you've settled on the food truck scenario?" Susan asks. "I saw the schedule posted on the wall in there. I didn't realize you'd made that decision."

She is wearing her work clothes, which I thought was an odd choice for coming to pick out flowers. She didn't even change out of her heeled, shiny gray pumps. Her gray slacks are topped with a tailored, long-sleeve, white blouse, and her hair is back in a tight bun. Not a ponytail or a messy bun, but an old-fashioned, tight topknot. As she marches toward us, it's like the principal has caught us playing hooky—Silas in his dusty jeans and work boots and me in shorts, tennis shoes, and a T-shirt.

His chin juts out. "I've made a lot of decisions that I tried to run by you. Do you want me to officially call it all off? Is that it? You want me to take the blame? Okay, it's all my fault. There. You are released from your servitude. Released from this awful, unpleasant alliance." The end of the porch has a two-foot drop-off, and he jumps down it. "I'll have your order loaded in your car, Carolina. I'll talk to *you* later," he shouts as he strides down the hill.

She takes his place beside me, and we watch him approach the plants I'd left in a tray by one of the greenhouses.

"Did you come here intending to break up with him?" I ask.

She snorts in response. "That? Oh, that's just him being dramatic. But we do need some space."

I turn to her. "Space?! You call that getting some space? He's really upset, Susan. Besides, you've hardly been seeing each other. How can you need space?"

"I'm just really busy right now."

"With what?" I practically shout. "What are you so busy doing? You're certainly not telling me!"

She pulls back in surprise. "I do have two kids to take care of and, well, lots of stuff." Then she leans aggressively toward me. "And work! There's talk of layoffs coming. I'm a single mother now. I can't lose my job. I know you and Laney enjoy playing at your shops and whatever else you do, but I'm on my own."

Now I'm the one to pull back. "Susan! I had no idea you were concerned about money. I thought you were fine with Griffin helping and all." I swallow my hurt reaction to her comment on mine and Laney's playing shop. I'll deal with that later.

She looks at the porch floor, then shakes her head as she walks away. "Never mind. I'm fine. "I've got to go."

I hurry after her, but I don't get too close; she still seems really mad. "Are you okay? Seriously, can I help with anything?"

When she looks up at me, she's guilty and unsure. It's the first time today she hasn't looked snotty and superior.

"Hon, what's going on?" I ask, pleading this time. "I'm your friend. You can talk to me."

She closes her eyes. "Just ignore me, okay? I need to go. I just need to…" When she opens her eyes, she doesn't look at me. She just turns away. We met here earlier, and her car is parked in the main area while mine is down near the greenhouses.

I watch her silently walk away. Then I turn toward my van, which has been loaded with the two flats of annuals I'd picked out for pots at the house. Again I'm struck by how Susan, who I thought when we moved here was the most stable of people, is now a complete mystery to me.

What is *not* a mystery is how Laney will react if her mysterious sister tries that line about "playing around and doing whatever it is we do" on her.

No mystery at all.

Not that I don't disagree with Susan concerning Laney. But don't tell either one of them I said so.

Chapter 24

"Figured it's a good way for us to save money on food," Jackson explains. We're standing in our kitchen, watching a tractor plow up the garden space, and then some, in our backyard. "Alex is going to parcel it out and oversee everyone taking care of their plot."

"How many people are going to have a plot?" I ask.

"I don't know. Alex is handling all that. Well, he's got Delaney and Phoenix on board too."

I'm having trouble knowing where to stare, at the tractor or my husband. I'm less likely to start yelling at the tractor, so I focus on the red machine.

"This is never going to work," I say, even though I'm inclined to think that, with the three folks he just mentioned in charge, it's going to work really, really well. "And I don't have to do anything?"

"Not a thing. They'll just share some of the bounty with us, so we'll save money on food, right? And the B&B guests might like spending time in the garden. I've seen places where that's actually part of the attraction. Also, I told Colt we have to ratchet up our business, so we made a decision to hire Cathy."

"Oh, really?" Now I know where to look. "You're hiring Cathy Stone? How *smart* of you to lead off our talk with the community garden venture."

"She'll only be around here while we get her acclimated. Will's going to catch her up to speed. Now that he's going to be teaching, he's not going to have time to be our bookkeeper."

I fold my arms. "I don't like the idea of Cathy and Will spending time together at all, but if it has to happen, I want them meeting right here at our dining room table."

He grabs me and squeezes me in a hug. "Exactly what I knew you'd say, Mrs. Jessup! And you'll get extra time with Francie 'cause it'll probably be while Anna is working."

"Oh. Well, yeah then. Okay. That'll work." I guess I forgot about the babysitting component. We settle into our hug, mostly because he won't let me loose. I groan. "It's going to be even more like Grand Central Station around here! Sounds like you did a lot of thinking when you weren't sleeping last night."

"I did." I feel his arms tighten ,and he rests his chin on the top of my head. "I don't want to go back to engineering full-time if I don't have to, but I did tell the office I'd work a few more hours. There's a project not far from here that needs someone to act as inspector a few times a month. I told them I could handle it."

Oh. Now I know why he tightened his hug. "So that'll involve being out of town?"

"Just a bit. But, uh, it'll be on weekends."

"You mean our busiest times with the B&B and Blooming Books."

"Yeah," he says with a sigh, "but it's all for a good cause, right?"

A good cause? Oh, right. Our daughter's last-minute college decision. "Right," I echo, though it sounds hollow.

Jackson lets me go, then moves away suddenly. "Looks like Jim's done with the tilling." He heads out the back door, then jogs down the back deck steps. I lay my forehead against the windowpane and close my eyes.

It sure is hard making things look easy.

"Do you think I should get a meal plan?" Savannah asks in the middle of dinner. She and Bryan are both home, so we're having tacos.

"Pass me the tomatoes," I say to her. "I looked into it today, and it's really different from when Will was at UGA. There are fewer dining halls and more options, so it looks very flexible. But it's also different for the summer. Are you sure you want to start so soon?"

She licks the taco sauce running down the side of her hand. "Yeah, it's the only way to be sure I can room with my friends."

"I'm getting a job this summer. A real job. Out at Silas's," Bryan says between huge bites.

Two kids at the table; two conversations. I shift my focus. "What? How will you get there? You don't drive. Have you even *thought* about studying for your permit?"

Jackson is coughing and waving a hand.

I turn to him, a little annoyed that he's adding a third conversation, and possibly an emergency, to my dinner. "Honey, are you choking?"

"No," he blurts out, then takes a deep breath as he glares at his son. "You already have a 'real' job. We've got several jobs lined up counting on you being out of school. We have to work around the summer football schedule, so it's good to have a job with the coach, right?"

"But that's working with my dad and uncle," Bryan protests. "That's not like a *real* job."

I pause with my taco in midair. "It's very much a *real* job. One you've committed to. I thought you liked it."

"I do, but everyone else is getting real jobs this year. Not just lawn-mowing and stuff."

Jackson growls. "It is a real job," he says again. "We pay you just like we would if we weren't related. Even when you had a lack of training, we paid you well. And you are getting training."

Savannah nods at her brother. "I see what you mean. As long as it's with family it's hard to see it as a real job. I bet it'd be fun out at Silas's. I know several kids getting jobs there for the summer."

He perks up at this show of support from an unexpected source. "Oh yeah? Like who?"

"No!" Jackson insists. "Colt and Will and I need you, and like your mom said, how would you get there? You can't drive. Your mom and I, our plates are already full." He smiles and turns to Savannah; the Bryan conversation dismissed, his voice is bright. "How about we go down and see the apartment before it's time to move in?"

"Why does she always get whatever she wants?" Bryan grouses and shifts in his chair. I think he's going to leave the table, but there are taco shells left, so he just reaches for another one and drops it onto his plate.

I hold up a hand toward Jackson, who is preparing to engage his grouchy son. "Ignore him. What do you think, Savannah? I'd love to see it all."

With a little back-and-forth, we land on a time we can all three go. I start stacking empty bowls onto my plate and setting anything with food still left in it in front of Bryan. "So we have a couple of graduation parties to drop in on this Saturday, but of course the big one is Laney's. I mean, Jenna and Angie's."

Savannah stands. "I'm spending the night at Amanda's Friday, and then Saturday night, there's a party after Jenna's at the lake. Nathan's throwing it."

Bryan is filling the last shell with whatever is left as he adds,

"I'm not going to Jenna and Angie's party on Saturday. I have another party to go to."

"And where might that be?" I ask.

"We're still working on it," he says before filling his mouth.

"Who's this 'we'?" Jackson asks.

Our youngest shrugs and never lets his mouth get close to empty. Savannah rolls her eyes and takes a load of dishes to the sink. I make eyes at Jackson, letting him know he's to get more information from the boy while I join Savannah in the kitchen.

"Hey," I whisper to her. "Don't encourage this 'real job' thing with him. Dad is trying to get the construction business going and needs him."

"Oh, I know. I just thought I'd try and be nice to him so he doesn't keep asking to move into my room. Because he's not." She's running water over the dishes, then loading them into the dishwasher. "I have a project to work on for the cheerleaders, and then Gregory is finally in town, so I'm going to go down and see their house later."

"Does he know you're leaving? Moving?"

She keeps working but doesn't answer, which is its own answer.

I rearrange the upper dishwasher rack to make more room. "Their house is neat. Right beside the river. You'll like it. So, how did Andy take you quitting?"

She sighs and turns to lean against the counter. "He's talked me into still doing some computer work for him. Cataloging and stuff. I guess I was planning on having some kind of a job, so it's fine."

"Oh, that is good. It's nice to have some spending money."

We finish in the kitchen, and she heads upstairs. Bryan brings the dishes in, then takes the dishrag to wipe the table. When he brings it back, I tell him to take the garbage out. "And then you'll be done."

"Okay. I'm going to walk down to the river. Then I've got homework to finish."

Jackson is still at the table, doing something on his phone. He says, "Hey," when I walk back into the dining room.

"Hey, yourself. Work emails?"

"Some. Also Dad wanting to know about Laney and Shaw's party. I guess Shelby's freaking out about gifts for the girls. Dad says money would be best, but Shelby says that's not polite." He raises his eyes to peek at me. "She's going to call you."

"Great." I wait until he hits send and lays his phone down. "So? Bryan's party?"

"Doesn't sound like a big deal. Just some of the guys?"

"Where? What guys? Are there going to be girls?"

He shrugs. "I didn't get the details. Like I said, it doesn't sound like a big deal. I think it's just a reaction to all the senior celebratory stuff. They want something of their own. Listen, I need to go downstairs and answer a couple of work emails. Won't be long." He gives me a quick peck on the forehead as he passes.

The house is still light; I love the longer days. My two flats of flowers and the pots are on the front porch. Maybe I should go work on those and enjoy the quiet, warm evening. Everything I need is already out there, and there's really nothing else I need to do. I grab a bottle of water and head in that direction, anticipating some flower therapy. However, just as I walk out of the kitchen, my phone rings.

Turning around, I sigh. Will I answer if it's Shelby? Or Laney? Or Susan? Or, well, anybody?

It's a telemarketer, so I end the call. Then I turn my phone off completely.

I've heard that's good for the battery, to completely power it down occasionally.

It's all about taking care of the phone.

And me.

Chapter 25

"It's a guy. I knew it!" Laney hisses at me when I get out of my car Wednesday morning. She'd apparently been sitting outside of Blooming Books, waiting for me to pull in. I wasn't completely surprised because she'd texted me where to park.

"What? I can't hear you." The big machines fixing the pipes are roaring early today, and the air is already thick with dust. "Why are you out here? Let's go inside."

I start across the road, but she grabs my arm.

"Too many people in there already." She looks around, then pulls me to her big SUV. "Get in."

We climb up into her plush, new vehicle—one of the benefits of having a car dealership in the family. She immediately starts messaging someone on her phone.

"I thought you wanted to talk," I say. "I'm supposed to be at work. Bonnie has meetings with clients all morning, and Danny and Shannon are leaving for a doctor's appointment soon."

She doesn't look up. "I have to tell Cathy I'll come inside soon. She's waiting for me at our table. There." She puts her phone down. "Now. I dropped in at Susan's office yesterday. Not the one at the park, but the one they gave her last fall in the main building at the power company."

"I didn't know about that. Sounds like her job is going well."

She nods. "So well that they gave her an assistant. Maybe

he's not exactly her assistant, but they work together, and he's so cute. I mean, *Silas* cute."

"You met him?"

"Yep. She's never even mentioned him, and there he is *in her office* when I showed up. He's tall too. Taller than Griffin for sure. Paul... uh, I don't remember his last name."

"And he's not married?"

"No ring. When I asked her about him later, she got all flustered and was blushing." Laney presses her lips together and shakes her head. "What has she got that has all these hot guys after her? She never even dated anyone but Griffin. Now it's just one after another?"

I choose to ignore this last bit. Instead, I muse, "That could explain what happened when we went out to Silas's place yesterday."

"About that," Laney says pointedly. "Why didn't you call me back last night? I was dying to tell you this and find out what happened."

"I was outside. Didn't have my phone. Anyway, she provoked him into breaking up. Just kept needling him and was really rude. I've never seen her like that. So you think she's really interested in this Paul guy?"

"He was sure interested in her. And before she knew I was there, I saw them laughing. It just makes sense. Right?" She opens her car door. "Come on. While I'm sitting here, I've ignored three texts and a phone call, and I can't do anymore. Makes my skin itch to not answer!"

We get out and hurry across the street. It's highly unpleasant outside with the noise and the dust. Missus has been laying low, so none of us can get any answers about how the work is going, but speak of the devil, if we don't open the front door to the bookshop to find Madam Mayor standing there, front and center.

"About time!" she snaps. "Sitting out in the car like a couple of teenagers. You're grown women, business owners. Start acting like it."

Laney brushes right past her, but I stop. "As a business owner, can I ask how the work is going? When will it be done?"

"I've been told 'soon,'" she says, and that's that. "Now, about Anna and Will's new house. Where are they looking?"

Okay, that's officially the last thing on my mind. "I have no idea. Why?"

She closes her eyes. "Oh, Carolina. Young people need guidance, help. They can't possibly know what to look for in a home or where it's best to buy. What about financing? We don't want them to get swindled or end up buying too much of a house. Surely Jackson is involved on advising them on construction issues, right?"

"No. We trust them. If they need anything, they know they can ask." I walk past her to the counter, then turn back. "Seriously? With everything you have going on, you have time to worry about this?"

"I *always* have time for my family," she spouts from atop her high horse.

That gets an eye roll and a turn back to the counter, where I look to make sure everything is ready for business. Bonnie is here, but she just peeks at me from her office door. I give her a thumbs-up, and she goes back to talking on her phone. I told Danny and Shannon to have an early lunch out after their ultrasound appointment, so they won't be in for a bit.

"Let's have coffee," Missus says as she marches past me.

"Can't. I'm watching the shop. But you feel free."

"You know I don't dillydally around, drinking coffee and gossiping. I need to talk to you about another matter of importance." She's made her way back to me. Now on the other side of the counter, I get the feeling this is what she's really here to talk about.

"I can't leave the register." I look around the space. "But we're slow, so talk."

She swallows, then folds her arms and leans in, as much as it is possible to lean with a steel rod for a spine. "That Sally Blankenship woman. Is she back in town?"

"Uh, I don't know. Gregory is back, but I don't know when they're going to start working together. Why?"

"We have to get this street open. Peter can't work in his offices, those beautiful offices Bonnie created, and so he's been working from home, and well, that hasn't been good for his relationships."

"His relationships? Like with you? With Delaney?"

"Exactly. You'd think he'd be around more, but he seems to be missing at the oddest times. I need to know who he's spending time with when he's not at home."

"Oh." She's leaned closer and closer as she's talked, so I take a step back. "Where do *you* think he's going? And when is he doing this sneaking around?"

"I didn't say 'sneaking around.'" She glances over her shoulders, one at a time. A couple of people have come in while we're talking, but they've gone straight back to Ruby's. She whispers, "Evenings. Nights. It's very concerning. It's not normal for a man and wife to be together all day and then also get along all evening as well. It's completely understandable that he needs some space, but it must be fixed. I will not let this marriage fall apart."

"But weren't they working together in his office all day?"

"But not in the same room! And not where I could hear them bickering." She actually looks sad. "I just want him to settle down and be happy. Delaney is crazy about him." Then some of her old sass rears its head. "Maybe she's *too* crazy."

Something evil unfolds over Missus's face, and she pulls off her gloves, which should've my first sign that something's up. "What if we started a rumor that she's having an affair? That'd stop him in his tracks. He's always been the cheater, never the cheat-*ed*."

I've got to halt this crazy train. "Missus—"

"Carolina, please. I'm thinking." She scans the tables in Ruby's part of the store. "Shaw Conner is a possibility. He's her age and still good-looking. Or what about Cathy Stone's husband, that teacher Stephen Cross? His mama is the only one who ever thought he was something special, but he's younger and handsome and plays the field, I believe. We should be sure to leave Jackson out of any talk."

"Oh. Yeah, naturally," I say with not a little sarcasm.

She spins back, at first I think to admonish me, but Missus has other ideas. "Wait! Jackson, that's it!"

"No—um, what—"

"Jackson's brother, Colt! He'd be perfect."

Perfect for what, I don't know, but I'm still relieved this has nothing to do with my husband.

Though Missus seems to be making perfect eye contact with me, she's really off in her imaginary, philandering world. Then she comes back to earth and actually winks at me. "Great idea, Carolina. I'll get started now." And she's once again marching back to Ruby's, leaving me at my counter with my mouth hanging open and my head spinning.

I know I have to stop this and stop it now. But well, *maybe* it could work in more ways than one. Phoenix might take it seriously enough that she'd talk to Colt. And, honestly, I have never seen Peter jealous. It would at least be interesting. I shake my head. What is wrong with me? Missus's wink must've enchanted me for a moment.

I hurry back, but Missus is already seated with Laney and Cathy. Their bugged-out eyes turn to me, and Laney grabs my arm. "Did you know about this? Delaney and Colt?"

I deny, deny, deny. "Absolutely not. That is not happening. Missus is completely making it up."

Missus's look of concern melts into one of sympathy. "It's okay. We understand, Carolina. Colt is family. Imagine my shock. Delaney is *my* family."

Cathy has already picked up her phone to text someone. When Missus sees this, she throws a glance full of triumph at me.

Laney leans back, shaking her head. "Doesn't surprise me at all. What's good for the goose is good for the gander. I've never been sure which is the goose and which is the gander, though? I mean, it's Mother Goose, right? And yet it sounds like the goose is the man, right? So is the gander the woman?"

We stare at her.

Missus pulls on her gloves and stands. "Well, I have town business to see to. I appreciate you keeping Peter and Delaney in your prayers. I'm sure they'll make it through this rough patch. It might even make their marriage stronger." She walks away but gives me another wink as she passes me. I'm still standing. Because, you know, I'm actually in charge of the bookstore.

I lean down to Laney. "I have to go back up front, but listen, she made that up. Made it up not even five minutes ago, talking to me right up there. Do *not* believe it."

Cathy might as well be rolling in melted chocolate as satisfied as she looks. "I'm not surprised at all," she echoes Laney's earlier statement. "No one will be. Colt is the catch of the day. I wondered how long he'd put up with Alison and her snotty attitude. Although he seems to like them snotty, look at how the high and mighty Phoenix dropped him. Oh!" she says as she picks her phone back up and her fingers start flying.

Laney and I look at each other.

"Oh?" I say.

"That's probably why Phoenix dropped Colt. She knew Peter was available. I don't think she was ever really over him. Wonder if Shannon will put her hat back in the ring for our philandering attorney-at-law now that he's free? No way he'll stay with a cheater."

A woman shouting, "Hello?" from the store counter pulls my horrified eyes from Cathy and her phone.

"I have to go. Stop her," I implore Laney.

As I apologize to the shopper and ring up her purchase, I try to just breathe. Breathe and not think about soap bubbles escaping an overfilled washing machine. Or yeast dough escaping its bowl. Or that movie *The Blob*. Doesn't it expand and, like, destroy a city? You know, I don't think I've actually seen it, but you get the picture.

Laney is waiting when I finish bagging the woman's books. As the customer walks away she demands, "So what was all that about?"

"I told you!" I moan. "She made it up. She's worried because Peter and Delaney are fighting, and she thinks this will make him jealous. It's crazy."

"Whatever. But seriously? We just sat out there in the car all that time and you didn't tell me about Colt and Delaney? I thought we were friends. This is really big news. Everyone I've texted is shocked." Her eyes sparkle. "Just think. All of them, Peter and Delaney, Colt and Phoenix, even Alison, they'll all be at the party Saturday! Can you say fireworks?"

I give up.

Chapter 26

"It's a girl!" Shannon announces as they walk in the front door of Blooming Books later that afternoon.

"Aww, babe," Danny says in disbelief. His whole body droops. "You told them."

"Yes, I did," she says with a tone that tells him not to say another word. "How have things been, Carolina? I hope the florist orders haven't been too much. We went to lunch like you suggested, out at the Mexican place out on the blacktop, and it was wonderful."

I greet her with a hug. "Congratulations. You, too, Danny."

His big, brown eyes look to me for some comfort, so I pat his shoulder. He sighs loudly and walks back toward the stairs to their apartment. "I had it all planned." On the stairs he says, "I'll be down in a minute. Gotta use the bathroom. Our bathroom."

"Okay, what was all that about?" I ask my business partner.

"The bathroom? Well, uh…"

"No. The other thing. Why's he so sad you told us it's a girl?"

"Oh, that. He and my parents are bound and determined to do some elaborate gender reveal thing. Totally out of control." She eases onto the stool at her table. "Did you know my dad has a cannon?"

"A cannon? Like a *real* cannon?"

She rolls her eyes. "Oh, yes. He's into all the Civil War re-enactment stuff—not to actually do the reenactments; he provides the weapons. It's kind of his thing. Anyway, they were trying to engage his cannon in a gender reveal party, but I do *not* need to be on the Atlanta news for killing someone with pink marbles or whatever they were going to shoot. So I fixed it. I'm telling people." She takes a moment, then settles into her smile. "A girl. A baby girl. I really wanted a girl." She gets busy with reading her list of floral arrangements as she says quieter, "Even though Peter wants a boy, he can't always get what he wants. But he won't be sad."

I wait for her to look up and realize she said that out loud, but she doesn't. She starts humming and collecting her materials. Could Shannon and Peter be talking? Is that where he's disappearing to in the evenings? I mean, they live less than a block apart. It'd be easy to meet up, even here in the shop. Danny probably sleeps like a log, and no one else would chance see them. I don't think they've rekindled their romantic relationship—and I certainly don't think they should—but it would be good if they could talk before the baby comes.

A woman clearing her throat stops my daydreaming. "Yes, ma'am. Be right there," I say as I hurry forward and force myself to focus on the shop. The lunchtime shoppers are either beginning to leave empty-handed or lining up to pay.

And sure as you can say "enchilada," Lord knows when Danny will be available.

"Alison is threatening to cut my, well, you know, my you-know-what off!" Colt is pacing our back deck while Jackson sits at the outside table, his back to me. I just got home and am hiding in the kitchen. I didn't get home fast enough to tell

Jackson the real story. The shop was super busy, and I kind of forgot—until Jackson texted to say Colt and Alison got into it in the high school parking lot.

I tried calling Missus from the moment I left work, but she never answered. Hopefully she's putting out her own fires and telling the truth. Jackson's phone is here in the kitchen, so I can't text him to come inside for me to explain. I just have to bite the bullet.

"Hey, guys. I'm home," I say as I walk out onto our deck. "What's going on?"

Jackson jumps up. "Hey. You knew about this?"

Colt explodes. "Knew about what? There is nothing going on! I told you that!"

His brother defends himself. "I meant about the rumor."

"I did hear about it this morning, but I didn't think much of it. It's just a crazy rumor, right? Just something someone made up."

"But why? Alison caused a huge scene at the high school. We sometimes meet in the parking lot when she's done at the elementary since I have fifth period for planning, and we, uh, we talk. I mean, at least we talked today. Okay… shouted." He steps closer, shaking his head, his thick, brown hair standing on end from how much he's pulling at it. "She said everyone knows I'm having an affair with Delaney Bedwell. She, like, *just got married*! I don't fool around with married women—well, uh, I mean, Phoenix was still married, but everyone knew she was unhappy. Delaney? I don't even think I've ever really talked to her!"

"Hey, you might want to keep it down," I say. "Is Bryan here? No need for him to know the rumor too."

Jackson cringes, and Colt falls back against the deck railing, crosses his arms, and says, "Oh, no worries there. I'm sure he's heard it all by now. The bus was unloading the kids that take courses at the community college. They got a great show. Not to mention the band kids practicing at the other end of the parking lot. Oh, there's nothing to hide here!" He drops his head, then reaches for his beer. "The only mystery is how long before I'm fired."

I whisper to Jackson, "Can I talk to you? Inside."

"Sure." He gets up and checks on Colt. "You okay, buddy? Why don't you walk down to the water? I'll meet you there with another beer in a bit. A walk will do you good."

Colt agrees and heads off down the hill. He's wearing his teaching clothes, khakis and a short-sleeve sports shirt. He doesn't lift his head as he leaves the porch, and it makes me want to kill Missus. Strangling her with one of her stupid gloves could work.

We get inside, and Jackson whirls toward me. "You knew about this? I was talking to Bonnie about one of her new jobs, and she said it was the talk of the shop earlier today. I'd've appreciated a heads-up, Carolina!"

"I was hoping it would die, just go away! Missus made the whole thing up, right in front of my face, and it went crazy. Like wildfire! It felt like that movie *The Blob*. It just grew and grew and grew with no one stopping it." (I looked it up on my own lunch break, and that is, in fact, what happened in that movie.)

Jackson points to our backyard, where his brother is walking sullenly toward the river. "He's telling the truth? He's not messing around with Delaney? I don't understand."

I pull Jackson to sit at the kitchen table with me. "No. She made it up. Completely. Peter is not staying home at night, and she wants to make him jealous. She as in Missus. Delaney knows nothing about this either."

Jackson's incredulous. He doesn't have a duplicitous bone in his whole body. He's not good at lying, and he doesn't play games, so this is as foreign to him as a blob from outer space.

As a matter of fact, he would probably understand The Blob better.

But he has become familiar with Missus. "Missus will never admit she did this, will she?"

"No. She's actually kind of pinning it on me. At least she did when she told Laney and Cathy earlier. I haven't been able to get a hold of her since then. Oh, yeah. Shannon's having a girl. That was kind of lost in all the rumor excitement."

He frowns at me. "What happened to the cannon gender reveal?"

"How do you know about that?"

"Danny's got the fire department guys in on it, and they told Colt and me the other day. Man, I was looking forward to that."

"Well, it's not happening. And I think the best thing for Colt to do is just deny and ignore. Let the rumor die."

Jackson stands up and goes to the refrigerator. "You think I should tell Colt how it started?" He pulls out two beers and pushes the fridge door shut behind him.

"I guess. I don't really know. Play it by ear, but it might help."

He shrugs, then gives me a bit of a smile before heading out the back door.

At the kitchen table, I lay my head on my folded arms. The house is quiet. I have no idea where either of my kids are. Grabbing my phone out of my pocketbook, I think about dinner.

Dinner comes way too often in my opinion.

I text both kids and wait. And wait. So I pull open the freezer door and think some more about dinner. Pork steaks on the grill, potatoes made somehow, and baked beans sound good. I pull the steaks out and put them in the microwave to defrost. There's enough for the four of us and Colt. If we end up with leftovers, they reheat great.

My phone dings, and Savannah says she'll be home for dinner. I take my phone upstairs with me to change clothes, and at the top of the stairs, I text my youngest again, this time adding a couple more question marks. That's when I hear his phone receive my text through his bedroom door. I knock quietly and say his name. Maybe he's asleep? When he doesn't answer, I open the door and slowly push it open. "Bryan?"

His phone chimes another notification, and I step farther into the empty room. Where would he go without his phone? Did he forget to take it to school today? His phone is still lit up from my text, and I walk toward it, where it's laying on his nightstand. Then I look at the chair beside the window.

Something yellow lying in the chair draws me in that direction. I don't think Bryan owns anything yellow. Especially not with little buttons like that. I pick up a blouse, not a T-shirt; not a sports shirt, a blouse. A girl's blouse, and it's not Savannah's. Then I see what's underneath the yellow blouse, and I drop it. I drop it, snatch up his phone, and get out of that room.

That room where some girl has folded her yellow blouse and neatly laid it on top of her bra and panties.

Chapter 27

Nothing. There's nothing on his phone that tells me one blessed thing! He rarely types, not like Savannah and her girl-friends who are constantly tapping away. His just has lots of one- and two-word texts. Lots of thumbs-up or thumbs-down emojis. He's a verbal kid. Reading and writing have never been his strong suits, and now that means there's nothing to give me a clue on his phone.

I get up from my seat on my bed and hurry back downstairs and onto the back deck. Jackson's phone is still laying in the kitchen, but Colt's isn't, so I text him to have Jackson call me.

My phone rings, and when Jackson picks up, he walks beneath the limbs of the weeping willow tree where I can see him.

"Is Bryan down there?" I ask him.

"Yeah. Him and some girl named Pilar. Swimming."

"Pilar? I met her one time, I think. Is she wearing a bathing suit?"

"What? I guess. What are you talking about?"

"Her clothes are upstairs in our son's bedroom. Her under-wear too."

He spins around, back through the weeping willow cur-tain, and I wait. I'd walk down there, but, well, I don't want to.

They'll be up here soon enough. I mean, she has to get dressed to go home, right?

Pilar? Yeah, I'm pretty sure that's the name of the girl that helped Kimmy get Ruby's set up that first morning. She paid Zoe and a couple of her friends to help. One was Michelle Walker, and the other was a freshman I didn't know.

Jackson's back on the phone. "Okay. Yes, she has on a bathing suit. She borrowed one of Savannah's. Savannah drove them home, gave Pilar a suit, and then left, so it's all good. Bryan wanted to know if she could stay for supper, but she said her mom is picking her up in a little bit. Do you know her mom?"

"No, but we have to tell those two this is in no way acceptable. I mean, what—"

"Honey, Colt keeps getting calls, so I better give him back his phone. Bye."

I've also ignored at least one call and a couple of texts, so after Jackson hangs up, I check them out. Susan just sent a string of question marks, so I guess she's heard the Delaney-Colt rumor. The call and the last text are from the same person.

Delaney wants to talk.

She doesn't even let me say hello.

"Just listen. Missus insinuated that you started this rumor, but that's not right, is it?"

"Right. It's not."

"She's delighted that Peter practically had a coronary when she told him about the rumor circulating around town. That was her goal, right?"

"Right."

Then she goes quiet. I can feel her thinking, so I stay quiet too.

She's less sure when she says, "What about Colt? Is he overly upset, you think?"

"He's more upset about Alison having a cow in the school parking lot and it being overheard by students. He's worried about his job. He said he doesn't recall ever really talking to you."

"Exactly. Okay, I'll make Missus fix things with the principal. Jed owes her for this pipe debacle. Tell Colt he doesn't have to worry about his job. Ask him if he wants me to call Alison—or maybe you should call her?"

"I could do that. I was there when Missus came up with the whole thing. You know, you can take some comfort in knowing that usually she's maneuvering things to *break up* Peter's relationships. She seems to want y'all to stay together."

Her smile comes through her words. "And that's exactly why I'm not really upset." She whispers, "And kind of liking how upset Peter is. Colt is younger, unmarried, and popular around town. The football coach! I have to say, Missus chose well."

As we giggle, I can see a car pulling into the driveway. "Hey, Delaney, I've got to go. Different fire here to put out."

I go inside and approach the front window to watch Pilar's mom walk up to the house. It turns out I do know her. She shops at the store. I can't remember what she buys or looks at, though.

"Hello. Come in," I say as she reaches the porch steps. "You're Pilar's mother? And you shop at Blooming Books, right?"

"Yes, I do, but I'm usually in a hurry, which is so not the right way to shop in a bookstore. I'm Regina; everyone calls me Reggie."

"And I'm Carolina. Nice to finally meet you. I met Pilar when she helped Zoe and her mom set up things for Ruby's to move into the back of the store temporarily."

"Yes, Zoe has been a good friend to Pilar. So, did they get to go swimming? I talked to your daughter who said she was loaning Pilar a swimsuit?"

We've walked to the back doors, and I open them, motioning for her to step out onto the deck.

"Oh, you talked to Savannah?" I ask.

"Yes. I was concerned there wouldn't be a parent home, but she told me her father was in the basement working and you were on your way home. It's been hard moving in the middle of the school year for Pilar, but your children have been very welcoming."

"I guess that's because they know how it feels to be the new kids. Not a lot of people move in and out here." I can see that two smaller figures have joined Jackson and Colt by the tree. "There are the kids. And that's my husband and his brother."

"The coach," Reggie says. "Our son is in seventh grade and wants to play football, so when we first moved here, we went to a couple of games at the end of the season."

We wait for them to join us, and the kids hurry inside to change clothes. I follow them. "Pilar, you can get dressed in my room or the bathroom." I try to make my words menacing, but neither she nor Bryan seems to notice as they rush up the stairs.

"She's not allowed to date," Reggie says behind me. "I told that to Bryan and to your daughter. They both assured me they are just friends."

Colt and Jackson join us inside, and by the time introductions are made, the kids are back downstairs. There's that cute, yellow blouse. Pilar is small and in some ways looks more like an elementary kid than a high school student. She has black, shoulder-length hair, which is wet and limp. There's no smiling or flirting or being bashful. As a matter of fact, she's not giving Bryan even a second look. He's frowning at me because I'm holding his phone, but he can tell this is not the time to test me.

Pilar thanks us for letting her come swimming and edges her mother toward the door. Reggie thanks us also and again stresses that it's good to have friends—since Pilar and Bryan are too young for anything more. She's very clear on that, and the kids nod along with her.

As their car pulls away, Colt applauds Pilar's parents for not allowing her to date. "I just see too much at school that shouldn't be allowed." He ruffles his nephew's hair. "You have your whole life to date."

"Sure, Coach," he says, and I can hear the total BS in his answer.

I hold out his phone, gripping it as I stare him down. "We will be talking about this." Releasing the phone, I move into the kitchen to get dinner started. I'm by myself, so I roll my eyes only for my own benefit, but I roll them real good.

I've come to the conclusion that telling your teen they aren't allowed to date just means you won't be told when they are dating.

"I didn't invite her! Savannah did."

Bryan's reply to my barrage of questions at dinner stops me in my tracks.

"What?" I turn to my daughter. "Why?"

Savannah shrugs. "She needs a friend. She's getting bullied by some of the kids in her classes. She's smart, very straitlaced, and completely naïve. She's a kid, and so I grabbed her away from these girls that were not being nice and told her to come home with us. We called her mom, and that's that. I thought Zoe could come swimming, too, but she was busy."

Here she gives me a very pointed look that I'll need to follow up on later.

I look at Bryan. "So you're not interested in her as a girlfriend?"

"No, I don't think so. But we did have fun today. I was kind of mad that Savannah set this up and then bailed, but it was okay. Pilar's kinda goofy, and we had fun. She's a crazy swimmer too."

Back to Savannah. "So, why did you bail? Sounds like her mom thought you would be here."

"I had to do something." She flips to her uncle. "So, what was all that with you and Miss Alison in the parking lot? A lover's quarrel? Everyone knows y'all meet to make out in your car every afternoon."

"Colt!" I jump him. I'm in a jumping mood. "In the school parking lot? You're not a kid!"

He tries to look confused, but that doesn't work with both his niece and nephew grinning at him. He frowns. "The kids at school know?"

"Cut it out!" I practically yell. "Missus is going to take care of any matter with the principal stemming from today onward. Find another place to meet up with Alison, okay?"

He nods. "Yes, ma'am. And thanks for dinner. This is delicious. I miss good meals."

Jackson finally adds something to the conversation. "I bet. Phoenix is one great cook." He grins. "Of course she probably wouldn't make out in the high school parking lot. So there's that."

Colt shoots him a dirty look. "I hear Dad and Shelby will be here on Friday for an extended stay? *That* sounds like fun."

"Oh yeah, we're all excited." I start collecting plates. "I'm going to the grocery store tomorrow. If any of you need something, make sure to write in on the list on the fridge."

"We're still going down to KSU on Friday morning?" Savannah asks.

Jackson and I check with each other, and he answers. "Sure thing. Looks like it's all coming together."

Colt's phone suddenly makes a bunch of noises. "Yikes! I turned it off while we ate, and now everything's coming in."

He reads for a minute, then looks up at me. "You talked to Delaney and she's cool?"

"Yes. She's got things handled there. How's Alison?"

"Not as mad. Wants to know if she's still my date for the Conners' party on Saturday." He whistles. "Hmmm. Lookie there. Been a long time since I've seen that name pop up."

Savannah has stood to help with the dishes, and now she leans over her uncle's shoulder. "Phoenix. You should call her back before you confirm with Alison for the party."

"Savannah! Hush. That's not nice," I say with a slap at her arm.

Colt shrugs. "Yeah, but she's not wrong."

CHAPTER 28

She's going to love it.

It's a beautiful campus with rolling hills, modern buildings, lots of greenery, and so many sidewalks and paths. *So* many sidewalks and paths, and I believe we traversed them all. I barely had the energy to fall into the front seat of the minivan for the drive home. I want so badly to join in Jackson and Savannah's excited chatter, but I can't keep my eyes open.

Yesterday was the longest day ever in the shop.

Shannon's mid-pregnancy feel-good period has ended. I mean, I guess that's what her mood was about. And good-natured Danny revealed another talent: he's a really good sulker. Guess I shouldn't be surprised. Sulking doesn't require much energy or dignity, so it's right up his alley. The power went out downtown midmorning due to the construction. We were supposed to be told about any planned interruptions to the power, but they just apologized and said they're working on it. None of the construction guys came in so we couldn't get any more details. However, everyone else wanted to know what was going on and that caused a big influx to Ruby's. I guess to drink lukewarm coffee and complain about having no power. Shannon had a big flower order in the non-cooling cooler, and the rising heat didn't help her stay cool either. The place was murky, with only light from the front windows to see by, and we had to keep track of all purchases with paper and pen.

In case you're wondering—shadows and low light enhanced the creep factor of the dolls by about a million.

The outage was fixed by lunch. However, everyone's attitudes took longer to fix.

Brittani, Bryan's old girlfriend, came in to help Shannon, and she chattered nonstop. That girl has always gotten on my last nerve. Her gossip didn't go so far as to include names, but I'm sure I recognized my kids in there several times. She did mention Pilar by name, and I get the feeling I know at least one of the bullies Savannah was talking about. Susie Mae also came to work—late. I couldn't—okay—I *didn't* stop myself from yelling at her in front of everyone.

Brittani especially loved that.

Susie Mae stormed off. Said she quit. Meaning I needed Danny to work.

Danny then got mad because he was supposed to be off the rest of the day for some fireman training. I didn't stop myself again. I told him I'd never seen a fireman that moped around and couldn't lift his feet off the ground to walk.

Yeah, and that didn't help Shannon's already sour mood.

Did I mention our air conditioner didn't come back on when the power came back? No? Well, it didn't, and it was hot. Kimmy's cream pies didn't do well in the heat, and so she complained to, oh… let me think. That's right: Me. She complained to me.

I lay awake all night thinking what I should have said. What I wished I'd said. First blasting everyone, then begging forgiveness. Then blasting them when they smarted off at my contrition. Then pleading for grace. Then blasting… you get the picture.

At a stop sign, Jackson reaches over and pats my hand. "Go

on to sleep. You're not missing anything, but you're going to break your neck with your head bobbing like that."

They both laugh, and Savannah adds, "I have to finish reading this, so we won't bother you. Go to sleep."

So I do.

"Well, if this isn't a fine 'welcome home' from my honeymoon!" Gertie says when we walk in the front door of the shop, straight from our tour of KSU. "Ya broke the air-conditioning unit."

Rejuvenated from my nap, I jump right in. "*We* didn't do anything. The power went out, and when it came back on, *your* heat pump and air conditioner didn't restart. And welcome home." As we neared Chancey, I woke up and turned my phone back on for the first time since we had arrived on campus. I'd turned it off so I could focus on Savannah and our tour. The calls and texts from the shop had gotten crazy, and Laney's party had a million and one things going wrong that she wanted my help on, so I turned my phone off. I'm getting good at that.

The first thing I discovered when I turned it back on today is that our landlady, Gertie, didn't want to call the guy who installed the air-conditioning unit and repairs it. She wanted to give it a look over first. Have her man take a look. Bonnie texted that Bill took a look, shrugged, and said he didn't really know anything about air-conditioning systems. So Gertie demanded that Jackson come take a look. Listen closely—you can hear my eyes rolling. But here we are as requested, joining the party in the very warm building.

But who needs air conditioning with all the cold shoulder I'm getting? Pie time luckily hasn't started yet, so there's no one to add their two cents' worth from the café tables. Bonnie tips her head at me to follow her to the back door, near where the looking over is happening just outside.

"What is going on with Shannon and Danny?" she quietly asks me. "Working with them reminds me of my days teaching junior high girls. They're sniping at each other between silent pouting sessions. Are they arguing over something in particular?"

"They're probably still mad at me," I admit. "I was a regular witch yesterday. I don't know what was wrong with me, but I yelled at them and at Susie Mae—"

"Finally!" she interjects. "Susie Mae has to know she can't just show up when she feels like it." Bonnie's back stiffens. "Good for you."

I shrug. "Well, I don't know about that. She quit when she stormed out."

"Really? Oh, I didn't want it go that far." Bonnie goes from stern to concerned. "She's really a good little worker when she's here."

"I know. I'll call her when school is out. Now let me go up front and apologize to those two."

Bonnie lays her hand on my arm. "I don't know. Feels like it's more than something you did." She sighs, then moves closer to the wall, motioning with her head for me to follow. "Something's up with Shannon," she whispers.

"Like what?"

"Like what? Come on. Peter."

I flinch and open my mouth with a little gasp. "Peter and Shannon?" Maybe I guessed right about them meeting. "How do you know?"

She's turned facing the wall, so I follow suit. I don't know who we're fooling, but we look like we're closely examining the concrete work. Her whisper is even quieter. "Last week I finished late at the house over on Oak. The couple invited me to eat dinner with them and talk about doing a renovation for their office area. They want something grand, stately. I thought of Peter's office, and so I wanted to pick up some pictures to leave with them. Real pictures in a folder are just so much more professional than ones on a phone, in my opinion. Anyway, by that time it was really late, but I stopped in to pick them up. Guess who was sitting at one of Ruby's tables?"

"Peter and Shannon?"

She nods emphatically. "Yep. So the next day I chatted with Danny and found out he's spending almost every evening at the firehouse, training and socializing."

"Did they see you?"

She quickly shakes her head. "I don't think so. I came in the back door, but only opened it a few inches. They were sitting facing the front of the store. I didn't tell you because I abhor gossip, but I decided you should know. Sure would be awful for all of us here if Danny and Shannon break up."

She and I turn to face the front of the store, and I watch Shannon at her worktable and Danny as he works on our front window. I bend toward Bonnie. "Thanks. I hope Peter and she are finally talking about the baby. I don't see them getting together, but if they are keeping all this a secret from their spouses, they may be doing real damage to their marriages." I shrug as we hear the contingent from outside coming back in. "For now I guess we'll just wait and see. Once they work out an arrangement they'll have to let their spouses know."

Jackson comes in first, looking at me with wide eyes. Gertie follows him, blustering about fishing in Alaska. "Who in the Sam Hill goes all the way to Alaska to fish when God gave every kind of fish to ya right in your own backyard?!"

Bill drawls, "Said somethin' about salmon. King salmon I believe he said. He's gonna call a couple of buddies to come have a look when they get a chance."

Our landlady pushes through the tables and chairs, still

grumbling. "All I need, another couple of bumpkins in here to look and tell me they ain't got no idea. What good is it to have a repairman if he's gonna up and run off when he gets a chance to catch some fancy fish way up north? I've about had it with this place."

Bill and Jackson are right behind her, and Bonnie and I bring up the rear. Behind my hand I say, "You'd think she'd be in a better mood after her honeymoon and all."

We giggle, but are composed by the time we get to the front.

"Well, don't worry," Jackson says. "Dad's on his way."

Gertie makes her way over to the couch. "I'm looking forward to meeting your old man. Gonna meet Hillbilly Hank himself."

I groan. "Aww, Jackson. You didn't."

He shrugs, hands out to the sides. "Can't hurt. He texted they were coming into town, so I asked him to swing by here."

"Shelby, too, probably," I mutter.

Shannon leaves her worktable to join us. She has a glow about her, and it's not a pregnant-woman glow. It's a mean-woman glow. "Oh, wait. Shelby, as in Jackson's first wife?"

Danny looks at me and laughs. "Mr. Jackson don't have no first wife. There's just Carolina!"

But then he follows the direction of my stare and lands on my husband. "What? You been married before?" With his long legs he's beside Jackson in about a second, where he stretches out his hand for a high-five. "Me too, bud!"

When my husband looks at me, his eye crunched in a cringe, I shrug and sit down across from Gertie. "You started it."

Chapter 29

You know those pictures showing how the US presidents age while in office? Well, I'm going to have to go back in my phone and pull up the pictures from just seven months ago when we went to Shelby and Hank's wedding. I haven't seen her since then.

Taking care of Hillbilly Hank has taken its toll on Shelby Jessup.

I can't say I'm exactly surprised, but still—this is a surprise.

Laney, Susan, and I previously nicknamed Shelby "Melanie" because she reminded us of Melanie Hamilton in *Gone with the Wind*. You know, Ashley's wife, Scarlett's nemesis, and her best friend? Porcelain skin, sweet attitude, quiet talking? Butter won't melt in her mouth, and she never says anything bad about anyone? Like Melanie, Shelby floated around on the periphery as long as Hank and Etta were married; she was always there but never in the way. She would float in for meals. Float in to do some paperwork. Float in from her little cottage, where she did whatever it was she did all day. They had let her live in the cottage on their property after her crazy marriage with Jackson ended. Shelby had no one else, so they let her float around, being sweet and innocent and vulnerable.

Except she was sleeping with Hank.

The cute, shiny bob from before is now shoulder-length,

straight hair with gray roots. Her skin is no longer like porcelain. I guess that's understandable since she's probably had to take over a lot of the farm duties. First that was because Etta moved out, but then Hank fell from a ladder and was laid up a while. And as for her skin being smooth, well, nope. Life with Hank, not as his mistress but as his full-time wife, has led to lots of wrinkles. She looks really tired and stressed standing inside the shop's front door.

Hank comes blustering in. "Cock of the walk" never described anyone as well as Hank Jessup. He's wiry, of an average height, with not much gray hair left, but even so, he arrives as the conquering hero, even when he's not done one blessed thing.

Shelby wearily smiles at us, then steps toward me. "Hey, y'all. Carolina, I love your shop."

Then her better half shouts, "But it's awfully warm in here! Where's that air-conditioning unit, son? Let's get these folks cooled back down!"

Jackson leads Hank toward the back with Bill in tow. Gertie sits frozen on the couch, undecided on whether she should follow the men for more of the Hillbilly Hank show or say everything that is already on the tip of her tongue. Gertie likes nothing better than ridiculing self-important men behind their backs. She'll do it to their faces, but she's best with an audience of women. You ought to see her imitation of Peter.

"Shelby, let me introduce you," I say after we give each other a quick hug. "My partner in Blooming Books, Shannon, and her husband, Danny. Danny also works here. Gertie is our landlady, and the tall man that went with Hank and Jackson is her new husband, Bill. Kimmy, come up here and meet someone. This is Jackson's dad's wife, Shelby."

Everyone is polite, but they don't say much. They've all heard stories in which I make fun of Shelby, and this sad, worn-out woman does not look like someone that should be made fun of. I don't believe I've ever mentioned her name without there being a story representing her as the wicked witch attached. Guess I have some making up to do.

Okay, just one quick thing, though: She got exactly what she wanted.

There. I'm done.

Bless her heart.

"Uh, I'm not just dropping off food," Phoenix says when I open up our front door late Friday afternoon.

"Okay. Come in. What's going on?" I'd ordered a meat loaf from her for supper tonight since it's a big family affair. "Let's put that in the kitchen. It smells delicious."

"It's one of my biggest sellers." She sits the box on the kitchen table, and I step over to turn down the potatoes I have boiling on the stove.

"I can't wait to taste it. So, what's up?"

"Colt invited me tonight." Her tone is telling me this information, but it seems like she's asking a question at the same time.

Trying to hold back my grin doesn't work. "Really? That's great. Are y'all back together?"

"I don't know." She folds her arms and walks back and forth beside the kitchen table. "I took him some food last night. Spicy chicken kabobs and rice. It was just a neighborly gesture, and well, we talked and stuff."

Nope, I'm not going to ask what she means by "stuff." I'm going to stifle this grin and just listen. "That sounds nice." I sit, then push out the chair across from me with my foot. "Want to sit?"

"Sure. For a minute." Phoenix perches on the edge of the

chair. "Should I come tonight? Is he really broken up with Alison? He wasn't ever with Delaney, right? I mean, I kind of knew that was a silly rumor. I don't think they even know each other, right?"

I nod. "Right. Missus started it. She wanted Peter to be jealous, but Alison seems to be the one that lost it."

"I know. Right in the school parking lot! It's crazy that she came to find him at his place of employment to cause a scene."

Okay, let's not mention why she usually showed up at the high school parking lot. "Yeah, crazy, but if it gets you and Colt talking…"

"No." She shakes her head. "I didn't tell him about, you know. I'm so afraid he'll *say* he doesn't want kids just so I don't feel bad when I do tell him. I don't want him to resent me later or to really regret not having children of his own."

Sympathy for all Phoenix is going through shivers through me. I place a comforting hand on hers. "Who knows? Kids are a lot. All this time with Alison's girls and being a teacher may have made him not want kids for real. Phoenix, you've got to talk to him. And yes, please come to dinner tonight. We've missed you."

She smiles at my hand atop hers, then gently removes it to stand up. "I'll be here tonight, and I will talk to him soon. I've missed being with all of you too. I have one more delivery to make, and then I'll be back. I saw the Kentucky plates in the driveway, so I assume Hank and Shelby are already here?"

"Yeah," I say, forcing down the accompanying eye roll. "She's taking a nap, and he's off somewhere with Bryan." I stand too. "I've got to say I'm glad he showed up when he did: he fixed our air conditioner at work. Now we just have to survive the next week of hearing him crow about it."

Phoenix stops to look in the mirror beside the front door and pulls her hair around in one hand. It hangs past her shoulders and she studies the uneven ends "I wish I'd gotten my hair trimmed, but I've really not been in a good place lately." She smiles, and her eyes meet mine in the mirror. "Although Colt didn't seem to think I looked that bad last night."

"Well, that's good." I hug her shoulders from behind. "I've missed that sparkle in your eyes. You and Colt are going to be fine."

I follow her onto the porch and wave at her as she pulls out of the driveway. The porch is looking good with the rugs washed and the furniture all wiped down. The flowers are still in a little shock from being planted, but by next weekend the pots will be beautiful. Now to finish dinner.

"Oh! You scared me," I say as I come into the kitchen. My father-in-law is sitting in the chair Phoenix just left. I walk past him to the stove. "Thanks again for fixing the air at the store."

"No problem. So Phoenix is coming tonight? Seems she went back to her stage name. Gave up trying to be Rebecca?"

"Uh, yeah, I guess so." I'd almost forgotten she introduced herself as Rebecca when she first came to town with Colt. Her Las Vegas past, not to mention leaving the older judge who'd brought her from Nevada to Kentucky when she ran off with Colt, made her want to drop her stage name. But Rebecca never felt right, neither to her nor to us.

As I spear one of the boiling potatoes to see if they're ready, I wonder what Hank is getting at. He's most definitely poking around about something. Wait, how does he know she's coming? What else did he hear us talking about? "Did you just come in?"

"A bit ago." He slowly stands and starts walking back toward his room in the B&B hall. "Came in through the basement door. Let me go get Shelby. Sounds like dinner will be interesting."

Great. He heard us.

Chapter 30

Shelby looks better after her nap, and she's been a big help getting dinner on the table. Will and Anna arrived with the star of the evening, Francie. Phoenix and Colt decided they'll arrive together instead of meeting here. I'm anxious to let her know Hank possibly, probably, knows her secret, so we can cut him off before he can let Colt know, but they aren't here yet.

"Uncle Colt texted that they're almost here," Bryan says, strolling into the kitchen. "Are we going to eat soon? I'm starving."

"Yes. Here, put the carrots on the table. And there's a relish tray in the fridge."

Shelby peeks in the oven. "Rolls are done. Want me to take them out?"

"Sure. Bryan, holler down to the basement that it's time to eat."

Savannah wants a shelf built for her dorm apartment's bedroom, so she's drawing out the plans in the basement with her dad and grandfather. Everyone gathers, and as we get the last dishes to the table, the front door opens.

"Sorry we're late," Colt says. "Hey, Shelby. Dad."

He gives them hugs, and I try to motion to Phoenix that I need to talk to her in the kitchen. I think she thinks I'm going to ask her if she had a chance to talk to Colt, but I have bigger fish to fry. Anyway, she brushes me off, follows Colt in giving out hugs, and then sits at the dining room table. I join everyone and draw in a deep breath, telling myself to just enjoy this. Just enjoy having all the kids together.

"I'll say it," I offer as we join hands to bless the food.

Jackson kisses my hand. "She cooks *and* prays."

I give him a grin and then close my eyes. "Thank you, Lord, for everyone being gathered here tonight. Thank you for Hank and Shelby's safe journey here and that he fixed our air conditioning." There's a small wave of laughter around the table and a hearty amen from Jackson. "I'm not through," I add. "Thank you for all you've done for us and the ways you continue to help us feel your presence even when we feel far from you. Bless us and this meal, and help us to see others the way you see them. Amen."

Phoenix spreads her hands across the full table. "Everything looks delicious! Thank you for inviting me."

"Anytime," I say. "Phoenix made the meat loaf," I explain to Hank and Shelby, "and I can't wait to try it. The rest was pretty easy to throw together."

Will is giving bits off his plate to his hungry daughter in the high chair that's situated between him and Anna. Francie's just started on some solid foods, and she's loving it. Between feeding his daughter and himself, he asks his sister, "So, how was the college tour? Isn't it a beautiful campus?"

Savannah lights up and then fills everyone in on all the details of her new home. Jackson and I meet eyes several times to smile at the joy in her voice. We'll miss her, but this is what we raised her for—to leave.

Dinner is pleasant and relaxing until Francie decides she's done. She suddenly starts throwing the food on her tray and catches us by surprise. Then when we laugh, she looks for more stuff to throw.

"Okay," her mom declares. "Dinner is done for you, Miss Lady!"

Anna scoots out to unhook her from the chair just as Hank raises his tea glass. "Wait, I have an announcement. Seeing as my oldest son is now having grandchildren and my youngest has apparently chosen to not have children, seeing as he's back together with Rebecca, uh, Phoenix—oh, whichever you prefer, dear. Well, anyway, with all that—"

Colt screws up his face. "What? What are you even talking about?"

"Oh, never mind me on all that. You and Phoenix obviously know more than the rest of us, except of course for Carolina. Here's to Shelby and me and our new creation. Yessiree, I'm going to be a daddy again!"

Now *I* feel like throwing food. Or maybe throwing up. Looking around the table, I know I'm not the only one.

"Well, it's better than announcing it during my graduation dinner. Shelby says that was originally his plan. Wonder what made him change his mind?"

Savannah and I are the only ones in the kitchen. Hank's announcements and innuendos scattered our family dinner. Phoenix shot a dark look at Hank and then at me, but I was able to say as she walked by me that I didn't tell him—he overheard us. She and Colt left the house by the back door and walked down the hill, I suppose, because I can't see them from the kitchen window.

Francie got very fussy at that point, and Will and Anna took that as an excuse to get while the getting was good. "She needs to get a bath and go to bed. Thanks for dinner!" was pretty much all they said as they gathered their things and fled. However, Anna texted me from the car to call her when I can. She added a string of crazy emojis stating their shock, curiosity, and blown minds to her text.

Shelby, in all the commotion, simply sat chewing her lip and taking small sips of iced tea, but then said she had to go. She jumped up and fled toward the B&B hall and the bathroom. Hank followed her.

That left the waitstaff—Jackson, Bryan, Savannah, and me. We cleaned off the table pretty much in silence, as we weren't sure who was where and could overhear us, but there were a lot of confused looks passed back and forth. Jackson left to take Bryan over to a friend's house, and Savannah and I are finishing up now before she heads out to spend the night at Amanda's.

Her comment stops me in my tracks. I turn to her as she dries her hands on a paper towel. "Wait, Shelby told you that? He was going to announce her being pregnant at your graduation dinner?"

"She didn't tell me what it was, just that Grandad wanted to make an announcement and she wanted to give me a heads-up." She throws the paper towel in the trash. "She was afraid I'd be upset. Is that why she looks so, you know, not good?"

"Probably. Maybe she's sick to her stomach a lot. Being pregnant can make you really tired. Some women just have a harder time with it." I wipe out the finally empty sink. "And she's not young. Not as old as Laney was when she had Cayden, but still, it's harder being an older mom."

Savannah's almost to the kitchen door, and she hasn't mentioned Phoenix or Colt, but then she turns back to me. "I don't know what's going on with Phoenix and Uncle Colt, but, well, I like them together. Funny how you can tell that some people just belong together." She shrugs and heads on into the living room.

Man, I'm gonna miss her.

Phoenix comes in the back door to find me sitting at the kitchen table working on a grocery list.

"Colt left," she says.

I smile sadly at her. "No worries. We can give you a ride home."

She slides into the chair across from me. "That's what I told him. It's not like he left me here stranded. He offered to take me home, but I told him I'd like to come inside, and he just, well, he just couldn't." She looks around, stretching her neck to look into the dining room and at the door to the B&B hall.

I can tell what she's thinking. "They went to their room right after y'all left, and we haven't seen them since."

She lets out a held breath. "Good. So you think he overheard us earlier?"

"I know he did. He was sitting here after I told you goodbye, and I could tell he knew something. I tried to let you know."

"Yeah, I know now that's what you were motioning about when we got here. Sometimes I'm just dense." She chuckles. "It was a nice dinner for the most part, right? Could Francie be any cuter?"

It's sweet that she thinks bringing up my granddaughter will distract me. "How's Colt?"

She screws up her mouth in response. "He's hurt. Angry. Confused. Needs to think. He's angry at his dad, but then appreciative to him because, well, was I *ever* going to tell him? How can he believe me that I really was going to tell him soon? You were right. I should've talked to him."

I reach out to tap her hand. "Hey. I'll tell him how hard it's been."

"Yeah, well, he's not happy with you either. And he thinks Jackson had to know."

"I'm not sure Jackson figured out right away that I knew and haven't told him. He had to take Bryan to a friend's, so I'm thinking by the time he gets home he'll have put things together."

She winces. "I'm sorry I put you in this position. But honestly, I am glad it's out." We sit in the silence for a moment, and then her eyes widen. "Shelby's having a baby. I never imagined that. Did you?"

"No, not really. I mean, it happens in books all the time when the old man remarries a younger woman. It's the main plot in tons of Regency and Gothic romances. You know, the new wife and new heir. But I thought Shelby and Hank liked having the freedom to roam around doing Hillbilly Hank stuff. And she's not some young twenty-year-old. She's not that much younger than Jackson and me. Explains why she looks so tired, though."

We hear Savannah come barreling down the stairs, and then she enters the kitchen, jingling her keys. "I'm leaving. Oh, hey, Phoenix. How are you doing? The meatloaf really was amazing."

Phoenix smiles. "Thanks. You're going out? Can you give me a ride home? Colt needed some time to himself."

Savannah offers a soft smile in return. "Sure. I'm going right past your house."

"Okay. I'm ready when you are," Phoenix says as she stands. They head out the door as Jackson is heading in—all before I have time to even stand up. Jackson comes into the kitchen. He doesn't say hi but grabs a beer, then, before closing the fridge door, asks, "You want one? Let's take a walk out on the bridge."

I shove my half-done grocery list away. "Sure."

He puts the beers in koozies, opens them both, hands one

to me, and then leads me to the front door, which he opens and motions me through. "So. What's been on your mind, Mrs. Jessup? Feels like we should probably catch up."

Oh, I'm going to need this beer.

CHAPTER 31

"Quiet morning at our house," I say to Susan as we meet on Laney's porch on the Saturday of the two big parties. "How are things with y'all?"

Susan shakes her head, but says, "Okay, I guess. But how was it quiet at your house? Aren't Hank and Shelby there?"

"Yes, but… Okay, I'm sure he'll be crowing about it today, so I might as well tell you. They're expecting. He told us last night. Everyone is still stunned, hence the quiet."

She blinks at me. "Expecting? Like, expecting a baby? Oh, for crying out loud. What in the world did Jackson say?"

"Oh, what *didn't* Jackson say? Here, want to sit down?" We move over to a wicker settee around the corner of the big wrap-around porch. Jackson and my walk on the bridge last night was a long one. He couldn't believe I hadn't told him what was going on with Phoenix. At the same time he understood why I didn't. He's not fond of having a divided mind. He likes things black and white which is why he's a good engineer. Besides, all of that paled in his shock over having another sibling on the way. All in all, as mad as he might get at me, I'm still his favorite family member. Of course I can't tell Susan about Phoenix and Colt so I jumped right into the Hank and Shelby news.

Parking for the parties is behind the house out beside Laney and Shaw's barn. The big tent with the tables and chairs is also out that way, so there aren't many folks up near the house. The party is still in its gathering stage, and we wanted to get here early to offer our help. Plus, getting out of our house early was a bonus. It was so awkward at breakfast. Jackson headed to the guys around the big barbecue smoker, and I'd come up to the house to find Laney when I spotted her sister on the porch.

"Jackson can't believe it, but Hank was just being Hank when he ended our dinner with a bang. Shelby seemed embarrassed. Darn if he didn't actually make me feel sorry for her."

Susan studies me. "Sounds like Shelby wasn't looking too great yesterday afternoon. Susie Mae said she looked really, really old. I guess I'd described her as being young and kind of stupid, so that didn't fit with what Susie Mae saw." She frowns. "It does make me feel bad. We weren't very kind to her."

"No, we weren't, but Susie Mae was right about how Shelby looked. Oh, and hey, thanks for helping talk Susie Mae into coming back to work. She's really a good worker, but she's just been hard to pin down lately. Do you know where she's been going? Or who she's hanging out with? It seems like maybe she was up at the winery that day we went after church."

"Susie Mae? No, she goes to school and work, and I'm sure she wasn't at the winery. I don't even think she's interested in anyone currently. We usually hear it nonstop when she likes a boy. She said she quit the job because you've been acting irrational. I told her it was probably just that Savannah is not only graduating but also moving, so you're emotional."

Okay, that does it. I've been holding it together and being polite to Susan—there are enough waves in Chancey right now; I don't need to make more—but this is the final straw. "*I've* been irrational? *I've* been emotional? Bonnie demanded I say something to your daughter weeks ago, but I held off. Danny is easier to count on than Susie Mae lately. And I've told you this!"

Susan draws back, frowning and surprised. "Oh. I, uh,

must've missed that. Hey, look, there's Laney," she says as she jumps up, completely ignoring me, and moves past me into the house.

I lean back and close my eyes. I did tell her, right? Am I not speaking clearly? Am I thinking so much about everything that I'm not saying anything? Last night on the rail bridge, Jackson said he feels like my mind is whirling so much that I can't get words out. Is that true? I sigh and look out at the bright blue sky. I breathe deep and let go another, deeper sigh.

It feels true.

Things are actually going pretty well, at least in my life, and I need to relax and appreciate it. I take another deep breath, letting it out so very slowly. As I open my eyes, the porch door creaks opens.

"Pig is off the roaster, and we're getting ready to eat," Laney tells me, her head sticking out of the door. "Come on. Let's get this party started!" She smiles wide and then lets the door bang shut behind her.

Another deep breath. Calm. No more drama, I decide as I follow her into the house. After all, it's a party. A celebration.

In the kitchen, I properly greet Laney. She's wearing a white sundress, and she's definitely been working on her tan. With its big skirt and flowy sleeves, she looks like the belle of the ball. Her shoulders are bare, and her dark hair just brushes the tops of them.

Susan looks like she's been shopping at her sister's shop; she's wearing a short, olive jumpsuit. The hemp belt emphasizes her small waist and matches her sandals. She's wearing her hair down, and she looks good, younger. I wonder if she's here with her new friend from work?

"I like your jumpsuit," I say with an apologetic smile. She nods and heads out the back door with her hands full of plates. I watch her go, then stop Laney from following her. "Listen. I think maybe she's following Griffin."

Laney stops, her mouth opened in a shiny pink circle as she stares at me. Then she shakes her head. "Following Griffin? Like up to the winery?" She squints and I know she's thinking what I am. "I did catch what she said about it. But, no. She knows better than to do something like that. I mean, that's crazy." We both turn to watch Susan talking to those at the table, then Laney grunts. "Could she be… ? No, listen we'll talk about this later." And she plows on ahead, plunging into the people happy to see her.

There's already nearly a hundred people here, I'd bet. The men have gravitated to where they are pulling the meat from the pig behind a small shed. I spy Jackson over there. There's a pickup football game going on in the side yard, and Bryan is there with some friends. His other party must've fallen apart as he told us this morning he'd be coming with us. Savannah and her friends, both boys and girls, are gathered up around the pool. I see Jenna but haven't spotted Angie yet.

"Hey," I call out to Laney, "Angie and Alex here yet?"

Laney points with her head to the tent. "They were over there, last I saw. I hired a caterer from Sandy Springs, and Alex is busy getting tips from them. That boy is always working."

I look but don't see Angie, but like I said, there are already a lot of people here. We set down what we'd carried from the house, and Laney waves us toward the drinks station. "Have some punch. See? There's the adult one and the kid one."

Susan and I say at the same time, "I want the adult one." We all laugh and move over to the shade of a big pecan tree, where lots of our friends are gathered. Susan is acting completely normal, so I will too. "Laney, it looks magical," I say. "You've done a great job."

It's not too long after that we hear a resounding clang, and I notice an old-fashioned, iron bell on a post near the shed. "Chow time," Shaw yells as he yanks the bell rope back and forth. The group from the football game stampedes in our direction. Up on the pool deck, the older teens also begin moving, but more slowly and calmly, as befits graduating royalty.

Susan laughs at the forming buffet line. "I guess smelling that pork cooking all morning has whetted some appetites. Hey, but before we get in line…" She turns to her sister. "Carolina was telling me Susie Mae's been acting a little erratic lately. You know anything about that?"

Laney opens her mouth and then nods. "Yeah. I mean, Carolina and Bonnie have said that. And then there are times I've mentioned her leaving school."

"But I thought that was no big deal. Her grades are fine. Besides, where do you think she's going? What could she possibly be doing?"

Laney and I look at each other. Then, ignoring my no-drama decision, I ask, "But, Susan, where have *you* been going? What are you doing? Are you making trouble for yourself? For Griffin?"

She pulls back. "Me? Trouble? I go to work and home. That's it. I already told you I'm a single mother now. I have a lot of responsibilities." She presses her lips closed and decides to leave it at that. "I'm hungry too. We better get in line. Listen, I'll talk to Susie Mae. I'm sure there's nothing to worry about." She moves off, her hands jammed in the pockets of her shorts and her head shaking in a terse, agitated way.

We watch as she joins up with some of our other friends, suddenly laughing with not a care in the world.

Laney hits my arm. "Maybe we're the crazy ones. Whatever, I'm tired of trying to figure her out. She's always been the steady one, so I'm sure she's fine." She stands and fluffs the full skirt of her dress before giving me a wide-eyed look through her lashes. "Besides, I'm not cut out for worrying."

We ate. The kids ate. Everyone ate. And it was delicious. As we wandered around or sat in groups with full bellies and topped-off drinks, we enjoyed watching the seniors on center stage. Many of the younger kids are sprawled where they'd been playing football. Some are kicking a ball around or messing with the volleyball court, but they are in our peripheral vision.

Our focus is directed at those gathered around the pool.

They are moving on, moving away, and this is one of the last opportunities to simply watch them. To have them in sight. From those days of sitting close to catch them as they learned to walk, to sniffling as they headed into their first classroom with a cartoon character backpack, our placement as their watchers and minders grows farther and farther away. When they climb into a car for that first solo drive, we watch with a lump in our throat until the car fades from view, and in that moment, we experience a whole new kind of watching. But now we're getting ready to watch them walk across a stage and finish something we had no idea would go so fast. And then they'll keep on walking off that stage, to the night they no longer sleep under our roof. The walk is taking them into a new place, a place they'll feel bad calling home in front of us, but that's what it'll be—their new home.

So graduation celebrations are one of our last chances to unabashedly watch, to give them center stage and take our seat in the audience. They are so young, so alive, so scared, so fearless.

It's a great adventure being young.

Even more so being a parent.

Chapter 32

So it didn't work exactly as Laney planned, with everyone staying around for a little rest and downtime between the pig roast and the dancing. You see, in *Gone with the Wind* they had horses and buggies and dirt roads. They couldn't just run home to take a nap and change for the dance.

We can. And we did.

I do think all the men stayed and played around on Shaw's new putting green, though. And of course most of the younger kids stayed to hang out and play in the pool. The older girls, like Savannah, Jenna, and their friends, congregated upstairs to get dressed for the dance. The older boys drifted off to go do whatever boys do on a hot Saturday afternoon. So when I say most of us went home, I guess I mean the moms.

Quiet, empty houses were a no-brainer.

Shelby hadn't gone to the pig roast, so I checked in on her when I got home, but she didn't answer my knock on her door. I assumed she was taking a nap.

Upstairs I rested, read a book on the deck for a while, and then got dressed for the evening's festivities. As I'm coming down the stairs around five, I decide I will definitely make Shelby answer the door before I leave.

She opens the B&B door almost immediately.

"Hey," I say, "I just wanted to check on you."

"I'm fine. Just getting dressed for tonight."

"Do you want a ride over? No sense in Hank having to come back here to take you."

"He's already here. He's taking a shower." She smiles at me, and I smile back.

"Okay. Well, see you there then."

All right, duty done. Hank was fairly quiet at the barbecue. I don't remember seeing or hearing much of him. I know he was playing croquet, and he does seem to be going a bit slower now that he's been here a couple of days. Maybe now that he's had all the fun of announcing he's still virile, he's realizing the hard part starts—having a baby at sixty-six years old.

"Look at you!" Jackson says as I do my best Laney sashay over to him.

I'd gone through my closet and matched a fitted, sleeveless black top with a flouncy, crinkled skirt I'd forgotten I own. It swings around my ankles and has bright pink, blue, and yellow line drawings against a black background, which goes well with my top and my black sandals. I pulled my hair up in a pink clip, and I have on big, dangly earrings I got from Laney's shop. (C'mon, I had to shop a little.)

Jackson leans in for a good kiss, and I'm glad all the frostiness from last night is gone. He understood why I hadn't told him what was going on with Phoenix not being able to have a baby, but he was still aggravated. But that's what it means to have Hank around—constant aggravation.

Plus, the sun and the beer have aided his ability to forgive.

"Look," he says, pulling me around. "They've laid out a dance floor under one end of the tent, and the DJ is already warming up." In addition to the music, white lights are strung over the trees, the barn, and the tent itself to create a party atmosphere. It feels like we're surrounded by twinkling stars. I'm so glad I went home and rested; this looks like it could be a long, fun evening.

Jackson pulled me out to the dance floor, and we got in a groove that didn't stop for about half an hour. After a slow song which we really enjoyed, I decided I needed a break.

Coming off the dance floor, I spot Phoenix at the food table.

"Hey, you!" I grab her in a hug. "I spotted you out there dancing, but it was too crowded to get to you. I can't believe how many people are here."

"Me either. So many people I've never seen. Do you know everyone?"

"No way." I get closer to her. "Are you here with Colt?"

She shakes her head. "No. He didn't ask, and I decided to just come by myself. Then I ran into Gertie and Bill leaving their house, so I rode with them. Patty and Andy didn't come; she's just so uncomfortable being so pregnant. Besides, a big party isn't really her thing even when she feels great. But that must not run in her family—Gertie and Bill haven't left the dance floor once."

As we turn to look at them, where they have claimed the center of the floor, Phoenix grabs my arm. "Look."

Oh, my word. She isn't pointing to the newlyweds. Closest to us on this side of the dance floor is Colt, and he's dancing with Delaney Bedwell. He winks at me, then gives Phoenix a nod. He reaches for Delaney's hand, entwines his fingers with hers, and they move a little closer. I look for Peter, but I don't see him. I do see Missus seated at a ringside table, and she is completely delighted, though it's not because she's looking at the dance floor. She has two gentlemen seated with her, older men I know from around town and their visits to the shop. Both are widowers.

Colt dips Delaney, and then after a quick hug, they part.

Delaney seems taller in black pants and strappy, black heels as she hurries over to us. "Y'all saw us? Couldn't resist rubbing my mother-in-law's nose in her rumor, but I don't think she even saw us." She flits a hand toward Missus's table. "So far I haven't been able to get Peter on the floor, but I don't care. I love dancing, so I'll dance with anyone who's willing!" She looks past us to the food table. "Oh, this all looks good."

"It does," Phoenix says, "but I think I'm going to see if I can find Colt, if you're through with him for a minute."

Delaney grins. "He's all yours."

We watch the lithe redhead make a beeline for Colt, where he is talking to one of the other high school coaches and his wife. Tonight, Phoenix looks more like she did when she moved here. She's wearing a tight, provocative dress, and her hair is hanging shiny around her bare shoulders. She approaches Colt so that he can't help but see her advancing. When I catch his look at her, I smile, realizing he never looked at Alison that way. He scrambles to get out of his conversation and meets Phoenix at the edge of the dance floor just as a slow song begins. They melt together and are soon lost in the crowd.

"I think she's decided what she wants," I say. "If he's smart, he'll let her have it."

Delaney chuckles. "There comes a time when a woman has to act on what she wants or just live never knowing. I know y'all wonder what in the world I want with Peter, but he's my other half. I'd rather do life with him than without." She leans closer, "And just for you to know, I do know where my husband is going at night. He and Shannon are working things out for when the baby comes. He wants it all settled before his mother gets involved." She gulps down the drink she'd been sipping and hands me the glass. "I think I'll go find him. He owes me a dance, whether he knows it or not."

While she was talking, Jackson has given me a questioning look: Do I want to dance? I shake my head at him and mouth, "In a bit." We've danced and talked to so many people on the dance floor, but I want to walk around and see who's out here not dancing. I'm delighted that Peter and Delaney are working around Missus. Now if he'll just not steamroll over Shannon and Danny. Poor Danny is too easy going for his own good, although he married Shannon knowing she was carrying Peter Bedwell's child so he had to know what he was getting into. I hope.

It's a warm night, but the fire pit is lit and giving a nice glow to the faces seated around it. I can see people up on the porch and around the pool. The older kids have left the pool for the dance floor. Other tables, like where Missus is seated, are a little farther from the music where you can hear yourself talk.

We old people like to hear ourselves talk.

Wandering up to the pool, with the light from it bathing everyone in an aqua tint, I find Augusta and Peter with another couple I don't know.

I tap Peter's shoulder. "Your wife is looking for you. She said something about this being your song?"

He tilts his head. "Is it?"

Augusta laughs. "It might be if you find her and make up for your mother's meddling this week."

He scoots his chair away from the glass-topped table. "Good idea. Here, Carolina, you can have my seat. Thanks!"

He hurries away, and I'm glad to see him excited to find Delaney. She'll be so happy to see him looking for her.

The other couple stands up. "We're not trying to be rude," the gentleman says, gesturing for me to take Peter's open seat. "We're Ben and Carol Davis; we do business with Shaw over in Canton. We didn't make it up here for the pig roast, but we've heard there's some pork left over on the food table, and it's calling our name." We shake hands, and they move on.

From our vantage point, Augusta and I can see over the whole party. We take it all in for a minute.

"So, how did Gregory take finding out Savannah is moving?" I ask.

"He was surprised. Were you surprised?"

"Completely. I still can't get my head around it, but we toured the campus and saw the apartment yesterday, so I guess it's really happening."

"And here I am doing the exact opposite. Gregory hasn't lived with me for four years, and now here we are, together in a new house and a new town. It's more than a little strange."

"So, what's up with Peter?" I blurt out.

I can actually hear Augusta's grin, but she doesn't say anything.

I prod her with my elbow. "You've been talking to him, haven't you?"

"His son, which he just found out about, does live with me, you know? He wants to stay on my good side."

I shift my chair around. "When I realized he and Shannon were talking, I thought you might be involved. You are such a good influence around here."

"Compared to his mother, who started a rumor on a whim as her idea of marriage counseling?" She gives me a saucy wink. "I'm finding being a good influence isn't really that difficult in Chancey."

"True, true," I say through my laughter. "Missus is a piece of work!"

"Although…" With a nod, she directs my eyes to the dance floor, where Colt and Phoenix seem to think another slow song is playing. They are wrapped together, ignoring the bouncy rhythm and bodies surrounding them. "Maybe it helped in that case."

"Maybe it did." I trace my fingertip over a water ring left in the glass-topped table. "You know, not long ago, I felt as if nothing was going to work out. For the last year, it's seemed like no one knows how to move forward. Or, at least forward in a positive way. I think I might've gotten used to the drama, but I'm trying to let it go. And now, sitting here watching everyone, well, I feel a kind of peace about things. You know?"

"It's a gift to be able to recognize peace when it comes around. Enjoy it; appreciate it. But it's an even greater gift to be able to recognize peace in the chaos. It's always there. Always available."

I give her a skeptical smile. "I don't know. You've not been in Chancey that long. You might want to rethink that after a while." We settle into watching the party. It's truly a beautiful night. Before long I lean forward. "Let's go join the fun. My drink is empty, and you don't even have one. Plus, the food table looked amazing."

"I do feel like moving around some." Augusta stands and smooths out her dress.

"Augusta! Look at your outfit! It's perfect."

"You like it? I've always loved clothes, but I really haven't bought anything for a while."

The dress is a medium purple with a light sheen to the silky fabric. It fits her well, accenting her wide shoulders by leaving them exposed. Then the sleeves start and cover most of her arms. It falls much like a sheath, except she has curves on which the expensive fabric rests so nicely. The hem just reaches her knees, and her silver sandals are a perfect touch.

"Well, I'm glad you started shopping again," I enthuse. "In a dress like that, you should be dancing! Bill and Gertie are here. Is his brother Jim around?"

"Oh, Carolina, don't be silly. That was just one date."

She's blushing, though, and it makes me smile.

"Come on." I take her arm, and we walk down the pavers

leading to the party tent. I lead her right to where Missus is still holding court, having now added a third widower to her audience.

"Missus, look who's here." I drop Augusta's arm. "Augusta, I'll get you a drink."

I'm leaving when I hear one of the gentlemen offer his chair to Augusta, but another interrupts and asks if she'd like to dance. I chuckle to myself, imagining Missus's face when she realizes she'll have to share the spotlight.

Oh, well, that's what happens when you start interfering in other people's love lives. Karma's a, well, you know...

CHAPTER 33

"I guess everyone can't be fixed at the same time," I say with a sigh.

Silas looks so sad sitting at a table by himself, both elbows fencing in his hands, which hold a watered-down drink. He's not moved in at least half an hour. When Jackson and I stopped and sat at his table a while ago, he didn't even brighten up.

Jackson tightens his arm around my waist as we stand at the edge of the dance floor. "I'm glad to hear that's his first drink. I was wondering if he should be driving, but he's just sad, not drunk."

The party has crested and is simmering nicely now. A grand cake decorated in Chancey High gold and black is being cut, and we've all been given extra-long sparklers to light in celebration of the graduates. I know the kids are ready to move on to Nathan's lake party, and most of us parents are ready to move on to bed. The day and the party couldn't have gone any better. Laney and Shaw have outdone themselves. They are standing arm in arm on the dance floor, and the seniors have been called up to stand behind them.

Laney has borrowed a microphone from the DJ. "We're going to light the sparklers and send the graduates off with a big cheer. Be sure and have some cake, and there's decaf coffee too." She looks around, giving a nod to those holding lighters. Sparklers begin to light around the circumference of the crowd.

"Excuse me," Alex Carrera says, striding up to Laney from his place in the audience. He reaches for the microphone. "Can I borrow that?"

Laney frowns at him and shakes her head no, but he already has it in hand and is taking a step away from her. Alex is probably the best-looking man here. He's not yet twenty-five, but he's definitely not a kid. His jet-black hair shines in the soft white lights as he moves to where Angie stands next to her sister, Jenna, in the line of seniors. He takes his girlfriend's hand, and as he begins to lower himself onto one knee, Laney gasps. Angie's eyes widen, and she grabs her sister's hand with her free one.

Alex kneels and pulls a small jewelry box from his pants pocket. "Angie Conner. I love you, and I want to love you every day of the rest of my life. Will you marry me?"

It's like a scene from a movie.

Right until Angie looks up at Laney and loudly moans, "Mom?"

Alex cranes his neck around to look at the woman who is, in his plans, his future mother-in-law. Then he slowly turns back to look up at Angie.

Jenna leans in front of her stunned sister, grabs a fistful of Alex's sleeve, and hisses, "Stand up. Come on, Alex. Stand up."

But his shoulders tighten and his back straightens as he remains planted. He says sternly, "Angie, just give me an answer."

Poor thing. Her face melts, and she squats a bit to be closer to him. "Oh, sweetie, I can't get married now."

Poor thing. His face melts, too, and his whole body follows. He stands, but it's like his bones are too weak to support him. The box, never opened, goes back in his pocket, and he turns away. At the edge of the crowd he's met by a tall, blond man who puts an arm on his shoulders and leads him away from all of us.

Silas to the rescue.

Our sparklers hang in our hands, sparkling for all they're worth. Shaw half-heartedly shouts, "To the graduates!" and we lift them and give a cheer that matches his half-heartedness. Then the girls form one big knot on the dance floor surrounding Angie. The boys up there slide off on each side and head into the dark, probably to the cake table—or to hidden flasks.

Jackson and I make our way to Laney and Shaw.

I whisper as I wrap my arms around her, "So, no idea that was happening?"

Laney shakes her head and pulls back. Angie comes out of the knot of girls and into her mother's arms. Jackson and I watch for a moment, making eye contact with Savannah, who grimaces at us.

Jackson nudges me. "Hey, the cake is cut. Let's head over there and give them some space."

I nod, and we move in that direction as the DJ plays a mellow song that works to cover some of the awkwardness.

"Well, that was weird," Jackson says under his breath as he guides me through the crowd, fingers lightly on the center of my back.

I agree. "Savannah told me Angie was thinking of moving back home. I guess Alex thought being engaged might keep her with him. Remember when we all worried *he'd* break *her* heart?"

"I don't exactly remember worrying about that myself. Chocolate or vanilla?" he asks as we reach the cake table.

"I'm good for now. Have you seen Susan?"

With his cake in hand, we move to the side.

"No," he says. "Now that you mention it, I haven't seen her since earlier."

"I should let her know what happened." I pull my phone out

of my clutch and walk a step away from him, but I'm back at his side shortly. "She didn't answer. I'll text her. Although she may not be answering my texts. We kind of had an argument earlier, although she didn't argue much. Just ran away as usual. I'll have to fill you in on that later."

Savannah dashes over to us. "Oh my gosh! That was insane. Angie was getting ready to break up with him." Her eyes are large, and she pulls me into a hug. "Poor Alex and poor Angie. She's a mess. And he looked so brokenhearted."

Jackson expresses his sympathy by offering her a bite of cake.

She takes her daddy's fork and has a taste. "Oh, wow. That's good." She keeps the fork and takes another big bite.

"Hey, come on! I let you have a bite. Give me my fork!" Jackson demands, but with a gruff smile. "Are you driving over to Nathan's? Who's riding with you?"

She smiles and looks behind her to where Gregory is standing. He takes her look as permission to advance. "Hello, Mr. and Mrs. Jessup."

Jackson pulls his cake to his chest. "You're not here for my cake, too, are you?"

Gregory lets out a breath and chuckles. "No, sir. Would you like me to get you another piece?"

Pointing his crumb-covered fork at his daughter, Jackson says, "See? He's a good example for you. But no, thanks." He takes another big bite, so I join the conversation while he chews.

"Hey, Gregory. You're riding with Savannah? Where's your car?"

"Aunt Aggie's driving it home. We rode here together."

"She looked beautiful tonight. Seems the local men noticed." After I gave her a nudge in the right direction, I saw a lot of Augusta with different dance partners out on the floor.

"Who was she dancing with?" Savannah asks. "I didn't see her."

I roll my eyes and laugh. "You were over on the other side and busy yourself. But it was a couple of men who come to the shop."

She wrinkles her nose. "Oh, the old men? They were dancing? She's not that old."

"Hey!" Jackson says, his mouth full of cake. "Old men can still dance. I was cutting it up out there."

Savannah gives him some side-eye but leans against his arm. "Oh, yeah. I definitely saw that. We're going to leave, okay?" she says this as she gives her daddy a flutter of her eyelashes and big, soft eyes. He obliges by giving her another bite of cake.

There's that pinch of my heart I keep getting when I look at her, but I swallow and ignore it. "Okay. Y'all keep an eye on Angie, all right?"

They nod, and as they walk off, Gregory puts a hand in the center of Savannah's back. Such a grown-up move. "When did you start doing that?" I muse to Jackson. "You know, putting your hand in the center of my back?"

Scraping the icing off his plate with his fork, he doesn't even look up. "When I wanted you to move along and stop talking."

I elbow him and push him back in the direction we just came. "Come on. You can get another piece of cake. This time, I want a bite."

He grins, and in the lights over the food tables I can see his teeth are bright yellow and black from the icing. I can't help but laugh. "You're a goof. But you're my goof. Now, try and get us a corner piece with lots of icing."

"Sorry to do this at this time of the night," Griffin says.

It's one in the morning, and he's standing in the stark light of our front porch.

Jackson and I had barely gotten to sleep when his phone woke us up with a call from Griffin. Jackson holds the door open for Bryan and Grant to come inside, saying over their heads, "You mentioned the police?"

Griffin nods. "Uh, yeah, but…"

I hug each boy, but I can see he doesn't want to talk in front of them. "You guys go on to bed," I tell them.

They trudge up the stairs, neither one looking back down at us. When we hear Bryan's door close, I grab Griffin's upper arm. "What is going on? You said Susan is in jail? What happened?"

He rubs his tired face. "She's lost her mind. I don't know what to tell you except thanks for taking the boys. I don't know how much they know, but they seem pretty sleepy. Sorry, but I need to get down to the police station." He backs away from us and turns once he's out of the door.

I follow him a half step, pushing the screen door open wider. "You're going to get Susan out? Bring her home?"

He turns his head toward me, and his mouth opens before he has something to say. Then he shakes himself. "No. I'm going to press charges."

Chapter 34

"I can't go to church. I haven't slept a wink. Besides, what would we tell people? We don't have a clue what's going on."

I stand up, pulling my robe around me and finishing the last bit of coffee in my cup. Jackson stands in the kitchen door, just watching me. He doesn't look like he got much sleep either, although I heard enough snoring to know he got more than me. I motion out the door with my head. "Let's go sit on the deck."

Being a good wife, I let him take a few sips of his hot coffee before I start talking. I've got a lot to say. And ask. My mind was reeling last night, and he was snoring before I knew what I wanted to ask. "What exactly did Griffin say when he called last night?"

"Just that there'd been a problem, or maybe he said an incident, and he needed to bring the boys up here to spend the rest of the night. He apologized for waking us up, and, uh, I could hear a woman in the background." Jackson takes a moment to think. "You know, that's who I heard say 'police' first. The woman. And then Griffin said, to her probably, 'Yeah, that's the police.'" He thinks again. "I don't think it was Susan's voice. Must've been Athena? She said, 'She belongs in jail.'"

"Yeah, you said that last night before you went to sleep. But just knowing that and nothing else has been driving me crazy.

I've been waiting until daylight to try and get more information, but now I don't know who to reach out to."

We sip our coffee and watch the sky light up. Beyond the trees at the bottom of the hill, the open air above the river is a warm, buttery yellow that catches the sun first. Quickly, the color progresses to a light gray, and then, suddenly, everything is a bright blue. There are no clouds on this beautiful Sunday morning. How is it possible that Susan is waking up in a jail cell on this gorgeous morning?

"I can't wait anymore. I'm calling her."

Jackson waits as I dial Susan's number. The call goes straight to her voicemail, but I don't want to leave a message. Before I can hang up, though, I see Laney is calling, so I hold up a finger to Jackson. "Hello. Laney? What's going on?"

"You tell me," she blurts out. "Grant's there? He's safe?"

"Yes. Bryan left the party with Grant, going Griffin's to spend the night, so when everything happened, whatever it is that happened, he brought both boys here. Have you talked to Susan yet?"

"She's here at our house. She's still asleep, but I thought I'd see about her son before she gets up. I assumed Grant was with his dad, so I offered to come get him, but Griffin said he was at your house. How are he and Bryan?"

"Fine. They were asleep by the time we went to bed, and we haven't seen them this morning. How is Susan? What happened? I'm surprised to hear you're on speaking terms with Griffin." That's as close as I'm going to come to saying that the last I heard he was pressing charges against her sister.

"Listen, you and Jackson just come on over. Alex is making breakfast burritos with the pork from yesterday. Bring the boys and we can all talk."

"Wait. Alex is there. *Alex* Alex?"

She laughs. "Yes. Alex. It's been a crazy night. Just come over."

I hang up and look at Jackson, who's heard all she said. We stare at each other, and then his stomach growls really loudly. He shrugs. "Pulled pork breakfast burritos do sound really good."

We woke the boys up and told them where we were going. They rolled down the stairs in the same clothes they wore in last night, and we were in the car in record time. I did change into a T-shirt and shorts, but that's about it. We look ragged, but we're here.

Alex and Angie are running the kitchen like they didn't have a huge emotional scene in front of us all just last night. I sneak a peek. Nope, she's not wearing the offered ring, but they seem to be fine, greeting us and telling us breakfast will be ready soon.

Jackson and the boys stop in the kitchen, but Shaw points me up the stairs. "They're waiting for you."

I find Susan and Laney in the sitting area of Laney's master bedroom suite. Cayden is sitting on the floor playing, and I bend down to tickle him and say hello first. Then I sit in the glider rocker across from the two sisters, who are seated in cushy chairs near the front window.

"So, what happened last night?" I ask.

Laney shakes her head and points at Susan. "You have the floor."

Susan is wearing black running pants and a navy blue turtleneck, which she waves a hand over. "You can see I've not been home to change. These are my, well, my Peeping Tom clothes."

Laney closes her eyes while mine pop wide open. "It *was* you!"

"Yes, I've been spying on Griffin and Athena. That's what I've been doing when I wasn't at work or taking care of my children. I've been spying on my ex-husband and his girlfriend."

"What? But why? That is so crazy!"

Her neck muscles are so tight, they look like they might snap. Every part of her hums with tension, and her eyes look a little crazy as she stares at me. "I was obsessed with the idea that he could be so happy. I swore he would be miserable when he didn't want to get back together with me, but he wasn't. I couldn't figure it out. How could he be happy with her? So I followed them places and snuck around their house." She looks down at the floor and makes a choking sound.

Laney prods her past the stall. "Then last night…"

"Yeah, last night, well, they left the party and, of course, I did too."

Her sister snorts. "Of course. Makes perfect sense. Leave your nieces' graduation party to play spy!" Laney's tension is more of a controlled explosion, with lots of energy rumbling around, wanting to escape. She's agitated and can't sit still in her chair. "I'm still in shock that you thought this was, what, normal?"

Susan gives her a nod and swallows. "Well, anyway. I followed them home. They had a babysitter for Athena's kids. I waited until the babysitter left, and then I went around to the back deck to watch the happy blended family."

I interrupt. "When did you get changed into your Peeping Tom clothes? Your outfit for dancing last night was so cute."

"Thanks. Of course it came from Laney's shop."

Laney sniffs. "Those might be the last clothes I ever sell you. This is not the kind of attention my club wants."

Susan dips her head in guilt, then, after a sigh, says, "I changed while I was waiting for the babysitter to leave. I, uh, keep them in my car so I'm always ready."

Laney looks at me as if to say, "See? She's crazy."

Susan continues. "Usually I don't go up to the upstairs deck because, well, that's where the bedrooms are, and there's no need to, you know, see more than is necessary." She turns to her sister. "I know, I know. None of this is necessary. Yes, I can hear myself."

She takes a deep breath. "But last night I did. I went up there for just a minute because, well, I don't know. I felt like I needed to. Anyway, since I'm not as familiar with the furniture and stuff up there, I tripped over something and fell, making a racket. Well, of course they heard me. Then down on the lower deck, someone screamed."

Laney looks ready to explode. "Not just someone. *Who* screamed?"

Susan doesn't even look at her as she answers. "Susie Mae. She was trying to distract them."

"Distract who? Wait, Susie Mae was there?" I look from one sister to the other. "You took Susie Mae with you?"

Susan has the audacity to look offended. "Of course not! I wouldn't take my daughter along to do, you know, that sort of thing."

Laney picks up Cayden, who has crawled over to her. Poor thing probably wants to soothe his mommy. She talks in a baby voice, "Oh, no. Your sweet auntie Susan would never dream of taking her little girl out spying with her. Not like she already knows her little girl spent last fall spying on all of us." Her voice hardens. "I guess it runs in the family."

She looks at me. "Susie Mae has been spying on her mother all this time. While we've been so concerned, so worried about her. About both of them. Susan's stalking Griffin, and Susie Mae is stalking her mother."

I'm finding it hard to draw a breath. "So that's where she's been going? You didn't know she was following you?"

"No. I was busy, you know, watching, uh, her dad. And Athena."

"Okay, give me a minute," I say. "You fall on the upper deck, and it's loud, so Athena and Griffin hear it. Did they come out there?"

"Not right away, but they turned on the bedroom lights and some other outside lights up there. Susie Mae saw that and screamed to get them to focus downstairs. That's the first I knew she was even there. I jumped up and ran down the stairs to her. Which caused her to scream again. The boys then came out of the basement, saw two people fighting, they thought, and yelled for Griffin. That's when the police got called." She slumps back, the tension sliding out of her. "I can't imagine what they thought. Athena called 911. I mean, I understand her being scared, but you'd think she'd settle down when she saw it was just me. And Susie Mae. So, how are the boys?"

I close my mouth, lean back, and set the glider in motion lightly. Shaking my head, holding back the many things I want to say, I answer her. "Okay, I guess. Neither of them had anything to say this morning. Granted, we just got them out of bed and said we were coming over here, so they were half asleep."

Susan leans forward, elbows on her knees. "Griffin told them it was me and Susie Mae and just a big misunderstanding. He told them to not worry, that he'd handle everything. I don't think they saw me being put in the police car."

"Oh, Susan," I groan. "Please say they found y'all back there before the police arrived."

"Yes, but just barely. The emergency response time was really good, which is good to know. The boys ran back inside when they saw us, but didn't know it was us, so they were all hunkered down in the house. I didn't think we should go running across the yard because I know Griffin has guns at his house. I didn't think he had a gun at Athena's, but what if he did? I got to thinking later... what if he'd shot one of us?"

"Yeah, what a great thing to finally think about!" Laney shouts, though she stops when Cayden's face clouds into a frown. "It's okay, sweetie. Mama's not yelling at you. She's yelling at your idiot aunt." All smiles, with her voice full of sunshine, she continues. "Sneaking around in the dark, peeping in windows in Georgia, is a real good way to get your silly head blown off, isn't it, Cayden?"

"I know," Susan says. "I am an idiot, but I just couldn't believe he was really happy. But forget all that. Anyway, I called his phone and told him it was me out on the deck. The police arrived about that time, and, well, I guess we got put down in the books as the strangest domestic dispute in the history of Chancey."

I move forward in my seat. "Susan. You are one step away from a stalker. No—actually, you are a stalker. Do you know how you sound? So, did Griffin, uh… did he press charges? That's what he said he was going to do when he left our house."

She exhales. "No. Thank God. And I've learned my lesson. Susie Mae could've been arrested along with me."

"Or shot," her aunt plugs in.

"Or shot. I will never do anything like that again, and I am going to counseling."

I scrunch up my forehead. "So, the winery? Folks have said they saw you there, and Gertie swears she saw Susie Mae."

Laney looks shocked; Susan does, too, at first. Then her face folds in on itself, and she nods. "Yep. I followed them up there. I didn't know Susie Mae was there, though." She groans and bends double. "She told me she didn't want to go to Six Flags because she got a stomach ache right as they were getting on the bus. She said she went home and slept all afternoon. Poor thing. Instead of having fun with her friends, she was chasing me all over North Georgia."

It takes a while for me to process all this. The only sound for a while is Cayden softly babbling to his mommy as she rocks him.

"Where's Susie Mae now?" I finally ask. "I didn't see her downstairs. Wait. Speaking of downstairs, Alex is here?"

Laney and Susan share a look, and Susan draws in a deep breath, straightening up as she does. "Griffin didn't press charges, but he did let me take a ride in the police car to teach me a lesson." She stops just short of rolling her eyes. "I needed a ride home, but he said he was bringing me here. I have a key, and I was planning on slipping in and sleeping on the couch; no need to wake everyone up in this house too. I'd convinced Griffin not to call Laney since we knew they had to be exhausted. When I snuck up on the porch, Alex was asleep in one of the porch chairs. He woke up, but, well, I didn't know it was him, and I, uh, screamed. Guess I was a little on edge."

"Scared the life out of us," Laney says. "We started turning on lights. Shaw got *his* gun. I was ready to call 911, but then my phone rang and it was Susan. Downstairs with a traumatized Alex."

She cradles a sleepy Cayden in her arms, and staring at him, a smile creeps up on her face. She talks softly, "Angie didn't go with the girls after the lake party, so she was here for all the excitement. She came down and heard Alex apologizing to us for springing the proposal on her and saying that he realized he needed to give her some space. He was spilling his heart out about how he thinks her moving back home, or to her own place, would be a good idea. That they need to slow down and he wants to give her time to do her own thing. That opened her up a bit, and I think they ended up talking downstairs most of the night."

Susan stands up and stretches. "Of course, by the time Alex had said all that, Shaw and Laney were realizing I shouldn't be here, so then I had to tell my story." She walks to the window and looks out. "Griffin offered to take Susie Mae to your house with the boys, but she wanted to stay with Athena until he got back. Then she spent the night at Griffin's house with him." She turns around to face us. "I owe them all a huge apology."

We hear someone coming up the stairs, and then Shaw sticks his head in the door. "Breakfast is ready. Y'all want me to bring something up?"

"No, we'll come down there," Laney says quietly. Cayden has fallen asleep in her arms, so Susan and I follow Shaw into the hall, leaving Laney behind to put her boy into his crib. Near the bottom of the stairwell, Susan turns to look up at me.

"You know, now that it's over, I can't believe I was doing all that. It was like an obsession. Like watching a TV show you can't get enough of. I just couldn't stop. You know, he's a totally different man with her. Totally." After an extended frown, she turns to continue down, muttering, "So strange." After the last step, she abruptly stops and turns back to me, surprise all over her face. "Maybe, uh, maybe I'm supposed to be totally different too?"

I have nothing to offer her. Nothing but a shaking head and an open-mouthed shrug. She's a self-proclaimed Peeping Tom. Being "totally different" from what she is now could only be a step in the right direction.

It definitely can't hurt.

CHAPTER 35

"This is no longer fun," I tell Danny. "My head is pounding already."

At first the chatter and dish clatter from the temporary Ruby's was pleasant, lending the shop a nice atmosphere and a welcome uptick in sales. But that was before all the patrons came back. We apparently did too good of a job making everyone comfortable with the change. Ruby complains she's selling as many muffins as before, but now she has to slog them over here. Keeping the coffee going in this makeshift setup isn't working well at all, as Libby constantly reminds us. Kimmy doesn't complain like the other two, but she has mentioned that carrying everything back and forth is getting old. Real old. On our side of things, the bookshop and floral customers seem to have become as annoyed with the noise and traffic as we are.

Like I said, this is no longer fun.

Danny nods in agreement. "I miss our quiet mornings. That back door starts banging before me and Shannon are even up. I never thought it'd get as busy as the real Ruby's was."

"Me either." I reach under the counter for my purse. "You hold things down here, and I'll be back in a bit. I'm going to go see the mayor. We need some answers."

Early Mondays used to be my favorite time in the shop, reveling in the quiet as I checked in the books from Andy's weekend scavenging. Now, the place is busy when I get here. The bookstore has to be open since customers have to walk through it to get to Ruby's, so Danny is pulling those early hours. Revenue has stalled, and I think it's because our customers are no longer milling about, enjoying their time here and spending more. They get in and get out. The acoustics of the high ceiling mean it's hard to hear yourself think, much less concentrate on a book. Shannon is doing more business over the phone, which also cuts down on impulse purchases and adds another level of noise as she tries to communicate, mostly on speakerphone so she can keep working. So while we're happy we could help Ruby out, it's not good for our businesses. Or our headaches.

The sidewalk is quiet, a welcome contrast. AC's doesn't open until eleven o'clock, and the other end of Main Street is blocked with construction equipment. At the end of last week we heard some rumbling that the work would be done soon, but no one has any real information. Missus wouldn't discuss any city business at the party on Saturday, and the rest of the time she's basically been in hiding.

I cross in the middle of the block and head straight toward the gazebo in the park. The mayor's office is just past the library. Usually I'd walk on the sidewalk around the corner, so this is one benefit of the construction—a stroll through the park. It's not a straight-to-the-point walk, more meandering, so it takes longer, but I guess that *is* the point of a park. The paths from the gazebo wander around, and I resist cutting across the grass and dirt to save a couple of minutes.

Even with all the tumult of the weekend, I feel things are working themselves out. Susan apologized to everyone last night. Susie Mae came up to the house last night to apologize and to promise she'll be on time at work from now on. She seemed relieved and more like her old self. She did end up in the basement playing video games with Bryan. I'm not sure how I feel about that, but... there's nothing I could really say.

Angie moved back home yesterday afternoon, and Alex helped with the move. It'll be interesting to see if they end up back together for the long haul. Laney was over the moon to have all three of her kids under her roof for one last summer.

I'm trying not to be jealous.

Savannah is packing and shopping for her big move. I want to be excited for her, and I am, but it's all happening so fast. This last week is going to be jammed full of activities and people. There's not going to be a minute to just enjoy her still living at home. Hank and Shelby are already here with all their tumult. Etta arrives Thursday. My mom and dad are camping not far from here for the weekend before heading down to the Florida Gulf Coast for an extended stay. Our family dinner is going to be at AC's on Saturday afternoon. I can't help thinking it feels anticlimactic after Laney's huge celebration. Especially now that we know Savannah's actually moving away.

But no. I'm not going to do that to myself. I'm going to enjoy what we have. Savannah and I have yet another shopping trip planned for tomorrow. Today she's packing and actually going to hear her grandfather's Hillbilly Hank presentation at a senior citizens center near Dalton.

As I approach the police station and city hall offices, I slow down. They are at the opposite end of the park from the shop, and I've only been in either of them a couple of times. Is this where they brought Susan Saturday night? I guess there could be a holding cell or something in there. I think the whole thing really scared Susan and Griffin. They've both told us they are focusing on Susie Mae and Grant and making a real effort at communicating better. Lord knows it would've scared the life out of me!

The main door opens as I near it, and a gentleman just leaving holds it open for me as I scoot inside. It's warm this morning, so the cool, dark hall feels nice. It's not an old structure like many of the buildings in town. It's a utilitarian, one-story, concrete-block building with a flat roof. The center hall goes the length of the building, with the police department on the left side and the city offices on the right. The mayor's office is near the back and is rather small and depressing. There are no side windows in the building, just big ones at the front, where the reception areas for both sides are. After knocking on Missus's door, then finding the door is locked, I go back to the reception area and push open the glass door right inside the main front door.

"Hi," I tell the young woman standing at the chest-high counter. "I'm looking for Missus."

She frowns at me. "She's not been in yet today. I mean, the mayor, you know."

"Yes, I know. Do you expect her soon?"

She looks down and moves some papers on the counter. "I don't usually work over here, so I don't know. We aren't this, this unorganized over in the police department."

"Oh, you work over there?" I reach my hand across the counter. "I'm Carolina Jessup. I own Blooming Books."

"Oh, yeah. I love your store. Anyway, I don't know when the mayor will be back." She shakes my hand when I offer it, but then goes right back to shuffling the papers on the counter.

I pause and look around. "Can I ask you a question? Is there a holding cell over there?"

She looks up. "Yes. Why?"

"Just wondering. My friend was, well…"

She grins. "Mrs. Lyles?"

I nod, and she nods back at me. "No one can picture Mrs. Lyles in the holding cell. I could've sold pictures of it, but first, I wasn't working, and second, she never got that far. I mean, the officers know her ,and so they just brought her into the station and gave her some old coffee. Told her to have a seat.

Everyone likes her. I mean, everyone likes Mr. Lyles, too, you know. But, no, they let him take her home as soon as he got there. So no profitable jail pictures," she says with a little giggle.

She likes to talk; I wonder what else I can find out. Leaning on the counter, I echo her giggle, then ask, "Any idea when this construction is going to be done?"

She rolls her eyes. "Are you kidding? The mayor isn't telling anyone *anything*. The chief is fit to be tied. All the officers are too. Mayor Jed was pretty incompetent, but we could just go around him. This one…" She shakes her head. "There's no going around her. She's got everything locked down tight. I just hope the chief doesn't quit over it."

Her cell phone rings, and she jerks it up. "Yeah," she says into it. "Okay. Be right there." She comes around the counter. "Gotta go back to my real job. Lord, I hope they find someone for over here soon. They're wearing me out! Nice to meet you."

So, no construction answers here. Just an empty reception area looking for the next sacrificial lamb to work under Missus. Places like this tend to hire nice young women without a lot of experience. I'm sure she eats them alive. Wonder where I should look for her next?

However, I'm doubting I can get more answers out of her than the police chief does.

Back out in the morning sunshine, I discover I can probably track Madam Mayor by the trail of magenta papers laid out in front of me. There's two across the street on the library doors, and I can see another one on a telephone pole near Missus's house. The gazebo is now sporting magenta rectangles it didn't have only a little while ago, and all along Main Street I see her trail leading right to where I started this morning. There's no magenta adorning AC's door, so I bet she's in Blooming Books right now. I don't take time to cross the street and read the library's notice, but I hurry back, across the grass and dirt this time, to catch up with the woman herself.

"Is she here?" I ask Danny as I plow into our front door.

He gives me his confused look. Okay, his normal look. "Shannon? Sure. You need her to come up here? She's been real tired, so why don't you go back to her table?"

"No. Missus. Never mind, I see her." Passing, I give Shannon a smile, but she barely grunts at me. Missus is seated at a table in the center of the others, and I see the magenta papers lying all around her. I don't ask, but slide into a chair across from her. "Just the woman I was looking for."

"You no longer have a phone?" she simpers. "You can call me anytime."

I pick up a paper, but before looking at it, I smirk at her. "You don't answer my calls anymore."

"Impossible. So, what do you think?"

I throw up my hand. "What do you mean impossible? That's a crazy answer. What do I think of what?"

She sighs loudly and flicks the back of the paper in my hand. "Read it."

I look down, and I can feel my expression brightening. "Wait, this says the construction will be done this week? That's fantastic! So Ruby can move back into her café and Laney's club can open?"

"Of course. But what about the party? Any concerns about that?"

"Wh—party?" I skim down the page, and my heart sinks when I see a block party listed for Saturday night.

"I'm counting on the business owners to do their part," Missus says in her most imperious tone. "After all, I'm doing it *for* you. There'll be a planning meeting here tonight."

I crunch the corner of the paper in my fist. "But, Missus, this is graduation weekend. I don't have time to do this!" I drop the balled-up paper on the table. "Or to attend a meeting tonight."

She smiles and leans back as Libby approaches our table.

"Coffee, Carolina?" She pours before I can answer, continuing to talk up a blue streak as she leans over our table, nodding to the flyer. "Isn't it great? We're going to be back home in our place, and you'll have *all* this back to yourselves. We have enjoyed being here, but it sure has been an awful lot of work on *our* part. Y'all are now going to have to walk all the way down there for muffins and coffee. No more easy service. Ruby is tickled pink, or maybe I should say tickled purple like these here beautiful papers of Missus's."

Okay, maybe I'm still rattled by the block party that's been dumped on my overflowing to-do list, but I'm not sure I've ever heard Libby speak with such an edge to her voice. And it's directed at me?

"Here's your *last. Free. Muffin*," Ruby says, coming over and dropping a plate with a brown muffin in front of me.

As the plate hits the table, the muffin rolls and threatens to fall in my lap, but I grab it. "No one asked you to give us free muffins!" But then I find myself distracted. "What is this sticky stuff on top?"

"Peach glaze," Libby explains. "It's sticky but so yummy. The muffin is peach, and Ruby thought it was kind of bland, so she added the glaze." She bends down and whispers, "It's really just a bit of peach jam spread on top."

Ruby elbows her. "Hush, giving away my secrets. And you might not've asked for free muffins, Carolina, but we know we're the redheaded stepchildren. We know we ain't wanted."

What is all this attitude? I try to keep my voice down. "It was my idea! Of course we wanted you here. We wanted to help you out."

"Only 'cause we're the poor relations. Well, not anymore. We'll be out of your hair as soon as possible. Thanks to your fast work, Missus. You might not've been my first choice for mayor, but you're growing on me. You can count on all of my people to hold up our end of things at the celebration." She turns to look down on me, one bony elbow propped on one bony hip, every bony thing jutting in my direction. "And if it's okay with the queen here, we'll come to the meeting tonight too. I might even provide refreshments if you don't think that would be overstepping our bounds, Your Majesty."

I'm literally sputtering. "I don't know what you think I've said or am thinking, but you've lost what little brain you brought down the street with you! I'm going back up front." Shoving my chair under the table, I march up to my counter, where I realize I'm still clutching the sticky peach muffin. I shake it off into the wastebasket as Danny watches.

"Oh, man. That's a good muffin you just threw away."

"Shut up. What has happened back there? She wasn't mad at me earlier."

He shrugs, but doesn't look at me.

"What? What happened?" I demand.

"Shannon's had a rough morning," he mumbles. "She might've said some things."

"So? Be mad at Shannon, not me."

He thinks about that. "Yeah, but well, they were. Mad at Shannon, I mean. So, well, I might've repeated what you said this morning. About them being here not being fun anymore and giving you a headache." He gives me his sad puppy-dog eyes. "I gotta protect my wife. My very pregnant wife."

Well, that makes things clearer. Not better, but clearer.

Missus comes strolling by, her stack of magenta papers in one arm. "See you this evening, Carolina. If I were you, I'd go back and try to make up with Ruby. You really don't have the fortitude to deal with her as an adversary."

She adds, punctuated by a raised eyebrow as she looks me up and down, "We all know you like a muffin... or two."

CHAPTER 36

"Pawpaw is really good at this hillbilly stuff," Savannah says, sitting on the floor of her bedroom. I've ventured up to see how the packing is coming along. Her room is usually a disaster, but it's even more of one now.

"Really? Huh." I survey the destruction. "So, are you, like, making piles of what to take, leave... whatever?"

"Kinda. I mean, it's not like I won't be coming back here if I need stuff. It's just hard to know what to take."

"And you've not had long to really think about it." I have to give her that. The dormer windows make her room feel dark to me, but she hates the overhead light. "It's so dark. Why don't you turn on some lights? Can you even see what you're doing up here?"

"Yes, Mom. What do you want?" she says it lightly, but I can hear that edge creeping in.

I give her a fake chuckle. "Oh, nothing." I sit on the side of her bed closest to her. "So Pawpaw was interesting? I'm glad you had a good time."

"I did." The edge is gone. "The place had a potluck for him, and that was even fun. He's like a comedian." She looks up at me through her eyelashes. "A grouchy one. But it's actually funny, and Shelby is, well, she's nice to everyone, and the old people love that." She goes back to pulling things out of the drawer. "It's going to be strange having Meemaw here at the same time as them, isn't it?"

"I think so, but they all want to be here for you. We'll just have to not let it be too strange." I look around. There's so much I want to say, but none of it feels right. It feels too heavy, too—just too much. "So Angie moved home. How are she and Alex doing?"

"The same, I guess. I'm going out to Angie's after dinner. She has a pillow she made for me."

"Oh, that's nice. So you had fun with Gregory on Saturday? How's he liking Chancey?"

"He likes it. Nathan's was fun, but I'm kind of glad I won't be here all summer."

"Really?" That surprises me. "Why?"

"Everybody's so sad. Like they're never going to see each other again. Or they keep talking about how they can't wait to get out of here. It's just so much drama."

Okay. That makes perfect sense and actually relieves some of my anxiety about her sudden decision. She's ready to move on and not make a big deal about it. I stand up and walk to her. I place a hand on the top of her head. "It's good that you realize that. You're going to love college, and it's going to be a crazy, but fun, week. Anything I can help with?"

She looks up at me, her blue eyes so clear, even in the shadowed room. "No, Mom. I think it's all good. I can't wait to have that chicken casserole for dinner. Did you make those carrots I like?"

"I sure did. It'll be ready in about thirty minutes." I pat the side of her face and make my way through the piles.

"Love you, Mom. Thanks."

"Love you, too. You know I'll do whatever I can to help. Just ask."

At the bottom of her stairs, I open the door to the hall and am flooded with late afternoon sunshine. Guess I might as well go to Missus's meeting tonight. Bonnie and Phoenix said they'd cover for me, but there's really no need to stick around here.

Savannah isn't going to be here, and well, she's doing fine.

This time, Missus has claimed Shannon's worktable for her podium. She's sitting behind it, and because of Shannon's supplies, which no one who's seated could see over, she has sole occupancy of center stage. Almost every chair in Ruby's temporary café has been claimed, and we have been served coffee and cookies. Well, some have been served; I had to get my own.

I might apologize to Ruby and Libby eventually, but right now I'm kind of enjoying my black sheep status. Someone being mad at me used to really upset me, which makes living in a small town hard. I sweetly call out, "Ruby, these cookies are just delicious!" with nary a smidge of bitterness in my voice. I'm getting good at this.

She snips, "Thank you," at me, and just like that, I look like the bigger person. Shannon hasn't learned this as she's shooting arrows at both Ruby and Libby. She looks like that angry dwarf in *Lord of the Rings*, all hunched-over, lumpy, narrowed-eyed, and mean.

It's not a good look.

Missus has found a linen suit in the same magenta as her proclamation papers. It's crisp and actually a good color on her. She clears her throat and hands a stack of proclamations to the table nearest her. "Here are the plans for Saturday. I believe you'll find I've covered everything and made appropriate assignments."

I gush and practically bat my eyes as I take mine. "Oh, Missus, I'm sure you've thought of everything!" Everyone, including Missus, looks at me. Maybe they're searching for sarcasm?

Possibly insincerity? However, I beam eternal goodwill and serenity over them all.

Bonnie rolls her eyes and says out of the side of her mouth to me, "Mary Sunshine, you might want to tone down this Mother Teresa act until you've read the plans."

"Oh, you're right. Got carried away." It's quiet while everyone reads, but so far there's only murmurs of agreement. I scan the sheet first, then go back for a more in-depth read, and well… it actually looks pretty straightforward. I know I'm as shocked as you are, but yes, I'm fine with it.

My tablemates and I look at each other, then look around the room. A sense of unease is growing as our drinks grow cold and the cookies lose their taste.

Missus's plan? Everything looks good. Reasonable. Doable.

We've obviously missed something. Nothing with Missus in charge can be this easy. Murmurs grow. People start to shift in their seats.

Madam Mayor knocks on the table with one gloved hand. "Let's come to attention. Any problems with what you find here?" She looks around, then back down at the page in her hand. "Ruby is providing the cookies and coffee tonight while Blooming Books has opened their doors for this meeting. Bill Purdy and his band will be playing Saturday evening. Phoenix and AC's have agreed to provide a few treats, cookies, and veggie trays. Bedwell Attorneys at Law will provide all drinks, which we are keeping to non-alcoholic. I will make a short presentation and cut the ribbon to the reopened street, there will be forty minutes of music, and then the event will conclude. Any questions?"

A lot of blinking eyes meet her gaze. Then she says, "Oh yes. One more thing." We brace ourselves. Here it comes. It's got to be a lighted vehicle parade with rented motorcycles, or fake snow falling during the announcement, or a mountain of ice for sledding next to the gazebo. Nothing can be this easy with Missus at the helm.

"We will need assistance in moving all this back to Ruby's," Missus states. "She's informed me that will be happening Thursday afternoon after pie time at four o'clock so she can open Friday morning. If there are no other questions, that will be all. Good night." Missus closes her folder, and the meeting is over.

I haven't even eaten a whole cookie.

Bonnie bends forward to talk to just our table. "Laney isn't on the schedule for anything! Hers is the only business left out."

Shannon and I quickly study our papers. Danny is busy finishing another cookie.

Shannon's eyes narrow even further. "You knew Missus would screw *someone* over. Carolina, have you talked to Susan or Laney today?"

"No, I was trying to give them all a break. Maybe that's all that's going on. I wonder if Laney knows about this meeting? It never dawned on me to tell her."

Bonnie shakes her head. "What's with Missus becoming efficient? Is this kind of a sudden change even possible? Maybe she's had a stroke?"

"I'm so busy this week with family coming in and graduation stuff, I'm not even going to question it." I fold my sheet and tuck it in my purse. "I'll call Laney, but I'm sure she'll be fine. They had a crazy weekend and have a busy week too. Wow, we don't have to do anything except enjoy Saturday night. I'm more than good with that!"

Gertie comes over to our table as we are standing, and we all chat for a moment. It's the first time in a long time—try ever—that we're leaving a meeting with everyone in a good mood. I could get used to this.

Then Peter calls out from across the room, "Gertie, I just thought of something. Is your name now really Gertie Purdy?"

Gertie laughs. "Been waiting for folks to notice that!"

It takes a moment, but then everyone is laughing.

Now this is what it's supposed to be like living in a small town.

Chapter 37

We made it.

Well, those of us with tickets.

A typical spring storm this afternoon didn't move out like it was supposed to. Lightning kept crossing the western sky, threatening to come our way, so graduation had to be moved from the football field to the high school gymnasium. Everything is in place here, with magnolia arrangements on the stage along with teachers, school officials, and the featured speaker, Madam Mayor. She looks very official in a black suit with gold piping around the lapels. She's also sporting a magnolia on her lapel, which matches her cream-colored gloves.

Each graduate got four tickets, which means my original five Jessups are together again, except for the one sitting in the midst of all the other black robes and mortarboards. I'm letting the guys figure out which one is Savannah while I drink in the day. The week. It's been busy as promised, but not bad at all.

Wednesday night was the baccalaureate at the big Baptist church out on the blacktop. It was really moving with songs and prayers. I remember when Will graduated the baccalaureate was more emotional and thought-provoking than the actual graduation and diploma ceremony, so I paid closer attention this time. Two seniors sang an original song, the class advisor talked about their four years at Chancey high, and the pastor's prayer was heartfelt and made me cry. It was all perfect.

Etta arrived yesterday, and, having been forewarned about Hank and Shelby's news by her favorite daughter-in-law (I really am), she was all grace and congratulations. It's a testament to the content of Etta's character, though, that this would have been expected from her even without the forewarning. My parents got to the campground yesterday as well. They came over for lunch at the house earlier today, and all four grandparents, and whatever Shelby is, are back at the house now, where we'll gather for dessert after the ceremony.

"See her, Mom?" Bryan is sandwiched between me and Jackson, and Will is on Jackson's other side. "By the guy with that hat thing pushed way back. You can see her hair."

"Oh, I see her." She's turning, trying to find us, and then Will lets out a short blast of a whistle. Her head whips around. She searches for a moment, and we can see the moment she finds us. She waves and smiles, then turns back to her friends and the important matters at hand.

She knows we are where we are supposed to be, so she can forget about us.

As she should. This is her day.

"It hasn't hurt that Shelby's not feeling well and is all hunkered down in the corner of the couch."

My mother is squirting dollops of whipped cream from a can onto bowls of my homemade banana pudding. My meringue didn't work out. I assume this is because the dessert was for company. If it had just been us, it would've been the kind of meringue they serve in heaven. Whatever. I'm not bitter.

I'm scooping out the pudding ahead of her, but staying close to her so she can quietly fill me in on how things have been going up here at the house while we've been at graduation.

She counts bowls, then continues. "Etta and I have been playing with Francie, Anna is nodding off over in the rocking chair, and Hank and your dad are competing on whose stories can be told and retold the most times!"

I laugh and bump her arm. "Even when either one of them comes up with a new one, it feels like I've heard it before."

Mom rolls her eyes. "At least Hank is making money with his. This camping means a whole new audience for your dad every place we stop. I'm going to lose my mind."

I lick the serving spoon, then drop it in the sink. "Coffee will be ready in a minute. So. where are you headed when you leave here?"

"A lake in South Georgia for a week, then on to the coast. I've been thinking you should come stay a few days; either place would be a break for you. We could check out thrift stores in the area and relax. Bryan can come too. I figure Jackson isn't keen on staying in the camper with me and your dad."

I consider my mom's offer. A couple of days camping could really be nice. I'm gazing out the window over the sink, but I can see myself beside a lake reading or drinking coffee next to a campfire. "You know, that would be wonderful." Then I remember, and turning to her, I frown. "Jackson's going to be traveling some with work. I'll have to cover the B&B. Won't have Savannah here to help either. But I'll look at the calendar."

Mom rubs my back as I look back out the window. "You'll miss Savannah being around. Try and come down for a day or two. You really need a nice break. Ready to serve this?"

"I can help," Etta says, coming into the kitchen. "I heard y'all talking about you trying to get away for a couple days, Carolina. That would be really nice. You deserve it. Graduation is hard on a mom, especially one as busy as you. Jackson said y'all are planning on getting down my way at the beach this summer."

"Trying," I emphasize. "But now Bryan says he wants a 'real' summer job. He has no idea how hard it is to get time off when your dad isn't your boss."

As Etta carries bowls into the living room, she calls over her shoulder, "Only one way for them that are hardheaded to learn… experience."

Mom and I nod in agreement and follow her into the living room with our trays.

Savannah's silky, cream sundress perfectly matches the magnolia flower tucked behind her ear. It's the school flower, and there are at least a dozen of the flowering trees on the high school campus. Each of the girls was given a blossom with a bright yellow-gold ribbon tied around it. It was so striking held against the black gowns. The wide ribbon is now tied around her wrist, and she looks so happy sitting on the footstool near my dad. There's a pinch, a hard pinch, of my heart to think of letting her go. Of not seeing her every day. With my tray empty I turn back to the kitchen for the last two cups of coffee. I take a minute to compose myself, then take the final cups into the living room.

I set Jackson's cup down for him and blow him a kiss when he says, "Thank you." My bowl of pudding waits for me on the table at the end of the couch, so I sit down, blow on my coffee, and take a sip. I try not to stare at my daughter; that last pinch hurt too much. Then I notice the way Etta's eyes rest on Jackson. When I look at my mom, her eyes meet mine. Was she watching me?

Oh.

We might move to the audience to watch our kids, but we're still on our parents' center stage.

My eyes fill with tears, and I'm not sure I can eat or drink right now. It's all so lovely. So sweet. So sad.

236

"Hey," my dad says loudly. "Didn't you used to put home-made meringue on your banana pudding? Resorting to canned stuff now?" He clicks his teeth. "Not near as good as the real thing."

Well… parents gonna parent.

CHAPTER 38

God must like the new and improved Missus. It's a perfect night for her street reopening party. There's a slight, warm breeze, a clear sky, and every flower along Main Street and in the park is blooming. Lights are on in all the businesses, and there are even some white lights strung up in the gazebo. We're having one of those early summer nights where it feels like it's never going to actually get dark and the air is silk against your skin. No raised voices or drama disturb the peace. Even when I called Laney to let her know she wasn't on the agenda, she didn't have a problem with it. She's just happy to be able to open her store and very happy her epic graduation party is over.

Our family lunch today was perfect. We had the large, circular table at AC's, and everyone got along. Just saying, but I think we need to have all our family gatherings in public places from now on.

Even when Colt made his big announcement, Hank behaved. Colt called us last night, asking if he could bring Phoenix to lunch. What he didn't tell us is she'd be sporting a big diamond ring!

So, yes, Colt and Phoenix are now engaged. Hank even ordered a bottle of champagne. Well, now that I think about it, Shelby ordered it, then handed it to Hank. Of course he acted like it was all his idea. Shelby has always known how to pull his chains and push his buttons. It's hard not to bristle at it, but I guess we should just let them do them. He loved nothing more than being the big daddy making a toast. Etta sat between my mother and Savannah, and you'd never imagine she was once married to Hank. She's a saint.

Bryan had his favorite spot, between his grandfathers. While I'd claimed my granddaughter and daughter to sit between, Jackson had stuck close to Colt. After their dad wasn't nice to Phoenix at our house, he'd said he was going to make sure Colt knew he had his back. Jackson is a really good man, isn't he? I liked sitting across the table from him, where I could watch him and occasionally make eyes at him.

Alex made sure we had the absolute best service, and now I'm thrilled we didn't have a big party with lots of people up at the house. Getting to spend a whole meal sitting beside my beautiful graduate filled my soul. There was no more hurtful pinching of my heart; at least not today.

We'll see how moving goes tomorrow.

But first—tonight. The party, with Missus actually cutting a big ribbon tied across the patched-up street, is in full swing. Our parents opted out of this. Hank and Shelby are at the house. Etta actually went out to stay the evening with my parents in their motor home. We'll all gather for breakfast in the morning before the big move begins.

"We sure have a beautiful night," I say, walking up to where Missus and Peter are talking. "And I like the choice of colors for the ribbon."

Missus nods once. You know, like the queen being complimented. "Of course we had to use the school colors of gold and black since it is graduation weekend. Especially since I was the speaker for commencement."

"You did a really great job," I say. Honestly. "Peter, did you get to hear it?"

He smiles big but doesn't laugh. He's obviously holding it back, but I don't know what there is to laugh at. "Oh, yes. I was there. But…" He draws out the word with a side glance at his mother.

"But if anyone did miss it," she says, her voice raised and enunciating a bit more than usual, "it's on you tube dot com. That's all you have to do, look up you tube dot com." She says each syllable like it's a word by itself. "It's all right there on your computer or even your phone. You tube dot com but you spell out the 'you,' and there's no space before the 'tube.' Then 'dot com' like normal."

Now Peter's having to bite his lip to keep from laughing. I have a feeling she's been giving this spiel all day. Missus is all seriousness. Delighted seriousness. "We're going to have to look into this you tube dot com. "Let others know about it. I need to make the rounds. Do my duty. Enjoy your evening," she says as she hurries off.

"You can laugh now," I tell Peter. "She did do a good job, though. And this street reopening is really going well. Maybe she's turning into a good mayor."

"Or has some good help…"

"Okay, Peter, you've been a great help to her. So great." I roll my eyes at his arrogance. "But listen, while we have a minute. You and Shannon are talking?" I speak quietly and make sure we can't be overheard.

"Yes. We need to, I think you'd agree. I believe things are beginning to straighten themselves out." He looks around at the gathering crowd.

"Really? That's great." But then, something isn't sitting right with me. "Like what?"

He stares at me. No laughing. No smiling. "It's best not to talk about it all yet. Why? Has Shannon said something?"

I stop myself from saying no and shrug. "I think I'll go find, uh, Jackson." I walk away, fighting down my sense of unease. I walk through the crowd, which is moving toward the micro-phone and speakers, until I find who I was looking for.

"Shannon, there you are. Glad you found a place to sit. I don't think there are many chairs since it's such a short pre-sentation."

She peers up at me from the metal folding chair she found near our shop. "Yeah, I grabbed this one, and I'm not giving it up. Danny went to get me something to eat, and then I'm go-ing back up to the apartment. We were really busy at the shop today."

"That's what Bonnie said. Hey, so you and Peter are talking?"

"Some."

"You know, if you start talking about things like custody you might want to, I don't know, talk to an attorney?"

I guess I look like I just fell off a turnip truck. That's how she's looking at me, anyway. "Duh, Carolina. I'm not stupid."

"Okay. Just checking. I mean, you know, Peter's not exactly been all on the up and up recently."

"I believe I know Peter better than you do," she sniffs.

I chuckle. "That's true. So you know exactly what he's capa-ble of."

Our conversation stalls, and then Danny arrives with a plate of goodies and two drinks. "Uh, I didn't bring you any, Carolina. Sorry."

"No worries! I just wanted to stop and say thanks for cover-ing so much for me this week and today at the shop. We've had a great graduation week with the family."

Shannon finishes taking a long drink of punch. "She really wanted to warn me about Peter."

"I just wanted to make sure you were protecting y'all and the baby. Danny knows how confusing custody matters can get, right?"

"Righto," he says. "Oh, look, Missus is getting ready to talk."

"Oh, I want to move up closer. I'll see y'all Monday at the shop."

As I walk away, I can hear Danny talking to his wife: "Yeah, me and Alison had to pay a lawyer a lot. We're lucky Peter is a lawyer. Gonna save us all a lot of money."

With a groan, I keep moving. I guess you can't save some people from themselves. Missus is having trouble getting the microphone to work, so I have time to get up to where Jackson is talking to Gertie beside Bill's band.

"The music was nice," I say. "This is great, having our own bluegrass band around."

Gertie crosses her arms across her wide chest. "Yeah, I'm liking this marriage thing. Not sure how long he's going to be happy living in my apartment at the store. It's kinda disconcerting having Andy wandering in at all times of the day and night. We can't be containing our ardor to that little space when we got a big ol' house with all those rooms to explore." She gives me a wink as she nudges Jackson's arm with her elbow. "Y'all know what I'm talking about. Got all those B&B rooms to try out. And now Savannah's leaving you a whole new space to have fun in! 'Course, ya still got Bryan wandering around, so you know what I'm talking about with Andy. Just makes it hard to be spontaneous."

She stares at our frozen faces, then laughs. "Law, you people are funny! Anyway, saw you talking to Peter. He tell you about the house?"

Jackson and I take a minute to get our voices back. I shake my head. "What house?"

"The house he's renting from me that's up the hill behind the Bedwell place. Right down the street from the church and the apartments. It's just another property I've owned for a while. The last renters left at the end of the year, and Peter contacted me. He's going to put Shannon and the baby there. Cut a path through the back of his property, and it'll just be a hop, skip, and a jump."

She's silenced us again.

Jackson looks down at me. "So he's admitted finally the baby is his?"

Gertie answers for me. "Why, he was just getting things in place, I'm thinking. Contacted me about the house months ago. Got it looking right cute. He tell you when they're moving in?"

Jackson clears his throat awkwardly. "Did you, um, did you know they are moving out of the upstairs apartment, Carolina?"

I shake my head. I'm thinking too much to say anything.

Gertie's eyebrows raise. "Well, yeah. About that—" She's cut off by the squawk of the microphone.

I look up at Madam Mayor, giving her half of my attention. My mind is swirling. Peter never had any intentions of letting that baby out of his control, especially not after what happened with Gregory. He'll get them in that house, and they'll never be out of his grasp. I'm sure he'll have a nursery in his house, and what do you bet he's the only lawyer involved in drawing up the custody papers. Shannon will give up all her rights without ever asking a question. That's why Peter's being so nice. Surely Shannon can't be this naïve. She knows Peter!

I clap along with everyone else, but as Missus continues talking, I keep thinking. I'll just have to make Shannon see sense. Maybe her folks can help, although they don't seem to be the most logical people. I grunt in disgust. Why did I think Peter was going to let Shannon and Danny ride off into the sunset with his child?

Jackson bends down. "What? Are you okay?"

"Just frustrated. Has she said anything important?"

"Not really. But she said she has an announcement, so you might want to listen up."

I shake my head to clear it and focus on the mayor thanking everybody. She sounds genuinely grateful. That's different. I don't know what has caused her to turn this new leaf, but I'm all in favor of it.

"Now, I'd like to introduce you to someone who needs no introduction, Susan Lyles. Susan, wave your hand."

There at the end of the stage is Susan. I hadn't seen her earlier. I wasn't sure she'd even be here. Folks were too surprised that she was the Peeping Tom to actually believe it *was* her. In our collective disbelief, we all dropped the subject overnight. Weird, but that's how it is in small towns. If the story doesn't hold up to the preconceived notions of the people, then it probably didn't happen. If the story fits the preconceived ideas, then it's as good as gospel.

Missus taps the microphone. "Now for my announcement. Susan Lyles is my new executive assistant. Let's all congratulate Susan!" Missus claps, but the rest of us aren't so sure this a feat warranting congratulations. More like condolences.

It does explain all Missus's recent efficiency.

"I'll be right back," I say to Jackson and start in Susan's direction while Missus wraps up her talk. I get to the new executive assistant at the same time as her sister, who was listening to the speech from just outside her shop. One look at Laney, and I know she's as surprised as I am.

I let Laney take the lead. "You're working for her? Why on God's green earth would you do that?"

Susan rears back. "You two are the ones saying I was neglecting my kids. Now I'll be right here in the middle of everything. She called me her executive assistant, but mainly I'm going to be the city office's receptionist. I just sold myself to her by helping Missus plan this. Plus, I'm cheap, so the city couldn't resist. What do you think?"

My eyes are stretched in disbelief. "I think you're crazy. She's impossible, and you're going to be stuck in that depressing city hall building? You can't possibly make what you're making now." I shake my head and cross my arms. "You're crazy. You could still work with Silas. Even part-time. Apologize to him. I saw how sad he was at the graduation party! He'd take you back in a heartbeat."

"And I'd be just as distracted as ever. Silas and I are just too much together." Susan shakes her head. "It's too distracting. I don't want distracting. I want normal. That's all. And as for my current job, I was given my walking papers this week. Sneaking around, spying on another employee, even though he's my husband, made cutting my job pretty easy for the higher-ups. But it's fine. This way, I'm stuck right here in town with y'all. I can focus on my kids," she repeats, then adds with a shrug, "and I can handle Missus."

"He's your ex-husband, you know," Laney says. She and I share a look, but Susan's mind seems to be made up.

"Whatever." Laney looks over her shoulder toward the lights of her store. "Y'all are not going to believe who is in my shop right now spending a blue million."

We look but can't see inside past all the people. "Who?" I ask.

"Sally Blankenship. She says she's back for good this time." She wrinkles her nose. "Our famous author who thinks the South is full of degenerate, sex-starved hillbillies is back. At least I only have to deal with her when she's shopping. Not like you."

Susan and I look at each other. I have a bad feeling, but ask anyway, "Not like who?"

Laney tilts her head, her eyebrows scrunched down. "You. She says she's moving into the apartment above the shop."

My mouth drops open, even as Susan chirps, "Uh, where are Shannon and Danny moving to? I hope they're getting a bigger place with the baby coming. Though I'm not happy for you having Sally Blankenship in residence." She shudders. "I'll take working with Missus any day."

Gertie comes lumbering up to us. "I heard Sally's name. I was gonna tell you, Carolina, but Missus started her speech. You know how hard it is to rent that apartment, so I had to jump on Sally's offer. I'll be looking for another place for her, but she seems quite excited about living in a bookstore, seeing how she's an author and stuff. Who knows? Y'all might just hit it off!"

"Oh, I can't wait! A brand-new best friend." I drop my fake, trilling voice. "I'm going home." I turn and make my way to Jackson, who is at the refreshment table, where Phoenix is consolidating platters.

My sister-in-law-to-be quickly asks, "What'd Susan say? Is she really going to work for Missus?"

"Yep. Wants to be around town for the kids."

"Well, that's what you wanted, right?" Jackson adds.

I give him a shove. "Not like this. Not with her working for Missus for pennies. I mean, okay. It'll probably be fine. It's just a job."

Phoenix leans across the table and whispers, "And did you see Sally Blankenship is back in town?"

"I haven't seen her yet, but I've heard all about her plans." I heave a heavy, heavy sigh. "She's moving into Blooming Books' upstairs apartment."

Phoenix and Jackson give me the appropriate gasp of horror, which I very much appreciate. "Yeah, I know. I can't imagine what work's going to be like now." I pat Jackson's arm. "Let's go home. Savannah has already gone to Amanda's. Have you seen Bryan?" I ask Phoenix.

She pulls back, her mouth shut tight but her eyes wide. "What?"

She slides her eyes to her left. Just above the table and close to herself, she points in that same direction. Jackson and I both turn around to look. I don't see anything, but then Jackson grunts and strides past me. I follow him, still not seeing anything until he approaches a little red car parked in front of our shop with the driver's side facing us. Through the half-opened driver's-side window, I can see someone in the passenger seat.

"Bryan!" Jackson barks.

Suddenly the one head in the passenger seat becomes two faces turned toward us. One is Bryan's. He's sitting in the passenger seat of Susie Mae's car. Susie Mae is also sitting in the passenger seat—straddling our son's lap. She waves and smiles as she leans over to look out the open driver's window. So we can chat, I guess. Then she leans back to where she was, lying on my son's chest, running a finger along his chin.

"Hey, y'all," she drawls. "Missus got boring, and there were no chairs out there. I can give Bryan a ride home later if you're ready to leave." Did I mention she's *lying on top of him*? Just shooting the breeze while she's on top of my son.

Bryan coughs, then speaks up as he opens the passenger door. "Nah, my grandparents are visiting. I better go."

She moves just enough to let him slide out. Slowly. Her shorts are so short and her shirt is so small, she might as well be naked. Okay, I might be exaggerating. But barely. She follows him out of the car and stands with one elbow hanging over the door, her other hand grasping the tail of his T-shirt. She tugs it and causes him to look back at her. "Okay. See ya at church, Bryan."

She turns her smile onto us, still holding onto the shirt I bought, washed, dried, and folded. Of course he just stands there. On his leash. Her voice chirps, full of joy and happiness, "Love that dress, Miss Carolina!" Then she takes in the others on the sidewalk. "Oh, hey, Carl, tell your mama that book she ordered is in at the store. Tiff, I'll see you tomorrow night. Be at your house at seven sharp to babysit, right?"

With another playful tug, she pulls Bryan toward her, letting his shirt fall out of her hand so that he stumbles a bit. "Call me later, babe. You want to babysit with me tomorrow night?"

He nods, then eyes flying to me, shakes his head as he turns to walk. He's trying to look casual, strolling down the sidewalk with us following. His head is hanging, and his hands are plunged in the pockets of his khaki shorts. On both sides of the sidewalk, I can see the smiles, and smirks, of those who saw the action going on in Susie Mae's car. They must've caught the aftershow too.

Stop me if you've heard this before, but…

I hate small towns.

Chapter 39

This is more than déjà vu. It's like a slow-rolling dream where I move between two scenes that are far apart in time but are so, so similar nonetheless.

But I'm awake.

Which is a good thing since I'm driving. Savannah is seated beside me, chattering incessantly, her music blaring through the speakers like it did when we first rolled into Chancey, but this time, she's not complaining. She's excited. I feel pretty much the same as before. My stomach is churning because, despite my feelings that this doesn't feel like a good idea, I know it's happening.

Just like when we drove to our new home in Chancey two summers ago, we are on a trip, taking Savannah to her new home at Kennesaw State. She and I are in the van, following her dad and brothers in his truck like we did that day. Both vehicles are loaded down again, and I'm already tired out by the prospect of the full day still ahead of us.

Driving through Chancey this time, though, we are flooded with memories. We know what's behind every door, every window on Main Street. Jackson honks at Peter and Delaney, who are walking up the sidewalk toward church, and they enthusiastically wave back at us. We know most of the people on the church steps, who also wave.

Savannah's chattering stops. We pick up speed as we pass Silas's greenhouses, where there are already several cars in the parking lot. Soon they are behind us too.

For the life of me I can't remember my parents taking me to college. I'm sure they can. I remember every minute of taking Will, though he's told me it's now all just a blur for him. He even asked if Jackson and I both went. There's so much new stuff for kids to think about and discover when they first set foot on campus that their parents must fade into the background. Not a bad thing, I guess. But still…

"I'm glad it's just you and me in the van. A little bit of quiet in the day," I say as I pat my daughter's leg and give her a smile.

"Yeah," she says, releasing a held-in breath. "But it's really weird, isn't it?"

"Yeah, it really is. But it won't be weird for long. You're good at making yourself at home wherever you are. And it's a bonus that you know your roommates already."

"Uh-huh." She straightens up in her seat, then picks at the hem of her shorts. "I'm kind of nervous about not having my car."

"You'll be fine. There's plenty of transportation options." I don't say out loud what has already been said—several times: We don't want her to be able to run home on a moment's notice. At least not for the first few months. She'd already talked about being home on the weekends for parties when we shared that she wasn't taking her car. "We're picking you up in two weeks for the weekend home. And Anna's made plans to come down and take you to lunch when she's here next week, right?"

She nods, then reclines her seat a bit. "It'll be okay, I guess. You know, maybe I'll try to close my eyes. I didn't sleep well last night."

"Sure. That's a good idea."

I reach to turn the music down and then look at her. Her head's laid back, tilted in my direction, and her eyes are closed behind her sunglasses. She's so grown-up. So much my girl. So…

Nope. Can't do that.

I have to drive.

"Remember that elevator in my dorm? It was so slow and tiny," Will says with a laugh. We're all, along with empty boxes and suitcases, in the big elevator of Savannah's building. "And my first room was on, like, the twelfth floor."

Jackson shakes his head. "And we were moving you in with everybody else at UGA. All four hundred thousand students in triple-digit temperatures. This is a cakewalk compared to that."

Bryan scowls in thought. "There's that many people at UGA?"

Will bursts out a laugh. "Oh boy, you are too, too gullible to be let out on your own, little brother. Dad's joking. Although that dorm did get awfully hot."

Jackson and I meet eyes over Bryan's head. We've put off discussing our youngest's gullibility, especially with girls, until we get home. One kid's problems at a time.

Will's right, though. Moving his sister in has been a breeze. We pulled into the quiet, empty campus a couple of hours ago. We parked right near the building, in the unloading area, and had unfettered access to the elevator. Savannah was moved in in record time. Two of her roommates were around to help, but then they left to play tennis before it got too hot, so it's just us five, heading out for lunch. Anna opted to stay home with Francie, as we didn't think having a baby along would be helpful. This ain't our first rodeo.

I put my arm through Savannah's as we leave the elevator. "Your choice for lunch."

She shrugs. "Y'all know there's a Mellow Mushroom here, so there's no decision to be made. And I'm ordering a buffalo pizza. I don't care what the rest of you want!"

All three guys groan, and Bryan makes gagging sounds. I, however, am eating buffalo pizza with my daughter. Yes, it's unnatural to have chicken and bleu cheese on pizza, but if that's what she wants, then that's what I want.

As we pile into the van, the guys are discussing which pizza they'll order. I lay a hand on Jackson's shoulder as he drives, and I listen to the three kids lightly bickering in the back. I still can't comprehend how it will feel to have only one child in the house. But like so many things, I'll think about that later. I don't want to waste one minute thinking about the past or the future when the present moment is so full of... of... just so full.

I thought we laughed a lot over pizza, but that was nothing compared to our time helping Savannah stock up in the grocery store. It's been such a long day that, punch-drunk, I couldn't even remember what we were laughing at by the time we got back to the apartment.

But now we can't seem to buy a laugh.

The refrigerator has been stocked with Savannah's yogurt, drinks, and leftover buffalo pizza. She has two boxes of Little Debbie oatmeal cakes, one of which she's keeping in her bedroom. The other box and dry goods are in her designated kitchen cabinet. The goodies for everyone, including a box of muffins from Ruby's, are on the counter to share. Her bed is made, the TV and computer are hooked up, and her room-mates are back from tennis.

It's probably time for us to leave.

Will and Bryan are antsy, and their jokes aren't as funny as they were earlier. Jackson is sitting on a barstool, arms crossed, staring into space.

I push up out of an armchair in the living area and walk over to him. "Well, Mr. Jessup, I guess it's time we got out of here. Let the girls get on with their afternoon."

"Yep," he says as he slides off the stool. "Everything looks good."

Savannah is leaning against the wall that leads to the kitchen. She doesn't move.

Will puts his arm around Bryan's neck. "We'll go on down. Mom, I'm driving the van. You're riding with me." Will drags his brother over to Savannah, and she moves away from the wall to give them hugs. Watching them, my throat closes up, and Jackson slumps back onto his stool.

As the boys clumsily cross to the front door, the girls from Marietta tell them goodbye and quickly come over to give me and Jackson hugs. Then they scurry down the hall to their rooms. Their doors close, the front door closes, and we're left alone with our girl.

I tug on Jackson's arm, and he follows me over to our daughter, who is still reluctantly hugging the wall. "I really like your apartment," I enthuse. "You're going to have so much fun getting your room fixed up."

"Yeah. Thanks for everything." She slowly grins at me. "And wasn't the buffalo pizza good?"

"Okay, it was good," I admit. Then I grab her up in a big hug. "I love you. You're going to have a blast at school. I'm so proud of you." I talk into her hair and hold her tight, just for a few more moments. Then I let go, and she does too. I step away and take a couple of deep breaths as I keep walking. Okay. I wasn't sure before, but this is okay. I'm going to be okay.

At the door, though, I look back, and I can see that Jackson isn't okay. Tears are running down his face. His chin is shaking, and his eyes are screwed up tight as he holds Savannah. He smooths his hand down her dark hair and then pulls back a bit. "I'm going to miss you. Miss knowing you're up in your tower." He laughs, and she laughs with him. They hug once more, and then he steps toward me, his arm around her shoulders.

Jackson's tears threaten to undo me, but I focus on our daughter as they walk toward me. She's not a little girl anymore. In her eyes I see the growth of the past couple years. When we moved to Chancey there was a lot of faking-it-till-she-made-it, I realize now. Blustering past insecurity and awkwardness to arrive at this place of confidence.

She's taught me a lot.

At the door we all hug again, but this hug is faster, easier to break from. I open the front door, and Savannah's fourth roommate is standing there, startled to see us.

"Oh, you're still here? Um, I, um, have ice cream, and, uh, some friends are on their way over." The elevator dings, and a half dozen boys and girls spill out into the hall. They are carrying grocery bags, all talking and laughing, until they come upon us.

Then one young man steps forward. "Hey. I'm John. We're the welcoming committee for the floor." He shakes my hand, then Jackson's. He turns to Savannah. "You're Savannah, right? Since you didn't get the full-on freshman ice cream social, we're having one just for you!"

Before we know what's happening, the kids have slipped in around us and in front of us to surround our girl. She's smiling as she surveys the different ice creams and toppings. One of the new girls, with a shaker of multi-colored sprinkles in one hand, has her other hand on the door and she looks at us.

"We'll take good care of her," she promises. "She's going to be fine."

Savannah looks up at us and waves, her eyes bright, but not with tears now. "Chocolate mint is my favorite!" she exclaims before turning away.

The girl with the sprinkles smiles as she slowly closes the door.

The hall is really, really quiet.

Grabbing Jackson's hand, I head toward the elevator. We get in, and the doors close. Behind them, we just stand and breathe for a moment.

Jackson reaches out a hand and pushes the first-floor button. The gears churn into motion, and we move. At the bottom the doors open onto the sunny entryway, and we step out, but that's as far as we get before we stall out again. I feel as if I left all my thoughts and feelings and energy upstairs. I'm empty, and the parking lot looks so far away. I'm glad Will offered to drive me home.

We each take another deep breath. Then I laugh a bit and lean my head against his arm. "Well, Mr. Jessup. Now what?"

Sign up for my newsletter and check out all my books at
www.kaydewshostak.com
I love being friends with readers on Facebook.
Thank you for your reviews on Amazon!
The twelfth book in the Chancey series will be coming
next year in 2024, but the sixth in the The Southern Beach
Mysteries series releases later this year.

Books by Kay Shostak

The Chancey Books

Next Stop, Chancey
Chancey Family Lies
Derailed in Chancey
Chancey Jobs
Kids Are Chancey
A Chancey Detour
Secrets Are Chancey
Chancey Presents
Chancey Moves

Florida Books

Backwater, Florida
Wish You Were Here

Southern Beach Mysteries

The Manatee Did It
The Sea Turtle Did It
The Shrimp Did It
The Shark Did It
The Gator Did It

Printed in the USA
CPSIA information can be obtained
at www.ICGtesting.com
LVHW030557070823
754339LV00006B/624